The Brotherhood of Time: Dawn

For G and Q

The loves of my life

Thank you for always motivating me to be better

Prologue

Time is a funny thing. When I was a young child, I felt like time was never ending. That was bad for me, because my life was not a happy one. When I grew older and my life became one that I wanted to live, time had a way of escaping far too fast. As I sit here remembering how I stumbled into the greatest adventure, and the greatest love, that I could have ever imagined I realize that no matter how much control I thought I had over time it will always win. Mortality is inescapable. What matters is how you use the time you have between your first and final breath. I am disgusted to think of the times when I tried to hasten my final breath, and grateful for the hands that were there to pull me back.

We all get one life, some of us are blessed from the beginning and some of us get lucky and find our blessings. Regardless of how long we live, we all have a dawn, an eventide, and a witching hour. As I sit in my final stage, preparing for the inevitable kiss of death, I am indeed scared because after all that I have seen, I no longer believe in the Gods. If there is something next I am unable to see it.

But more than being scared, I am grateful. I am grateful for everything that has happened in my life, the good and the bad. Every moment, every event, led me to this exact place in time. My dawn may have started dark and cloudy, but it opened up into a warm and beautiful eventide. And in my witching hour, I get to set my own terms for the final darkness.

Finding my prince was the start of my life. Not my first breath, of course. But I had never truly lived, I had no idea what a real life was, not until my prince touched my soul and showed me. I will always wonder what he saw in me, a simple boy with boring dark hair. I wasn't tall, I didn't have much in the way of muscles, my eyes were a boring shade of brown. My nose was too large for my face. But whatever he saw in me he loved me fiercely, and I him.

No matter what comes next, my love for him will never die.

1

I often think of my first time meeting the prince. I was sixteen and I had snuck into the castle gardens one day after training with my father. That was where Prince Tomren found me. I had no way to know that that day would change the rest of my life. My father, General Mikhail Rorthan, was the most trusted of the king's generals, and often spent time with the king while the prince listened, learned, and was groomed to one day take over the throne. In truth, I was jealous of the prince at that time. I wished nothing more than that my father would allow me to learn of the kingdom. Hell, I wished that the general would just spend time with me at all. But, I suppose keeping the kingdom safe was an important job.

I wasn't exactly lonely. I spent five days a week in learning, and my father had insisted that I spend two of those days training my body after my classes. One day a week I was to just watch the army train. "There is much to be learned from simply watching the king's men train, you would do well to learn the strategies that they employ," my father had said. I may have done well to have him explain the strategies to me, or even for him to assign one of his men to explain them to me, but to just sit here watching the grown men did little to teach me. I brought this up to my father one day. "You will not be one of these men," he had said looking out over the soldiers, "you will be their leader one day. And as such, you need to get used to just watching over them." I had tried to further argue my point, but my father had curtly dismissed me.

So I was both busy, and physically exhausted more often than not. Yet, I had managed to excel in my classes, and I was grateful to have the opportunities that I had. Many children in the kingdom were lucky if they could even go to learning, often having to help their family's earn coin to survive. But, I wanted to learn like Prince Tomren did. I wanted to know of the conversations that were had in the throne room, and even more so of the conversations that were had behind the closed doors in the deepest parts of the castle. I wanted to know of the lands around us, and how they lived. I wanted the education that the prince was getting, but, I suppose there was no need for me to have that education. I was, after all, just the son of a general, and had no need to be taught as a prince. I was jealous just the same.

"Father," I asked over our dinner one night, "do you think perhaps I could follow you one day?

I would be silent, I just would like to observe what you do."

My father looked at me for a moment. It was rare that he was home, I had been surprised in fact when the door had opened. I had simply made myself some fish, fish was plentiful with the kingdom being mostly coast lands. When I saw my father come into the home, I had quickly given him the fish I had made and began eating some of the bread and cheese. I wasn't that hungry anyway. "Most of what I do cannot be seen by you. Many things must be kept secret, and that means even from you. When you are older, your time will come. If you study and train diligently, you will one day know of all that I do. And, I dare say, mayhaps you will know more than me."

I nodded. "I will continue to prepare myself for that day," I said, hoping that I was successful in hiding my disappointment.

"I know you will, your mother would be right proud of you," he smiled, "'Mikhail, that boy is going to be just like you one day' she had told me," a hint of sadness creeping into his eyes. "Well, I'm not one to argue with your mother, that was a battle that was never to be won."

I never knew my mother. She had survived my birth, but barely by a sennight. The healers said that she lost too much blood, and despite them doing everything that they could, she fell asleep forever, holding me, and my father holding her. The king had sent many to watch over me as I grew, his lead general being given every possible assistance in raising the child that had cost him his wife.

I knew rationally that no one blamed me for her death, at least no one other than my father. He wasn't a bad man, and he did love me I was sure. But every year, on the day that she died, he would go into his chamber with more wine than was needed for ten men, and he would close his door. I would sit silently outside of his door and listen. On that day was the only time I would ever hear my father cry, and not just cry. He would go between uncontrolled sobbing, and wailing loud enough to be heard from anywhere in our home. He would mumble, and say her name. One year, when I was only eight summers old, I heard him ask her ghost the question that I had wondered from the day I realised that I wasn't like other children. "Why, Eleanor," he had asked angrily, "why did it have to be you? That cursed child should have been the one to die, not you. We could have made another. I needed you, not some red bottomed child that was a stranger to me. I cannot look at him and not see you, my love. I see you in every single thing that he does, he is very much your son. He's not like me, he's soft and loving like you. He is no man."

Well, at least I wasn't the only one that wondered why I lived and my mother did not. And, he wasn't wrong, I was no man. I was only a child. Did he expect me at eight summers to be leading armies, as he did as a grown man? That night, I had snuck out of our home. I knew that he was so deep in his wine that I could have slammed every door in the house and screamed that I was leaving, and he still would not have heard over the sound of his own blubbering and grief. But, I had been silent as I left and found my way to the edge of the cliffs. Turning back I could see only the lights of the castle in the distance. The town was dark. I had sat there for what felt like a lifetime, although I'm sure it was, in earnest, only a few hours. I debated jumping over the edge. My father certainly would not care. And, the only other people in my life were ones that were obligated to be there. The caretakers that the king would still send to ensure that I was being raised well. The preceptors in the classes that I took. But, no one that actually loved me. Hell, no one that even ruddy chose to be around me. I was alone. And if I had killed my mother, why should I get to live?

I stepped to the edge of the cliff before me. I could hear the water crashing into the shore down below, but I could not see that far. The sky was filled with dark clouds, and the moon was hidden behind them. I did not exactly want to die. But, my father blamed me for his wife being gone. And he wasn't wrong. If I had not come into this world, my mother would still be in it. And she had many friends when she was still alive. Many folks loved her, and she was always out helping others in the capital, or so I was told growing up. But even those that she had called her friend did not come around. I was sure it was because they too blamed me for killing their companion. My life served no purpose, and it came at the cost of a life that had.

I sat down on the edge of the rock, mentally exhausted from the night. Hearing one's own father say that they wished that you were dead instead of the mother that you never knew had a way of draining you. I closed my eyes, feeling the wind blow around me. I swayed a little in the wind, but I wasn't scared of falling, in fact I almost hoped that the wind would take my balance and push me over the edge. As I sat there, I relaxed and my head began to nod. The morning surely would be here soon, and I needed to either return home before my father awoke, or end his suffering and make sure that he never looked upon me again.

With my eyes still closed, I leaned forward. I could feel my weight begin to shift, and my balance begin to take me over. I was slipping, and I felt no fear. I'm not sure exactly what I felt, mayhaps only some sort of relief. But, just as I could feel my weight begin to take me down to the rocks below, a strong hand grabbed my collar.

"You bloody fool," I heard a voice from behind. I did not recognize the voice, but it was deep and raspy. "Are you trying to waste your life so young?"

As he pulled me from the edge and dropped me, I slumped and turned to look at the man. He seemed like a giant of a man to me, though I was only eight, and I was scared, and it was dark, and I was practically laying in the grass, so in reality he was likely no bigger than any other man. "My life has brought nothing but sorrow, regret, and death to those around me," I said flatly.

He studied me for a moment. "True as that may seem, you have a life, and there are many who do not have that luxury. Your mother dying was tragic. Perhaps, she wouldn't want you to waste the life for which she gave her own to create?" His voice had lost the angry edge that it first held, but it was still stern.

"What difference does that make," I asked. "She is not here. The only person that is here is my father, and he would gladly trade my life for hers."

"Your father is a damned fool for being so careless as to let his hurt be heard by you," he said firmly. "However, his words when he is drunk on wine and pain are not necessarily his true feelings.

He has lost much, and he tries as best as he can to keep you from suffering."

I looked at him, knowing that my father likely did not hate me, but that took none of the pain away. This stranger wouldn't listen if I explained though, so I simply looked at him. He wasn't as large as I had thought at first. He was tall, certainly, but barely taller than any other man I knew. His muscles looked strong in his clothes, but not overly bulging. His face held a scruffy beard, and bright green eyes. His hair was shoulder length and dark, with large looping curls. His clothes, while not fancy, certainly did not appear to be those of an average worker or farmer. "Who are you, and why do you presume to know anything about what my mother would have wanted, or what my father does or feels now," I asked, a bit harshly.

The man sighed. "My name, young Rorthan, is Arthur, and I cared very much for your mother. I once knew your father very well, though that bond has long been broken," he said, looking almost saddened by his own words. "You and I have never met, at least not that you would remember. I have, however, continued to be very interested in the man you are becoming. And, I am highly disappointed," he said looking directly into my eyes, "highly disappointed indeed."

I snorted a gruff laugh, "Well, that certainly seems to be right in line with everyone else around me."

I expected some sort of retort, some sort of smart remark to put me in my place. I did not expect, and thus was unprepared for, a slap across the head that was so hard I saw stars. I looked at him, tears of anger and pain forming in my eyes, but no words forming clear enough in my mind to speak.

"Stop feeling sorry for yourself," he said, practically shouted, actually. "This world doesn't feel sorry for you, and it won't start now. I stopped you from ending your small life, but I will not again. You can jump, the edge is right there," he said, gesturing behind me.

"I...I wasn't trying to die," I stammered, "I was simply". My words died in my mouth, as he cuffed me again.

"Do not lie to me."

I was mad now, and I was thinking much more clearly than I was after the first strike. "How dare you strike me! My father will have you in shackles in the dungeon by the end of the day, you bloody fool." I seemed to forget that I was only eight, and that he could pick me up and throw me over the edge of the cliff if he desired.

The man laughed. Not angrily, not sarcastically, just a genuine laugh. "I highly doubt that, and what will you tell him? A man named Arthur, who claimed he was friends with him once upon a time, stopped you from taking your own life? Do you even know or believe that that is my real name? Perhaps I am just a man who was walking along the cliffs and saw you?"

I looked at him. He was right. It sounded crazy, and I would have to admit what I had planned on doing to my father. I turned to look back to the edge. "So, you won't stop me then?"

He didn't answer. A second later, the sky lit bright with lightning, but I heard no thunder, and when I turned back to look at him, he was gone. Well, that was strange. But, I suppose he was right. I was only eight, and someday I would be my own man, so I should probably just let life play out a little longer. My father wasn't bad to me, and I guess in the end, he probably did love me and maybe he didn't even really feel the things I heard him say. But, he did say them, and I would never be able to forget the words.

What I did not know was that eight years later I would meet the prince, and my life would change forever.

2

One day after my training, I had gone to change, and instead of going home after changing I decided it would be a good idea to explore. All of the guards knew that my father was the general, and I had never been stopped when walking through the castle. I suppose part of that was the fact that every other time I was in the castle, I was supposed to be. I wasn't sneaking around, trying to explore. But most of the people around were just going about their business, whether they were servants or guards. As long as I didn't go anywhere that was off limits, or cause any trouble, I had confidence that I would be undisturbed.

I left the training area like normal, but went deeper into the castle instead of leaving. As I suspected, the people scurrying about doing their business paid me no attention. I ended up outside, and walked through the gardens for a short time. There was no one in the gardens, at least not that I could see or hear. The grounds were very well kept, and I found myself being relaxed just by the smells and sounds. These must have been the infirmary gardens, as they smelled of fresh herbs, particularly pleasant was the mint and fennel that hung in the air. I found a small bench, and I sat down to breathe in the aroma. The sun was lowering, but it was still quite warm, and there were hours of daylight still ahead. My father was likely still here somewhere, and would be until well after dark. I would have plenty of time to get back to our home and prepare dinner before he arrived. I closed my eyes, feeling the warmth of the sun on my skin, and relaxed. If anyone bothered me, I would just tell them I got lost. I was certainly allowed to be in the castle, and the only ones likely to be in the gardens would be the healers, so I was sure they wouldn't make a big deal of my presence. I had no reason to be on guard, and I must have relaxed too much, because at some point I was rudely awakened by the feeling of steel on my neck.

"You don't belong here," said a firm but young voice.

I opened my eyes, but did not get up. The blade was pressed to my throat, and the person wielding it was behind me, out of my sight. "I am the son of General Rorthan, and unless you want to be put in the dungeons, I suggest you lower your blade immediately," I said, wishing that my words had not come out with a distinct squeak.

The man laughed, "I'm not scared of the general. I suspect he would not dare put me in the dungeon."

I felt the blade move away from my skin, and I leapt up, whirling around to face the man. "And why in the ruddy hell wouldn't," but I stopped short of finishing my sentence. It wasn't a man. I hadn't recognized the voice because I had never really heard the prince speak. But, I certainly knew his face. I dropped to one knee. "I...I'm sorry, Prince Tomren," I stammered, "I did not know it was you. Forgive me, I shouldn't be here, I was just resting, I meant no disrespect."

The prince took a step towards me, his blade pointed at my kneeling form. "You don't belong here," he repeated, "and, you may have meant no disrespect, but you have offered it just the same."

Before I could respond he began laughing. "I'm only jesting," he said, extending his hand.

I looked at the prince for a moment, my gaze resting on his outstretched hand. His finger bore a golden ring with a large, heart shaped jet lignite at its center. "Well," he asked, lightly, "did you want to get up, or were you going to kneel here until dark?"

"Of course, your highness," I said, accepting his hand. As he lifted me easily, I took note of his features. He was muscular for his age, we were both sixteen, but he was built more like an adult. I felt small in comparison, despite our height being seemingly the same, I was perhaps just slightly taller even. His sandy blonde, shoulder length hair laid perfectly in curls at his shoulders. His eyes were as blue as the ocean. He had a small, stubbly beard that made me jealous given my lack of ability to grow facial hair. His clothes, while worth more money than I would likely see in years of laboring, were just a bit dirty, mud and dust clear upon them. "Thank you," I said as I got to my feet.

"Certainly," he said politely. "Your father is the general?"

I looked down, reminded of my earlier threat to him. When speaking of 'the' general, there was no doubt that the reference was to my father. The king had more than one general to be certain, however, there was one that was both respected and known above all others. "Yes, he is. I had finished my training for the day, and I came to explore. I meant no harm, I apologize for intruding," I said quickly, still not meeting his gaze.

"Intruding," he repeated with a small laugh. "There is no intrusion. It's just the gardens, and not even the nice ones. People come here all the time for all different sorts of reasons. I, in fact, use it as a shortcut to sneak out of the castle."

"Sneak out?"

The prince nodded, "Yes, I do so almost every day. I'm very busy, you see, being groomed to run a kingdom and all. But, I try to make sure that I have at least some time to myself to think each day. I find it both relaxing, and energizing." He looked at me curiously. "What is your name," he asked.

I looked down again. "Rorthan," I replied, softly.

"Yes, yes, you are the general's son, but what is your given name?"

I didn't lift my eyes, already emotionally compromised from first the fear of the blade on my neck, and then the fear of having threatened the prince, I was sure that my eyes would betray tears. "I am just Rorthan. My mother died from bringing me into this world, and my father never gave me a proper name. He calls me son, and everyone else just calls me Rorthan."

"That is terrible," the prince said, a slight tone of sadness in his voice. "Every man deserves a forename." I finally looked up to meet his gaze, noting that his eyes had a thin layer of water forming in them. "My mother died when I was very young as well. I don't really remember her. Sometimes I feel as though I hear her voice, or what I think her voice sounded like, and see her face in my mind. But I was so young that I have no way to know if her voice sounded as I suppose it did when I imagine it."

Everyone knew, of course, that the queen had gotten sick and died over the course of just a few moons. Rumor had spread that it was the black bile, but no one had ever actually confirmed that I suppose. I was surprised by the show of emotion from the boy I had just met. Surely it would be considered weakness in a future king. Before I could say anything, not that I even knew what to say in response to him, he quickly changed the topic.

"Would you like to go out with me on the morrow?"

"Go out," I asked, unsure of his meaning.

"Yes, go with me, out of the castle. I'll be sneaking out again tomorrow, and you could join me, if you please."

I stood there, not knowing how to respond. The prince had not only just invited me to spend time with him, but to do so by breaking the rules and sneaking out of the castle. "I would enjoy that I'm sure, your highness, but, if we were to get caught, would they think I had taken you?"

The prince laughed. "Taken me," he said with a humorous tone. "While it is true, you may be a little bit taller than me," he said, appraising me, "I don't think anyone would believe it possible that you had 'taken' me."

I flushed, whether with anger at being seemingly called weak, or with embarrassment at even having spoken the idea, I did not know. "Of course, your highness. I would be honored to join you then, sir."

"Splendid. Two rules. One, no one must know. I prefer not to have my adventures discovered. And, two, you must not call me 'your highness' again. My name is Tomren. If those are rules that you can follow, meet me here, on the morrow, two hours before the sun is at its height." He turned, and without another word, cut through the bushes that ran around the gardens, and was gone.

Well, this should be interesting, I thought. A day adventuring with the prince.

3

I could barely sleep that night. I knew that I could sneak out of learning and make it back to the castle in time to meet the prince. But, what if someone stopped me at the castle? It wasn't a day when I would normally be there. I could say I was coming to see my father about something, make up some reason why I had left classes to come to the castle. That would probably work. But what were we going to be doing? Where does a prince sneak out to? Hell, where does a prince sneak out to when he has the son of one of his fathers most trusted generals in tow? Would we explore hidden parts of the castle? Mayhaps there were things on the grounds to explore. I had no idea what to expect, and that was unusual for me. My days were damn near the same, and even a minor change to the routine was not something I was used to.

I must have drifted off to sleep at some point, because my father woke me. The sky was just starting to burn with morning light, and after only a second I remembered my plans for the day.

"I won't be home until after dark this night," he said, "I will eat my supper before returning. If I'm not home before you retire, I shall see you tomorrow. Do not forget, tomorrow morning you have training at first light."

How could I forget? Every Saturday was the same, early morning training. It had been so for years. "Of course, father," I answered. "I will be up and ready for the day."

He just nodded, turned, and left. He was not a warm man, and after the things that I heard him say on every anniversary of my mother's death, I doubted a little more with each passing year whether he even loved me. He was my father because it was his duty. It was expected of him, and his pride would force him to at least care for my needs, and train me up so as not to embarrass him.

My mind returned to the adventure I would be taking with the prince today. With 'Tomren', though I doubt that I would be able to bring myself to call him that. He was the prince, and I was not someone in a position to call him by his given name. Then, that made me think of something that I had not yet considered, and this was a bit surprising, considering I had thought of just about everything as I was attempting to fall asleep last night. What if the prince was having a joke at my expense? He had already embarrassed me the last time we met, though it seemed to be just a light hearted jest. What if he and some of his princely friends were going to be there, waiting to laugh at me and the audacity I must have to think that a prince would want to go on an adventure with the likes of me? My face reddened at the thought. While other young ones hadn't been particularly mean to me, I also didn't have any friends of my age. I heard the whispers behind my back, and knew that the other children were afraid of my father. I knew that they thought I was "odd" because I didn't play with other children. But, I had no time to do so. I spent my days either learning, training, or keeping the home proper for my father. Play was not a luxury I seemed to be destined to enjoy. Mayhaps this was just a way for the prince to entertain himself, by making me the arse end of his joke.

But the prospect of time away from my responsibilities was enough to make me go to the castle anyway. Certainly, I would have to work that much harder later in the day to finish my chores, though father had said that he would be home late, so supper would not fall on me to prepare this evening. And, if I was back before he returned, I'm sure that he would not even notice my absence.

I put on my "fine" clothes, as my father called them anyway, and walked towards the castle. It hadn't occurred to me until I was halfway there that if I was questioned at the castle, I would have no good reason why I wasn't in my normal training attire. I would think of some reason, though even my so called fine clothes weren't really that fine, and I suppose that anyone stopping me would probably not look twice at them. They certainly didn't look like the clothing of someone who would be having an audience with the prince.

As I walked through the capital, I got to the market that was just outside of the castle. I had watched the castle go from a distant, somewhat blurry building, to the beautiful building it actually was. My home was not in bad repair, nor was it considered small, but it was still just a humble home. The doubt crept into my mind again. Why would a prince that lived in a ruddy nice castle, and had beautiful people with beautiful clothes, want to spend an afternoon adventuring with me? I shook it off. I would find out, and I would deal with the reasons, whatever they were.

Too late I saw one of my fathers men coming the opposite way. He was walking briskly, but he saw me before I could slip out of his view. "Rorthan," he called.

I had tried to pretend to be looking at the wares of one of the shops in the market, but I turned. "Hello," I said politely, but quickly.

"Do you not have learning this morning," he said, eyeing me questioningly.

"I do, but I wanted to get a gift for my father, and the shops weren't open when I first passed them," I lied. "I'll be going presently, though," I thought quickly and it had occurred to me how I might escape from him telling my father of our meeting, "if you could not tell him that you saw me, I would like it to be a surprise."

The man, who I had only seen a few times, and who's name I didn't even know, or couldn't recall at the moment anyway, gave a small smile and nodded. "It is his year day?"

In truth, my father's year day was coming up, but it was still weeks away. I silently thanked the soldier for helping my excuse take shape. "Yes, soon," I answered, "I just like to be prepared and I knew today would be an opportunity to get him his gift. He said that he would have a busy day, so I took advantage of that fact."

The man nodded again. "Busy indeed," he said, his smile fading. "We have had an odd...incident." He seemed unsure of the word he was looking for, and then looked at me as though mayhaps he shouldn't have even spoken of it at all.

"Of course, so he said," I lied again, hoping to ease the soldier's mind. If my father did hear of this, I would have to explain my lies to him, and I was sure that wouldn't go well. Better that the man in front of me thought that I knew of what he spoke.

It seemed to work, as the soldier relaxed just a bit. "Of course," he said. "Well, good luck with the gift. Make sure you don't dawdle for too long."

"I won't," I answered, but to his back, as he had already turned on his heel and began walking away.

When he had distanced himself enough from me, I nodded at the shop keeper that I had just noticed. I saw disappointment in his eyes when I returned the bobble that I had pretended to be considering buying. I walked away without a word. A few moments later, I was passing through the castle gates, the guards not thinking anything of seeing me entering the grounds. I walked towards the gardens, and no one that I passed paid me a second glance.

I sat down on the same bench I had sat on the last time I was here. I wasn't early, I knew that, if anything I may have been even a bit late. Did the prince already come, and upon not seeing me, leave? Was the prince even going to show up at all? Or, if he did show up, would it be with a group of friends, as I had thought of earlier, to have a good laugh at me? I closed my eyes, and breathed in the scents of the garden once more. It smelled so pleasant that I felt myself quickly relaxing, my anxiety fading with every breath.

"You made it," I heard a happy voice say from behind me. I opened my eyes, and turned to see the prince. But he didn't look much like a prince. His clothes looked nearly as basic as my own, and the only thing that would make anyone who didn't know him think that he was anything more than an average child, was his ring.

"Of course, your highness," I said, giving him a small smile. "It's not every day that one get's the chance to go on an adventure at a castle, with a prince."

He frowned. "Tomren is my name," he said, his smile returning just a bit, though not as free. "And is that the reason you came? Just to 'adventure with a prince'", he asked.

I felt myself flush. How did he manage to always make me redden? "No, of course not," I said quickly. "But it is certainly an exciting prospect."

His smile came back full. "Well, let us see if we can't make it truly exciting then."

He began walking further into the gardens, towards the back of the grounds. There was a thick hedge wall that surrounded the gardens. I followed, not sure what to say to a prince.

"Does your father know that you are here," he asked.

"No," I said quickly, not wanting him to think I was untrustworthy. "Does yours?"

He chuckled. "Certainly not. He surely thinks I'm off learning from one meister or another. As long as I have returned by the time I am expected in my chambers, he will never know. There was some sort of," he started, "well, I'm not sure what it was actually. I heard him saying something about a storm that had struck at

Meretown and a fisherman and his wife had disappeared. I believe he sent a small group of his men to go assist in trying to find them. But," he stopped.

I looked at him. "But, what," I asked. Though I'm not sure that it was really my place to question a prince.

He seemed to think it over before finishing his thought. "But," he continued, "he was also discussing something with your father and Beltoch about a cave that, from what I could tell, had something mysterious happening at it that needed investigating. I believe they were going to go there this afternoon, though, I'm not sure."

I knew that my father and Beltoch Mowbray, a meister of science and medicine, seemed to get on well. Though, on the few occasions that I had met the man, I felt like he was a rather stuck up git. "Mysterious?"

"Yes," he said as he stopped walking, just in front of the hedge wall, a glint of excitement in his eye. "I don't know for sure what, it was hard to hear from where I was listening, but it sounded like they seemed to think the cave may have something to do with the storm, and the couple that disappeared in Meretown."

I looked at him curiously. "How could a cave, all the way out here, have anything to do with a disappearance in Meretown," I asked. Meretown was at least a full day's ride from the castle. I could imagine no way in which the two could be connected.

He shook his head. "I do not know. But, my original plan for us today had been to just explore the woods here on the grounds a bit. Now, though," he said with a sly grin, "I think we have a cave to find."

Before I could respond, he slipped into the hedges and out of sight. I wasn't sure that I wanted to go hunting for a cave, but, adventure beckoned, and I intended to answer it's call. I followed him into the hedges, and our adventure began.

4

"Your highness," I whispered. I'm not sure why I whispered, I didn't suspect there was anyone there to hear me, and we hadn't even left the castle grounds yet. "Your highness," I whispered again, just a bit louder.

A hand reached out and grabbed my arm. "This way," the prince said, pulling me along deeper into the hedges.

I followed his lead, and soon the hedges were at our back, and a large clearing was in front of us. I turned around to look at the castle, and was a bit taken off guard. I had never seen the back of it before. It was just as impressive as the view when approaching it from the market, but there were even more windows, and even a pair of turrets on either end of the building that one could not see from the front.

"Come on," he said, "we need to get through the clearing and into the forest before we are seen."

I glanced at him as we practically ran across the clearing, "Are we going to get caught," I asked, looking back to the line of trees that dotted the distance in front of us.

He gave me a quick smirk, "I haven't been yet. So, I suppose, if we are caught, it would be your fault."

I felt as though he was just playfully teasing me, though I reddened just the same. Curse my skin that always seemed to betray my feelings.

He must have seen my color change, because he said, "I'm just kidding, calm yourself. We won't be caught, no one will be looking for us, and if we move quickly we'll be to the forest in just a couple of minutes."

He was right, and soon we had entered into the woods. He paused, and pulled out a water skin. He drank, and offered it to me. I accepted and drank as well, not realizing that the run had apparently been more effort than I thought. "Thank you," I said, wiping my mouth with my sleeve and handing the container back to him.

"You're welcome," he said. "So, there are three caves here that I have seen. I haven't explored them, I really prefer not to enter caves, they are dark and a bit unnerving. I think we should explore the one that is the farthest first, and then next time, we can do the next furthest."

"Next time," I asked with a smile. "We'll be doing this again?" I was excited at the possibility, but also my mind raced through all of the work, and the risk, that it would take for me to sneak out again.

"Of course, we must discover the secret. It's our duty, a prince and his loyal friend."

"Loyal friend," I repeated, a bit sheepishly. "You've really just met me, and you don't know that I'm not some kind of nutty."

The prince laughed, "Of course I know that you're not a nutty person. You are the general's son, and you did not tell anyone of our adventure. Though, sneaking away with the prince may be considered by some to be mental, I suppose."

He began walking deeper into the woods. The trees were mostly oak, chestnut, and ash, I knew this from my learning. They formed a lovely canopy of shade, while we were able to walk easily through them. The sounds of the birds in the trees, and various critters on the ground was oddly peaceful. I had never really been able to enjoy such things. The sounds of bustling were everywhere in the capital, and while at the castle, there were always people running around, or the sound of swords and shields clashing in training. Even when I had been in the gardens, there was still the distant din of the castle's everyday noises. Here though, there was only nature, and our footfalls. "It's very peaceful here," I said, breaking the even silence that we had held for a few moments.

The prince nodded. "It is indeed. It's one of my favorite things about being out here, in fact. My 'adventures' typically consist of me coming into the woods, finding a place to rest, and just listening and thinking. I find it remarkably calming, and there is much contentment to be found in this place."

"Do you have a favorite spot," I asked, thinking that if he did I couldn't imagine what would make it more special than this amazing place we were already journeying through.

"I do, very much so, I do", he said with a warm smile. "In fact," he continued, "it is on the way, well, mostly on the way, to our cave. Would you like to see it?"

"Yes, I would love to."

"Then we shall make a slight detour, and perhaps have a bite to eat," he said with a glance to the tuck that hung over his shoulder.

"You brought food," I asked, even though I instantly regretted it. Of course he brought food, we were going to be here for hours, why wouldn't he bring food. Why had *I* not thought to bring food, or water?

He put a hand on my shoulder. "Of course," he said. Then, as if he had read my mind, though it was likely not hard to tell my feelings as my shade was undoubtedly darkened by my embarrassment, he quickly added, "my first time out here, I did not think to bring any kind of supplies. I really hadn't planned on being here long I suppose, but, still, I regretted the lack of provisions. There are several cool streams here, certainly, and the water is perfectly sweet, but it does little to fill a grumbling stomach."

I felt my skin cool, and was grateful that he had calmed my embarrassment. Often, when other young people sensed that I was uncomfortable, they would make fun of me, as though the goal was to see how dark my skin could get. "That's good to know. I suppose next time, I will be much better prepared for the adventure."

"Well, I could have suggested you pack some provisions, though I honestly didn't think of it until after we had parted ways. And, it was really nothing for me to grab a few extra things from the castle. We will have plenty for the day," he said, patting his tuck.

We continued on, and while I am good at direction and not getting lost, I felt like I would have been turned around many times in these woods if I were alone. "It is all so beautiful, but I don't think I would make it far before becoming helplessly lost."

He laughed lightly as we walked, not turning to look at me. "I did my first time. I was in here for at least a mileway or two before I realized I had not one single idea where I was. Thankfully, I began paying attention, and through the trees I followed the sun and was able to make it back to the edge of the wood. Though I was rather far from where I had entered the trees originally, and I could not even see the outline of the castle from where I stood."

"Were you not scared?"

He laughed a bit harder this time, "Oh, I was bloody well terrified. No one knew where I was, and that included me. I had no provisions, and even though the hour was not as late as my mind wanted me to believe, I was just certain dark would be coming soon and I would be lost in the woods. And," he added with a glint of mischief in his eyes, "there are wolves in these woods."

My face must have betrayed my concern, though I'm relatively certain that I did not blush, because he quickly continued. "I, of course, was fine. I was back to the castle long before dark, and no one even had noticed that I was gone. That actually emboldened me, I decided then to make it a regular thing to slip away, and now I prepare. I sometimes add things to my list of supplies, but I've gotten pretty good at making sure I have what I need."

I looked him over as we walked. The tuck looked like it did indeed hold a fair amount of supplies. But, I also noticed that something was missing. "No sword?"

"No, I don't particularly like swords, and I don't suspect that I'll be likely to need one out here. I do have," he said, pulling something from his belt, "my blade."

"I remember the feel of that on my throat," I said, recalling how the cold steel had scared me.

"Yes, well," he said, and this time I felt as though perhaps I saw a bit of a blush from him, "I wasn't going to actually do anything with it. I was simply protecting myself."

I chuckled a bit at this. "Protecting yourself, from an unarmed boy?"

This time, I was sure I saw him blush. "Yes, well, an unarmed boy who was trespassing in our gardens," he said, not unkindly.

"Fair point, I suppose I did-"

I was interrupted by his arm stretching across my chest to stop me. He was stronger than I would have expected. "Quiet, look over there," he whispered.

Somewhat nervously, I looked in the direction that he was indicating. I didn't see anything other than the trees. Just then, I saw a bit of movement. I jumped with a small yelp, and then flushed bright red yet again. A deer took off running.

The prince laughed. "It's just a deer," he said through his laugh, a laugh that I thought was a bit too strong, "I would think the general's son would be a touch more brave than that."

I reddened, both of embarrassment and anger. "Do not laugh at me," I practically shouted,

"I am not a joke for you to enjoy. I may not have your title, and your wealth, but I am a person just the same."

The prince raised his voice to an octave above my own. "I am Prince Tomren, and you will address me as 'your highness' and show me the respect I deserve," he hollered, as I instinctually dropped to one knee and bowed my head, "when we are in the castle, or in front of others," he continued, his voice lowering to it's natural volume. "When we are out here, or when no one else is around, you do not need to yell. Only say 'Tomren, you git, you're being an arsehole to me, and I'm hurt by it.'"

I looked up at him, unsure what to say. He closed the distance between us, and held out his hand. "Now get up, you look silly bending the knee in the wood. I am not your prince right now, I am just your friend."

I accepted his hand, and again was surprised by his strength when lifting me to my feet. "I'm sorry, I was out of turn," I began.

"No," he interrupted, "I am sorry," he sighed heavily. "Rorthan, I do not have friends. I have people who are either paid, or obligated, to be around me. They are either my servants, or my fathers men, and either way, all of them are expected to kneel and bow before me. I am not used to having a friend, nor am I practiced in how to speak to one." He took a moment and looked at me, his bright blue eyes conveying both genuine regret at having offended me, and a bit of, what I assumed was sadness, at not having friends. "I am sorry. I did not mean to offend, and I do not think of you as a joke. In truth, I am a little bit jealous of the fact that you get to go to a class room, and have friends, and live a normal life."

I returned his gaze, "'normal life'", I repeated with a humorless laugh. "There is nothing normal about my life. I also do not have friends. I am the weird child, the one who killed his mum coming into this world, and whose dad is a feared general. No one wants to be my friend. I simply go to class, go to training at the castle, and keep my home for my father."

The prince studied me, a look on his face that I couldn't really read. "Well, then," he said, straightening his tuck, and turning to continue our way into the woods, "I suppose we are each other's best friend then."

I had never really had a friend, so the idea of a best friend certainly was foreign to me. What do best friends do? And, I'm fairly new to this, but, I'm pretty sure that best friends have to be somewhat of equals. And I was definitely not equal to a prince. But, I simply nodded. "I suppose so," I agreed.

He smiled, and I returned his smile. "Well, then, on to the cave."

5

We walked along in an amiable silence for another mileway, before hearing the sound of horses. They were coming fast, and the prince pulled me quickly, and silently, down behind a fallen tree.

"Stay down," he said quietly after we were in hiding.

I nodded. We were huddled down, listening to the riders get closer. That is when I noticed his scent. The prince smelled lightly of sandalwood and citrus, lemon I believe. The smell was soft and pleasant. I became self conscious of my own scent. I'm sure that I didn't smell like anything other than sweat, even though it wasn't hot, I was still sweating from the walk, and the stress of now having to hide. I started to ease back a bit from him, but he grabbed me and pulled me further down to the ground, and closer to him, with a scowl and a finger to his lips.

The riders slowed. "I swear I saw someone."

"It was just your eyes, you git."

I recognized the second voice as one of my fathers men.

"What if it's one of them," the first voice asked.

"I saw no one, and there is no sign that any of them have come through," a third voice said, freezing my breathing and making my heart race. I leaned in closer to the prince, as though he could somehow make us invisible. The prince looked at me, and I'm sure that he saw a very pale face looking back at him. He knew the voice as well.

"Of course, General."

"Let's go, there is much more to do still. I need to update the king," my father said, and the riders took off in a gallop,

We stayed down until we could no longer hear the hooves, then the prince stood. "Do you think that means we chose the correct cave," he asked.

I shrugged, still a bit on edge. "I don't know. What do you think they meant that none of 'them have come through'?"

It was the prince's turn to shrug. "I'm not sure. Perhaps the cave has an entrance on the other side, and some spies or something have been coming through."

"Spies?"

"Well, yes, it's possible. I heard whispers a few years ago of the mountain people from the north possibly interested in an invasion."

I was taken aback by this. "I had no idea. My father often speaks of the going on's in the kingdom, but I don't recall him mentioning this."

The prince shook his head. "No, I would hope not. I should not have even known, nor would have, had it not been for my eavesdropping. I like to know things. I haven't heard mention of it in years though."

I looked around. "How far do you suppose it is to the cave?"

"Not far," the prince answered, readjusting his tuck and beginning to walk again.

I followed, a bit nervous that there were possibly some in the woods whom were a source of concern for my father and his men. But, more than nervous, I was excited at the prospect of an adventure. And so we walked on for another few moments, both of us seemingly enjoying the sounds of the forest. We saw the entrance to the cave, but posted outside were two of my fathers men.

"Bugger," I whispered as we crouched down in the trees, out of sight of the guards.

"I've got an idea," the prince whispered back, "and when they leave, run in, I'll be right behind you."

I hadn't been looking at the prince, and now when I turned to ask him what his plan was, he was gone. He must have moved not only quickly, but silently as I did not hear any sound from him. A moment later, the guards must have heard something, because they both turned and put their hands on the hilts of their swords. Then, they headed off, away from the entrance to investigate the sound. As soon as I felt they had gone far enough and I could barely see their backs, I ran into the cave.

The cave was well enough lit from the sun, openings in the roof far above letting in beams of light. But, there were still enough shadows, and so I ducked down into a space behind a large stone, hidden in the darkness. My mind began racing again, doubt and anxiety creeping back into it. What if they had found the prince, and were this very moment taking him back to the palace? What if I had somehow missed him, and he was already further on, waiting for me? What if I had gone too far, and he waited closer to the entrance for me? Oh, gods, what if he had indeed been caught and taken back to the castle? I had no idea how to get back, and the prospect of spending the night in a cave, or lost in the woods, without supplies was now pushing me further into a panic. I could feel my pulse racing, hear it thumping loudly in my ears in the silence of the cave.

A second later, the prince came into view. "Rorthan," he called quietly, passing the spot where I hid. I practically ran out of the shadow. I could've hugged him from relief, though I thought that one doesn't just run up and hug a prince. Not wanting to embarrass myself, I just said "here."

He turned, a bit surprised by my appearance. "I didn't even see you," he said. "The guards will be back, so I'm hoping that there is, in fact, another entrance. Because now that we've come in, I realize I'm not sure how we'll be able to sneak back out past the guards. Entering was the easy part, getting out again may be significantly more difficult."

I looked at him dumbly, panic again rising in me. It must have shown clearly, even in the relative darkness of the cave, because he just smiled at me. "You're with the prince," he said reassuringly, "and if we can't think of a way to sneak out, well then, I suppose we will just have to allow ourselves to be discovered. My father will likely complain, but I will take full blame and you'll be fine."

"I'm not so sure of that," I answered back, "my father will do more than complain, I'm sure of it."

"Well then, let us make sure that we do not get caught," he said, glancing back. He turned once more and faced the depth of the cave. The path seemed quite straight for a while, though in the distance it either turned, or the light ran out. "Forward, then, Rorthan. Let us have an adventure.

***

As we got closer to the darkness, and the light behind us began to fade ominously, I looked back. The entrance looked like the point of a seamstress needle in the distance. I stopped walking. I could hear no sounds coming from the entrance, but I whispered just the same.

"What are we going to do for light?".

The prince patted his tuck gently. "I have a torch," he whispered back. "But," he added quickly, "I don't want to light it until it is absolutely necessary. If the guards have returned, and happen to venture in just a few steps, they will undoubtedly see it. Let's get to the darkness first."

I nodded, though whether he could see me do so in the waning light, I was not sure. We continued walking in silence for a few moments more. The air was becoming heavy, thick and damp. Breathing was still easy, but it made the light sweat that I had worked up on the journey here become heavy. I could feel it running down my forehead, the back of my neck, I could feel the armpits of my underclothes soaked in sweat, and I'm sure even my tunic at this point was showing signs of wetness. Thankfully, the darkness would hide the sight of it, and mayhaps the damp scent of mildew in the cave would cover any odor that was surely developing. I found myself longing for the scents that the prince had access to, wishing that I could afford such luxuries.

"Slow, now," the prince's voice snapped me out of my self conscious thoughts. He grabbed my wrist, and felt along the cave wall. This made my pulse race, and my hands tremble I knew, but if he noticed, he did not speak it outloud. "A little further, and we will light the torch."

We reached a bend in the path, and he stopped, releasing my hand. "One second," he said, as I heard him rustling through his tuck. A moment later, there was a spark, and the torch came to life. "There," he said.

We both had to shield our eyes, as the darkness was penetrated by the bright flames. After a moment, I lowered my hand, and looked around. The cave was wide enough to allow at least four grown men to walk side by side. The walls were a dark grey, almost black, with lines of rust color running through them. Moss grew in patches over the walls, and along the edges of the path, though it looked as if the ground had been walked on enough that it had been worn off most of the way. I reached out and touched the stone of the wall, it was almost slimy, and as I ran my fingers over the veins, my fingertips turned a dark orange with rust. Without thinking I wiped my hand on my tunic. The path in front of us lit up as he held the torch above his head, and I could see that not ten feet in front of us, it sharply turned again. I now wondered if we would come to different paths, if it was a maze, and we would be lost.

"A simple enough path," he said, as if reading my thoughts. Somehow, it always seemed as though he knew what I was thinking. While I typically do not like to be read so easily, something about his ability to do so put me at ease, almost giving me a small thrill.

"Yes, and hopefully it will stay as such," I said simply. Then, my thought came out without my permission. "What is it you hope to find here?"

He looked at me sideways in the torch light. "Why, an adventure, of course. What more do you desire?"

I hadn't really thought about what the purpose of our journey here was, I had simply enjoyed spending time with the prince. "I hadn't thought about it, if I'm being honest," I said.

"Then, why did you come," he asked, not harshly, simply curiously.

I thought about how to answer. 'Because I wanted to spend time with you' seemed like a ruddy lame answer, and 'to get a break from my routine' seemed its equal. "I guess I wanted to do something different, and I did not want to turn down your invitation," I decided was the most accurate way to put it, without sounding like a complete git.

"Ah, yes," he said, "back to not being able to turn down the opportunity to spend time with a prince." I felt myself flush, thankfully easily unseen by him here in the cave. But, he had a slight smile, and I guessed he was jesting with me again.

I smiled as well, easily, naturally. "Of course not, one does not turn down the offer of a day with the prince," I returned his chide.

"Well, then, let's adventure."

6

We walked on quietly through the wide halls of the cave for another twenty minutes. The air, while still damp, had gotten significantly cooler, and there was a freshness to it. There also seemed to be a breeze gently blowing.

"Is it my imagination," I asked, breaking our silence, "or is there a breeze?".

The prince shook his head. "No, it is not your imagination," he said, stopping. He nodded at the torch he held in his still hand. The flame rose, but not straight. They blew softly back towards us. "We are headed to an opening of some kind, and the breeze has been increasing for at least ten minutes."

I hadn't noticed it before now, and I was a bit surprised that the prince had. "This is the first time I have noticed."

The prince nodded, "I assumed, but I had been a bit nervous about how far we had walked, and was concerned that maybe we were walking into a dead end and would have to turn back to face the guards," he admitted.

This made me smile. The prince had seemed as though nothing made him nervous, yet, here he was, openly admitting that such was not the case at all. I felt better knowing that I was not the only one that was growing concerned, though I felt as if he was no longer nervous with the breeze now blowing steady, albeit still gentle. I, however, was as anxious as I was at any point so far in our adventure.

The rust color veins that had run through the rock had now slowly changed to more of a grey color. I paused and rubbed my hand along the stone. "Silver," I asked, not sure if I expected a response, or if the prince would even know.

"No, not silver. If you notice when the air was heavy and particularly damp, the veins were a rust color. Now, however, they have turned silver in the lighter, drier, air. Notice, the stone doesn't have the same moss on it, and," he grabbed my hand, not forcefully, but firmly, "notice it's not wet to the touch." He rubbed my hand across the vein. "Iron."

A small shiver ran over me at the prince's touch, and my pulse quickened just slightly. "Are you cold," he asked.

"No, the breeze is just cool, and my clothes are damp is all," I said. In truth, I was still quite warm despite the cool breeze, and I wasn't entirely sure why the prince's touch had affected me. Probably because I was already on edge, anxious. I was sure that was it.

We continued on. "So, is this the first cave you've explored," I asked, tired of walking in relative silence.

He shrugged. "Mostly. I've gone into a few, but they typically end soon after you enter, some have one or two curves, and then a wall. Others," he said, dramatically lowering his voice, as if someone could hear us, "have wolves."

"Wolves?"

"Yes," he confirmed, "wolves. I entered one a couple of moons back. I was not really expecting anything in the caves, had not even considered the possibility in fact. I walked along, and then when the path turned, I came face-to-face with a mother and her cubs. The wall curved behind them, and they had been resting in the dead end."

I didn't like the idea of facing wolves. "And," my anxiety now going even higher, I swallowed, "how did you get out?"

The prince smiled, a proud and bold smile. "Well," he started, but stopped as we turned another bend. We both stopped in our tracks. The cave had opened into a vast expanse in front of us. There were openings in the ceiling of the cave, though they were as high above us as the castle was tall. Some soft light filtered down through the holes in the ceiling, and it was bright enough to see without the torch. The edge of the ground in front of us fell off sharply in all points except one. The path continued straight ahead of us at that one point, wide enough for the two of us to walk side by side. Probably. It also branched off to the left, wider still.

Straight, however, led down, and while it looked as though it would be easy enough to navigate, there were no stairs. And, down was not lit. Down was dark, undoubtedly damp, and not appealing at all.

The path to the left seemed to go around the vast drop off that lay in front of us. The gap between where the ground fell away, and where we could see the other edge, dimly lit in the light from above, was mayhaps fifty feet. Across, what was visible in the dim light was beautiful to me. There appeared to be some small green plant life, probably growing up from soil that had washed down through the openings above. And it was wide open, vast, and well enough lit for now. The breeze we had felt blew even stronger now, coming at us from the other side.

I turned, and began to walk towards the left. I had gotten only a few feet before I realized the prince had not done the same. When I turned back to him, he was only visible from the waste up, he had hopped down onto the path below. He was just staring at me. I felt my pulse race again. Was it possible to have a heart pop like a balloon in one's chest? And, if so, did it happen to people of only sixteen? My heart had been beating faster than normal most of the day, and it kept spiking to a much higher speed far too often for my liking.

"What are you doing," I asked, as if it wasn't obvious.

"Adventuring," he said, smiling a bit.

And so down we went. The light that had been filtering in from above was quickly gone. The torch lit the way once again, and we followed the way down for a few minutes. It was easy enough to traverse, though it kept winding back and forth, and it seemed to get steeper with each switchback. At the end of the final switchback, forward, or at least what I thought was forward from where we had stood above, was no longer an option. The path ended into a solid wall. To the right, we may have been able to squeeze through the cracks in the wall, though for how long we could do so I was not sure. The prince must have agreed with my thoughts.

"Let's go left," he said, gesturing with the torch, "right is far too cramped for me to take it when given another choice."

"We could head back, surely the day is getting along, and we have a bit of a return hike yet," I said, hopefully not allowing my trepidation at continuing to show through.

"So it is, and so we do," he answered. "But, I think just a little while longer, I want to see what becomes of this cave." He paused for just a second and added, "Now that we have gotten this far, if we do indeed have to turn back, we should return here again. Our familiarity will make it faster next time getting to this point, and I am very much interested in this place. I find it beautiful."

I nodded, he was the prince after all, and it wasn't my place to tell him what we would or would not do while here. I would find some excuse not to return to this place, because, despite his apparent love of it, and though it was beautiful, one trip was more than enough for me. "It is unique," was all I said in response.

And so we went off down the most open pathway. There were a few more moments of twists and turns, in the torch light every turn had me hoping it was a dead end and we would be forced to turn back, yet, everytime, there was a plenty wide opening for us to continue. Suddenly, the prince, who had been walking a few feet in front of me, rounded a turn, disappeared from sight, and gasped.

I raced forward, despite only being slightly behind him, and despite the sudden pounding of my heart in my ears again. I bumped into him, and I too gasped.

In front of us, the path opened up wide. I could barely see any other walls than the one that we stood next to. Before us, there were spikes of stone shooting up from the floor of the cave. Wet, and slimy looking, they grew in all different heights and sizes. Some were only as tall as our knees, others grew to be three or four times taller than us. They varied in circumference, some being barely as round as my arm, others were as big around as my body, or even larger I guessed, though the light only shone so far.

"Gods, it's beautiful," the prince said, with wonder in his eyes.

This time, I actually had to agree. I had never seen anything like this in my entire life. The boring stone of the cave, the never ending twists and turns of darkened pathways, was gone. We stood in a field of stone pillars. The colors that blended through the formations were shades of reds, oranges, and some deep black. They were absolutely stunning to behold. "It is, indeed," was all I managed to say.

We looked up, and on the ceiling above we could just make out matching formations growing down towards us.

We slowly explored the floor, touching the formations, gently so as not to damage them. We now stood in the middle of the expanse that, from above, stopped our progress. Neither of us could have known that this world existed down here. It had simply looked dark, and scary.

"What do you suppose they are made of," I asked, breaking our awed silence.

He looked up at the expanse, light could be seen coming through the ceiling far above, but it seemed to die before it filtered down to where we stood. "I believe," he began, "that the water drips down, and mixes with the minerals that are in the floor. I would imagine, the water dripping down brings minerals with it as well."

I must have looked impressed, because he quickly looked at his feet. "I don't know that myself," he said, almost ashamed, "I read it in some of the meister's books."

I put a hand on his arm. "Then I'm sure that is what it is. And," I added, crouching down just a bit so I would catch his eye, "books are a wonderful way of learning things."

He smiled just a bit at this, and looked at me for a moment. His expression was impossible for me to read, I couldn't tell if it was happiness, sadness, or a mixture. His smile looked both pained, and happy. As if he'd had some sad revelation at my words. "We should turn back," he said suddenly, his expression changing immediately.

We had found our way near the middle of the expanse, and looking up, the light that was in the distance of the cave ceiling was dimmer, and held an orange tint. "Evening," I said, pointing to the light.

"Bugger," he said, "we've lingered too long. You were right, we should have turned back."

I looked at him, and then around the cave. "And have missed all of this," I asked. "I would rather be late home, and face questions, than have missed this amazing scene."

The prince smiled again, and this time I only saw happiness. "I'm glad you like it," he said. "I, too, find it to be remarkable. I love this place, and am so very happy that we found it together. We must return, earlier next time," he paused, and a smile crept onto his face. "I wonder if we could possibly find some excuse to have an entire day here, and maybe camp out for a night."

The idea thrilled me, and scared me. I couldn't fathom how I would sneak away for an entire night. But, the idea of spending an entire day with the prince exploring this place, and spending a night in it's quiet majesty, was one I would try to find some way to make a reality.

I had no way of knowing that within that moment, our lives would change forever. Nor could I have known that we would never come to this place together again.

7

The soft, steady breeze that we had grown accustomed to had become much stronger, and was almost a full wind now. The prince and I both looked up to the slits in the distance of the ceiling.

"Do you think there is a storm," the prince asked.

The light that could be seen coming through was still orange, though it was getting more dull as the evening progressed closer to night. I shook my head, "I don't think so, the light is still coming through, so I doubt there are clouds out there." I was almost yelling now to be heard above the wind. Then, it all happened at once.

The wind howled, I could hear nothing over the sound of it. The torch suddenly was blown out. Before my mind could process that, the entire cave was illuminated with a bright, blinding light. The light came in flashes, almost pulsing. I could see the prince in the flashes, but only his outline, the light made it almost impossible to keep my eyes open long enough to adjust.

Then, there was a loud crack. Suddenly, it occurred to me that the light seemed to be lightning, and the thunder had just come. I had no time to think of how that could be possible inside of a cave.

"Gods, what was that," the prince asked, his voice, to my comfort, was still close to my side.

I reached out, and brushed his arm with my hand. I grabbed a hold, as I answered, "I do not know, but I think it was-".

I was interrupted by a rumbling, low and deep. Not like the thunder, this seemed to come from the earth itself. The prince pulled from my grip, and I could see a spark, followed by another. What on earth is he doing, I began to wonder, my mind still fuzzy. But then the torch whooshed to life.

His face seemed ashen, even in the orange glow of the light. "We need to go, now," he said, even as the floor began vibrating even more. It was becoming difficult to stand.

The prince grabbed my hand, and pulled me back in the direction from which we had come. As he did, something crashed into the ground right where I had been standing. "What was that," I yelled out as we were now running to the pathway. I looked up and saw that the formations on the ceiling, that we had been admiring only moments ago, were crashing down with the shaking of the cave.

The prince pulled me harder, and I lost my footing. I fell, and his hand released from mine. He stopped and turned back to help me. "Go," I yelled, getting to my feet. He didn't listen. He should have listened. Why didn't he listen? He was only feet in front of me, but those feet were all of the difference that was needed when it happened.

One of the formations crashed down, directly where the prince stood. I jumped back, losing my footing again, and landed on my arse. I saw one of the spikes falling directly at me, and I rolled to my side as it crashed down in the spot where I had just laid. Something struck the back of my head, and my world went black.

***

Waking was still like a dream. I was in pain. My head pounded, my body ached, I could taste blood, and though I believe I had my eyes open, I could see nothing. I felt myself pushing up onto my hands and knees. I shook my head, still no sight came. My ears hummed, but I could hear nothing else. I tried to call out, to say anything, but I don't know if the sound came out or not. I still heard only humming in my ears. I shook my head again. This time I saw light. What little sight I had was blurry, but there was bright light in the distance and it seemed to be getting closer, bobbing along as it did. I collapsed again.

***

My eyes fluttered, and I moaned. My head was pounding, and I could still taste blood in my mouth. But now I could see, not as well as I would like, but see none the less. And, I could hear.

"This one is coming to," I heard a voice say in a strange accent, and he shone a bright, pure white, light into my eyes from whatever torch he had been pointing across from me.

I felt a foot to my back as I attempted to rise. "Stay down," a second voice said. The voice to whom the foot belonged, I assumed.

The light shone back over towards...the prince. He wasn't crushed, though I could see blood and it looked like he had been stabbed by one of the stone spikes.

"Hey," the first voice came back, "this one is the prince I think."

The second man removed his foot from my back, and walked over to the prince, adding his bright light. What kind of light was this? There was no flame. There was no heat, at least none that I had felt when it was right in front of me. It was white, pure white, not orange like fire. My curiosity at the light however, faded when the second man spoke.

"Take him. The father may be able to use him. At the very least, he will want to question him". He looked towards me. "Kill this one," he said before turning on his heel, and walking briskly towards the far end of the cave.

A brief moment of disappointment struck me at the thought that we had not gotten to explore that far into the cave. The first man came back towards me, pointing something at me. The closest thing that I could compare it to was a crossbow. But it was much smaller. And it didn't appear to be made of wood, or steel. I don't know what it was made of, but it was dull black in the light. I looked behind him at the prince. He had come to, and his eyes were wide.

"No," he shouted.

The man spun, and I jumped at him. I had forgotten my pain, any injuries that I had were gone in that moment. I leaped onto the man's back. He spun, shrugging me off. I landed on top of the prince, and he pointed the thing in his hand at me again. My hand touched something in the prince's waist band. His blade. I grabbed it, and lunged towards the man, feeling the blade bite into his arm.

"Fuck," he yelled out, pushing me back down on the prince again.

The object in his hand flashed, and there was a loud crack. The prince screamed out in pain, and I again lunged at the man. This time, the blade caught the inside of his leg and stuck there. He dropped both the object and the light, using his

hands to grip his thigh. I grabbed the thing he had
held, and pointed it at him.

"No," he yelled, and raised his hands up
over his face.

The object felt strange in my hand. Not
particularly heavy, but it didn't feel like any
material that I had ever held. "What is this," I
asked, still pointing it at him, but waving it around
slightly.

He looked at me as if I was somehow
strange for asking. "It's a goddamn gun, what does
it look like?"

I didn't know the word. And I didn't like
his tone. He must have realized I was confused, and
it probably registered in his mind that I didn't know
how to use this 'gun'. He lunged. I had seen
crossbows at the castle that were released with the
pull of a trigger. This was no crossbow, and what
hit the prince had been no bolt. I squeezed the
trigger just the same. It jumped in my hand, and the
crack that had sounded before rang again. The man
didn't scream, he just crumpled to the ground. I
approached him, still pointing the gun at him. He
had a hole above his left eye, and the back of his
head was broken open. How had this gun done
that? I looked towards where the other man had
walked, but there was no light to indicate he was
returning. I dropped the gun. I looked back at the

man's mangled head. Is that what had happened to the prince? Oh, gods, the prince.

I spun. "Tomren," I cried out, and ran to him. I looked at his head, but he only smiled weakly at me.

"My shoulder," he said. This was the first time that I had a chance to really look at the prince. "My leg," he muttered.

His shoulder was impaled by one of the spires on the cave floor, the stone sticking a few inches out of his body. I looked to his leg. There was blood on his trousers, and the spot was growing larger. I quickly removed my shirt, and ripped off the sleeve. I tied it tightly around his leg, as I had seen men do to wounds. The prince groaned, but said nothing. I looked at his shoulder. "I'll have to lift you," I said, "I'll have to lift you off of the stone."

The prince smiled, "You don't look like you are up to lifting much of anything, and," he said, his smile growing and his voice lifting just a bit, "you called me Tomren."

I blinked. "What? When? What does that matter," I asked, all at once.

He continued to smile, though his pain was showing clearly. "Just now, you called me Tomren. After that man had...done whatever it is that that 'gun' does, to me, you called me Tomren."

I was still in shock that this was somehow relevant to him. But, his reminder of the gun and the man spurred me on. "We need to get you up, and we need to get out of here, before the other man returns."

The prince nodded. "Okay, I'll help you as much as I can."

I positioned myself above his head, and carefully, slowly, began to raise his body off of the spike. He tried to help, but he was in a far too awkward position to be of much assistance. I finally managed to get his shoulder free. He moaned loudly in pain, and I'm not sure how he didn't scream. I set him down as gently as I could. I went over and grabbed the lantern that the dead man had dropped. This too was made of the same strange material. And it did not burn. It simply was...light. As if the brightest star in the sky had been harnessed by this thing. "What is it," I muttered.

"Is it hot," the prince asked.

I shook my head. "No, it is not. It's just bright."

The prince smiled. "Good, then you can use that, as my torch is under the stone somewhere," he said, gesturing around the cave. "I will try to walk, but you will have to help me."

I walked back over, and picked up the gun. With the light in my left hand, and the gun in my

right, I supported the prince on my left shoulder.
We slowly made our way back towards the entrance
of the cave.

8

It was an extremely slow process going back through the cave. I was fairly strong from my training, but I had just been knocked unconscious, and the prince could barely walk. His bleeding was slowed thanks to my wrappings, but he was in pain, and still losing blood. We had made it about half way back to the entrance when he collapsed, pulling me down with him.

"I can't go anymore," he said through short breaths.

I tried to lift him again. "We have to go on, you need a meister."

He shook his head. "You have to leave me," he said, his voice seeming even weaker since his last sentence. His eyes closed.

"Tomren," I said, shaking him. His eyes opened barely, and he smiled.

"You did it again."

I flushed, this time knowing what he meant. Why, how, could he think about what I called him, as we were fighting for our lives? "Yes," I said, "now get up."

He grunted in pain as I lifted him, but we managed to again get on our feet. "We need to make haste," I said, knowing full well that we had no actual way of doing that.

He laughed at my words, and then moaned from the pain it brought him. "Don't make me laugh," he said with a small smile that I could hear more than see.

I started to respond, but I realized that we had reached a point on the way to the entrance that did not seem familiar. "Did we get turned around," I asked, looking about the hallway that we found ourselves in. I didn't remember any branches in the way we came, it was all one pathway. Yet, there was an opening on our right, and a bit further down at the end of where our light reached, there was another.

The prince looked around as well. His mouth opened, but he stopped as we heard voices. They were too far to hear what was being said, but they were growing louder. "Bugger," he finally said.

"Hold on," I said, as I guided us to the opening beside us. The prince moaned as we moved, and we both froze when the voices stopped. Footsteps could be heard coming our way, and I pushed him deeper down the path. "Quiet," I hissed.

We had gone a fair way down the corridor when I finally had to stop. I dropped the light and the gun as quietly as I could, and lowered the prince to the ground as gently as possible. "The light," he whispered, "extinguish it."

I looked dumbly at the stick in my hand. "I don't know how," I realized and vocalized simultaneously.

The footsteps were getting closer, and there was no doubt in my mind, and certainly in his, that if we did not extinguish the light now, they would see it and be upon us soon. I removed my shirt, one sleeve already missing from tearing it to bandage the prince, and wrapped the light in it as best I could. I could still see a faint glow, but I doubted that anyone from a distance would be able to see it, especially if they too had lights.

As if to confirm my thoughts, lights soon danced from the way we came. Then, they stopped steady. The prince put a hand on my arm, and my pulse jumped. How, when my heart was already racing, I do not know. I didn't have time to think about it. The lights slowly began to get brighter, though still very dim, and the footsteps closer. They had come down the same corridor that we had chosen. Their voices were hushed, and I could only hear the indistinct murmur of them. I slipped the shirt wrapped light behind the prince, hoping that any glow would be eliminated under him. I felt beside me, and found the gun. I pointed it in the direction of the voices.

Fear gripped at me as I prepared to again kill, this time knowing what I was doing would take their lives. It was easier to kill when I didn't know that I'd be killing. This was different. And having time to think about it only made it harder. I'm not a killer. I'm only a young one, for the sake of the gods. My hand trembled in the darkness. The only thing my eyes could see was the faint light at the end of the corridor.

"There's nothing there," a man's voice said.

"I heard voices," said a powerful, but clearly female, voice.

"Yeah, me too," the first voice answered. "But, they probably went back towards the beacon."

Silence. It felt like hours. In reality, it was probably only a few breaths. "The Brotherhood are not ones to turn back," the female said.

"Still, this path is dark and silent," the man argued, "other than us, of course."

The woman grunted, and based on their receding footsteps, it was a grunt of acquiescence. The light disappeared and only the faint glow from behind the prince was visible.

"Let's go," I said, removing the light from behind him, and lifting him up again. This time, he made no sound as I lifted him.

"It's cold in here," he said, barely audible.

I looked at him. He was as pale as snow, and though some of that may have been the light, he was burning up to the touch.

"You have a fever," I said, quickening our pace. "We need to get you back to the castle now."

I took a second to think about that. Even when we left the cave, the walk back would take hours in our condition. And, it was dark now. Beside the fact that I knew not the way back, at least not for sure, there would be wolves. And gods knew what else.

"Our fathers are going to be furious," he said with a chuckle.

Great. Something else for me to have to think about. I had no time to focus on anything other than putting one foot in front of the other. "Let's just worry about getting to the castle," I said.

We walked the rest of the way in silence, other than the shuffle of our feet, and the occasional soft groan from the prince. Finally, we rounded the last turn, and could see the moonlight creeping through the entrance of the cave. It felt like it had been days that we had been in this cursed cave.

I wrapped the light in my shirt again, unsure if there would be one of this 'brotherhood' that had tried to kill us, well kill me, already once today. Suddenly, there was light from behind us. And footsteps running. I whirled around. I hadn't heard the footsteps until now. Nor had I seen the light, until I dimmed our own.

"Stop," the woman's voice rang out.

I dropped the shirt wrapped light, and the corridor flashed to brightness. For a second, the two people behind us were taken off guard. I

reached for the gun, and pointed it at them. I didn't
think, I just pulled the trigger. The weapon went off
with a familiar crack. The man dove for the wall to
their right, and the woman for the wall to the left. I
pulled the trigger again, pointing it at the man after
a second's hesitation. The stone around him seemed
to explode, and he grunted. I pivoted to point at the
woman, and pulled the trigger. The stone didn't
explode this time. There was a thud, and she
collapsed to the floor. I pointed back towards the
man. This time, he had a gun in his hand.

"No," I heard a voice behind me yell.

I had no time to process the voice. To think
about the fact that it was not a stranger's voice. I
spun and pulled the trigger. Everything happened at
once

Crack.
Recognition of the man's face to me.
Shock in his eyes.
Him collapsing with a thud.
The room spinning.
Darkness.

9

I awoke with a start. I was in a large bed, and the room that I was in was massive. Or massive at least in comparison to what I was used to. My mouth felt dry, and I ached all over. I had no idea where I was, or how I got there, but the air smelled sweet, and the bed was soft. I started to drift back into sleep. And then it came back. All at once. The cave, the prince, the gun. My father. The prince. Gods, the prince!

I jumped out of the bed, and ran to the door. My body tried to protest, but I did not pay it any mind. I also failed to notice that I was dressed only in a plain tunic, made of rather light material.

"Tomren," I called out as I opened the door to the room and burst into the hallway outside. I now realized that I was in the castle, and the light was bright through the windows.

"Tomren," I repeated.

Guards came around the corner of the hallway, as well as a meister. "You should be resting," the meister said, putting a hand on my arm as soon as he reached me, guiding me back into the room. Though he was gray haired, he was a bit younger than I would expect a meister to be.

"Where is Tomren," I asked, weakly attempting to shrug off his hand. The man was stronger than I would have expected, or I just was even weaker than a boy my age would normally be. His hand did not budge.

"The prince," he said, accentuating the title, "is recovering in his chambers. Much as you should be."

When he had returned me to the bed, he fetched an ornate, silver scrolled mazer of cool water. It had ornate silver scrolling. I barely noticed it's beauty though as I greedily drank the refreshing liquid. My throat, I realized for the first time, had been screaming at me to drink.

"We cannot have you wandering the castle as you heal," the meister said, as I handed him back the bowl.

"I'm a prisoner," I asked, surprised.

"You are a guest," the meister replied. "A guest whom we must keep safe. You shot a member of the King's Men. Not everyone here wishes to see you recover."

"I shot a-", I started to ask the question, but then I remembered the woman I had shot. And my father. "Gods," I muttered.

The meister looked at me. He must have thought my lack of speaking to indicate a fear of those who did not wish to see me recover. "You are safe here, with the guards," he said, gesturing to the door. "The king has ordered that you not be touched, so if anyone dares to harm you, or try to harm you, it will cost them their lives."

I nodded. I didn't feel like explaining anything, especially with my head still aching and foggy. "My father," I asked, unable to look at him as I asked.

"Alive," the meister said. "He will be fine. You are not exactly a marksman."

"A marksman," I repeated, confused.

"Your accuracy with the gun was not exactly precise," he clarified.

I nodded as if that made sense. I was about to question him further when there was a knock on the door, and one of the guards came immediately in.

"The king has requested the boy's presence in the prince's chambers."

The meister nodded, and turned to me. "There are appropriate garments in the wardrobe," he said, pointing to the dresser. "Do you need assistance to dress?".

I simply shook my head, and he turned. "The guard will escort you when you are dressed. Don't dawdle."

When he closed the door, I walked to the wardrobe. It was fully stocked with clothes that looked to be about the correct size. I picked out a basic looking outfit, or at least as basic of one as there was, and dressed. It was a slow process, and every part of me ached. I saw no looking glass, so I just hoped that I was presentable, and opened the door.

A guard stood on either side of the door, and when they heard it open, they turned to me. "This way," one said, and began walking.

I followed him, and the other guard followed me. They did not want me running it would seem, as if I had somewhere to go inside the castle.

The walk lasted only a moment. The room that I was in was less than a minute away from the prince's chambers. The guard knocked. When the door opened, I was ushered in, and the guards took up their post just outside of the doors as they had at my room.

Inside, the king stood next to the prince, who was sitting in a chair near the window. My father stood in front of them, his face in a scowl. His arm was in a sling, and he had bandages wrapping up his shoulder. So, one doesn't always die when the gun is used. That explains the meister's talk of accuracy.

I approached the king and the prince, and kneeled. "Your Majesty," I said, looking at the king. "Your Highness," I said, with a look at the prince. His color had returned, though he too wore his arm in a sling. I noticed a walking stick next to his chair, and I wondered how his leg was healing.

"Rise," the king commanded.

I stood, and the king studied me for a moment. "How do you feel," he asked, and genuine concern seemed to show on his face.

"I am well, Your Majesty," I responded, quickly adding, "thank you."

"That is good to hear. I want to know what happened. All of it. From the beginning. I have already asked my son," he said with a glance at the prince, "but I would like to hear it from you as well."

"Of course, Your Majesty. I suppose it started-"

"Rorthan," the king said, causing both myself and my father to straighten. "Young Rorthan," he adjusted, "you do not have to address me as Majesty every time that you speak. Also," he smiled, "please sit, I know you have been injured." He gestured to a chair in front of him. I sat, and glanced at my father.

This seemed to make my father's expression sour even more. "Would you like some food?"

My father's face somehow got even more twisted, and I was certain that he reddened just a bit. Why was he so upset that the king was being polite to me?

"Mayhaps just something to drink, sire," I answered, bowing my head slightly.

"Beltoch," the king said, and a man that I had not even noticed in the far corner of the room approached. "Please get our young friend some refreshments."

Beltoch was a few years younger than my father I guessed, and his full head of short, dark black hair had only a very small spattering of gray mixed in. He wore his beard tight to his face, but full. His eyes were a bright amber color that reminded me of the honey served here at the castle. The skin on his hands was soft, but their wrinkles showed his age. His robes were a rich, dark blue, and they seemed to glisten in the light. He nodded, and left the room.

"Now," the king said with a gentle smile, "please, continue."

I nodded, and looked at the prince. Had the boy been honest with his father? I did not want to cause trouble by revealing details that the prince may have left out. I also did not want to lie to the king. The prince's expression was steady, and I decided on the truth.

"One day, after training," I began, "I went to the gardens instead of going straight home." I glanced at my father, and regretted it immediately. He was full on glaring at me now. My training would be doubled for sure.

"I had sat on one of the benches," I continued, "and relaxed to the point that I began to nap." I knew I had reddened as I admitted that, but there was much story still to tell and I steadied myself.

"The prince found me there, and as I tripped over my words, he politely calmed me." I spared a glance to the prince and he smiled, leading me to smile as well. "He offered to take me on an adventure, and I accepted. I met him the next day, and we went into the woods. We distracted the guards at the entrance to the cave, and we went in."

There was a knock at the door, and Beltoch brought in a small platter with cheese, bread, and fruit. Another man brought in a pitcher of water, and a cup. They sat them down on a table, made me a small plate of the food, and poured me a cup of the water. I drank quickly, and then continued.

I told the story to the king, and he occasionally asked a question about what time of day some part was, or how we had done this or that, but for the most part he just listened. His face maintained a polite smile, but as the story progressed the king stood and began to pace the room just a bit.

When I got to the part where I shot my father, I apologized. "I should never have went with the prince, Your Majesty. I should have," I thought about how to word it for only a second, "I should have suggested that we stay at the castle, and explore here."

I was surprised when the king looked at me for a moment, and then waved his hand. "Nonsense," he said. "It is not your place to question the prince, nor to tell him what to do." His words were not unkind, and though I bristled just the same, I nodded.

"You," he said, his smile growing, "saved my son. For that I am grateful. However," he paused, and his smile vanished, "you also shot Sabina. And," his tone darkened, "she may yet die."

I felt my face burn. "I thought that it was the same people that had earlier said to take the prince and kill me."

"Yes, and, that is why you yet live," the king said thoughtfully, "indeed, it is why my men will not harm you. But, there must be some recompense. I have thought much on what would be appropriate, as well as what would please those that serve with Sabina," he paused. "And, I fear I have more still to think on. I assure you, whatever I decide it will be fair and merciful. You have my eternal thanks for saving my son, the heir to my throne."

"And, is that not enough," the prince spoke up for the first time. "Is saving my life, not enough to pay for a...misunderstanding?"

My father grunted, and also spoke. "He shot at me. He shot one of my soldiers. He shot a King's Man."

I was shocked. I felt tears bite at the corners of my eyes, but I refused to allow them. This was my father. How could he not support me? How could the king seemingly be more understanding and compassionate than my own father?

"Yes, so we've mentioned," the king said. "And yet, he did so unintentionally. And his actions earlier in the day undoubtedly saved my son's life."

"Your son's life would not have been in danger if not for him," my father argued, pointing at me.

I reddened and this time tears did form in my eyes. Not at my father's lack of concern for me. Gods damn him for all I care. No, my tears were for my own feelings. Because, though his words were a shit thing to say about one's own child, I felt that they were correct. I had endangered the prince. I had not prevented the danger to him, I had instead assisted it. I nodded, both to my thoughts, and to the facts that my father presented.

The king walked over and put his hand on my shoulder. Gods, the king put his hand on my shoulder. The king was comforting me.

"The boy could not have changed my son's mind," the king echoed his earlier statements. "If your son had not joined him on this...adventure...my son may very well have been taken by the Brotherhood, or worse."

"He is no son of mine," my father said, and before he could say anything further, the king held up a hand. My father closed his mouth.

"Control yourself, Rorthan," the king said a few octaves higher than he had been speaking, and with as much edge as I had ever heard a man have in their voice. "Do not speak of that again. You, and your soldiers, these so-called 'King's Men' that you are so proud of, did not protect my son. None of you knew where he was, or that he had even left the damned castle. The guards that you had posted outside of the cave were tricked by a child, and left the way open for our sons to be in danger."

He looked at the prince, and then at me. "Perhaps," he said, his voice lowering back to normal, but maintaining the edge, and his gaze turning coldly to my father, "you and your men are the ones that need to pay recompense."

My father reddened, whether from embarrassment or anger I was not sure. That was the first time that I could remember seeing him so disarmed. He opened his mouth, as if to speak, but the king again raised a hand and he shut it.

"Leave us, Rorthan," he said. "Your son will stay here, while he recovers under my meister's care, and I will think on how best to handle this situation."

My father bowed his head, and left without so much as a word or a glance in my direction.

When the door closed, the king walked back over and stood beside his son. "I am sorry that your father said those things," he said. "But, you do truly have my gratitude, and I will not forget what you have done for my son."

He smiled at me kindly, and I smiled back weakly. "Thank you, Sire."

"Rest and recover. You will remain under our care, and anything that you have need of, simply speak and the need will be met."

I do not know what came over me, I should have kept my mouth shut, it was not my place to question the king. Yet. "Your Majesty, if I may," I started.

The king nodded, and I continued. "What sort of weapon is a 'gun'? And, who are the 'brotherhood'?"

His smile disappeared. "I am afraid that I cannot tell you more about the gun. You," he said, eyes seeming to burn into mine, "must speak of it to no one ever again on pain of death. Speaking of it is considered treason. I am not angry that you asked, and again, I am grateful for what you did for my son. But speak to no one of the weapon."

I nodded, and held his gaze, waiting for more.

"As for the Brotherhood," he said, "they are a very crazed branch of the Christian church. And they seem to want to do us harm. We ward them off whenever they appear, more often then I would like as of late. While not treason, I would ask you personally to never speak of them with anyone. Your discretion will do much to help us."

I bowed my head. "As you command, Your Majesty."

The king squeezed his son's good shoulder, and kissed his forehead. He walked to me, and put a hand on my shoulder and squeezed it as well. Then he left and the door closed, leaving the prince and I alone.

10

I stood and walked over to the prince. "Your father seems nice," I said, before adding, "and fair."

The prince smiled. "And yours seems," he paused as if searching for the right words, "an areshole."

We both laughed. And then, we both winced in pain. "Indeed," I said, "but, don't make me laugh."

"How do you feel," the prince asked.

"Like I went to war."

The prince smiled again. "We rather did, I'd say. And kicked some arse while at it."

I shook my head. "We were dumb. And I shot an innocent woman, a woman that would have done anything to protect you."

The prince still smiled, though it was smaller and it's tone more comforting than happy. "You shot our pursuers, ones that you had every reason to believe wanted me captured and you dead. There is no fault to be had."

I nodded, though I didn't feel as if his words were accurate. "What kind of weapon was that, that 'gun'? And, those men, the 'Brotherhood', appeared out of nowhere. How?"

The questions spewed from me, and I don't know that I really expected any answers. I suppose I just wanted to put voice to them.

The prince sat up straight. "From what I can tell," he started, "it has something to do with time. Those men were from the future."

"The future," I interrupted with a wry cough of a laugh.

"I know, but our fathers, and some of the soldiers were talking when they thought I was asleep. Somehow they come from the future, there is a time beacon of some sort in that cave. I think that the 'Brotherhood' are bad men, but I don't think that all men from the future are. And, I think we have sent men there as well."

"To the future," I asked, probably a bit sarcastically.

"Yes," the prince answered, not seeming to notice or care. "It seems as though we have been doing it for a while. They knew about 'guns', and much more, from what I could tell. I got the impression that we may even have some such things in our armory, though I've never seen them."

I shook my head. These weren't answers. And, if they were some form of answer, they simply raised more questions. "I don't understand."

"Me either," the prince admitted. He grabbed his walking stick, and started to stand. I rose and walked toward him, but he held up a hand.

"I'm capable," he said. When he stood, he looked at me with a smile. "Well, you are to be our guest for a while. Shall we tour the castle?"

The idea wasn't terrible, and in fact I rather liked it. But, I had so many questions that I wanted answers to. "Yes, that would be splendid, Your Highness."

The prince groaned and rolled his eyes, but did not tell me to call him by his name. Though, I do believe I heard him mumble "it's Tomren" under his breath.

I opened the door, and the guards were gone. "Are they not worried that I'll flee, and become a raider," I asked sarcastically.

The prince laughed, and I saw the wince. I need to stop making him laugh, I thought. But, I loved that I could make him smile and laugh. I seemed to have that ability with no one else.

"I don't think they regard an unarmed child as a danger," he said.

"A child," I said in mock shock. "I'll have you know, I'm a warrior."

"True as that may be," the prince smiled, "you are unarmed, and every guard knows that you are not to leave."

"That I'm a prisoner," I corrected.

The prince stopped walking, and rested on his stick. "Do you feel like a prisoner, Rorthan?"

He never calls me by name. Hell, he never calls me anything. I shook my head. "No, but still, I cannot leave."

The prince nodded, and we continued walking. "Not yet," he said. "Which you should be grateful for. My father will be fair. And in the meantime, you will be tended to by the finest meister's in our kingdom." He stopped again, and looked at me with a smile. I had never seen him smile so much, and the fact that he did so because of me made my pulse quicken. Granted, I didn't spend any real time around him until a few days ago, but still.

I returned his smile. "And I get to spend time exploring the castle with you."

The prince groaned in disappointment.

"I...I don't have to, Your Highness, I can go back to my quarters and stay there," I stammered and stuttered my way through the statement.

The prince shook his head. "I think you misunderstand me, I am quite pleased that we will get to spend time around each other, and I look forward to getting to know you better. However," his face turned into a frown, that came close to being a pout, intentionally over done I was sure, "I have nothing to explore here." He gestured around the castle.

I reddened. Of course I reddened. "I see."

"Do you?"

I nodded. "I do. But," I paused to look him in his bright cerulean eyes, "I have not explored the castle. So, mayhaps, spending time together, while I get to see things for the first time, will give you a new perspective and interest in the place."

He smiled again. "I hadn't thought of that I suppose."

"What is your favorite place?"

"Well, the gardens are nice, and the small wood that is within the castle grounds is nice I suppose. But," he smiled, a bit mischievously, "one of my favorite places is the dungeons."

"The dungeons," I started, "the place where I may very well end up, you mean?"

The prince laughed, a full laugh, "Gods, you really think that that is where you will end up? As a reward for saving me? No, my father will not send you to the dungeons. I will continue to remind him that I am here thanks to you. By the time you have fully recovered, I would be willing to guess that he will actually give you a reward, rather than punishment."

I shrugged. "Very well, then, lead the way." I followed the prince, thinking about what would actually happen at the end of my recovery. When the meisters say that my body was healed, and I no longer felt pain when I laughed, or coughed, or did anything for that matter. I found it hard to believe that I would get rewarded.

***

We walked around the castle, and the looks that I got from everyone made it clear that I was viewed, at best, as a trouble maker. While the king may have believed that I saved his son, the people in the castle seemed more likely to agree with my father. I had been the one to put the prince in danger. The prince seemed not to notice the long glances I was getting, and after a half of an hour or so, I was sick of them.

"I should probably get back to my chambers. I need to rest, or so I was told," I said to the prince.

He stopped and looked at me for a few seconds, and then continued walking the way we had been. Further away from my room. "Ignore them," he said, as if he knew why I wanted to go back to my bed and hide under the most plush blankets I had ever seen.

"I can't. They think that I am, at the very least, a source of danger to you."

"Bugger them," he said, "I am the prince, and my father the king. If we are not concerned by your presence here, they can take their concern and bury it in their arses."

I chuckled, despite my sullen mood. "You really don't care?"

"Why should I," he asked. "I am the prince, and they do not tell me whom I can and cannot spend my time with."

"Well, I'm not a prince, and they certainly can say as they please to me," I grumbled.

"No," he said in a stern tone, "they may not. You are here as a royal guest. If anyone says anything inappropriate to you, or if I hear talk of it, they will find themselves quite unhappy."

I smiled. It was nice to have him come so quickly to my defense, and it made me feel...I'm not sure what exactly. It quickened my pulse, and made me blush just a shade. I had never had a friend really, and I supposed I wasn't used to being treated this way, least of all by the prince.

Finally, we reached a rather quiet, dull corner of the castle. There was a lone guard standing before a very solid, very worn, looking wooden door. I didn't recognize the man, and I thought that I knew most of the guards' faces, if not their names.

"Leofrick," the prince greeted the man, "how are you today?"

The man bowed his head. "I'm very well, Your Highness. Thank you for asking." He paused and looked at me.

"My friend, Rorthan," the prince said, putting his hand on my arm. There went my heart again, speeding up.

I nodded to Leofrick, and he nodded back. "A lovely day to visit the dungeons," the man quipped, his tone sarcastic but not unpleasant.

The prince laughed. "You know me, I love the quiet down there. Our guest has not seen many parts of the castle, and I am giving him a tour."

"No better guide," Leofrick said with a genuine smile. "Though, if I were you, young Rorthan, I would be thanking the gods that we haven't had many prisoners as of late. The more there are, the less," he paused as if searching for the right word, "pleasant, the odor."

The prince chuckled. "Yes, bathing is not exactly a luxury that is afforded to the prisoners. I do not visit when there are more than one or two."

Leofrick slid the bar from in front of the door, and swung it open. The smell of dampness, mildew, and an odor that I could readily identify, were immediately noticeable. The odor wasn't overpowering, and not particularly terrible, though the thought of that smell mixed with the odor of dirty flesh made me shiver.

"It's really perfectly safe down there," Leofrick said, mistaking my shiver for one of fear.

"Indeed," the prince said.

We passed the door, and Leofrick closed it behind us, though thankfully I did not hear the bar slide back in to lock it. There was a lit torch on either side of the hallway, and under each, there were another three unlit torches. The prince took one of them, and lit it.

We walked down the hallway a bit, and I was reminded of our time in the cave. The darkness was broken only by our torch. In front of us the wall curved to the left, and immediately began a spiral stone staircase, heading downward into the dungeon. The prince used his walking stick, and was able to traverse the steps with relative ease, though when we got to the bottom he muttered something about it being more difficult than he remembered.

At the bottom of the stairs, the hallway extended straight. If I hadn't gotten turned around on the stairs, then we were heading back towards the heart of the castle, though I couldn't be sure. There was one dim torch at the foot of the stairs, and one far off in the distance straight ahead.

As we walked, I saw that there were metal gates one each side, about six feet or so apart. The doors were staggered, so that the ones on the right did not look directly across to the ones on the left. The prince stopped at the first gate on our right, and opened it, stepping into the cell.

The cell was not necessarily dirty, but it was little more than an earthen floor, stone walls, and the gate. There were no windows, and I suspected that if not for our torch, there would be no source of light. The torches at either end of the hall would not likely reach into any of the cells.

"The prisoners are left in complete darkness," I half asked, half stated.

The prince nodded in the torch light. "Yes. They see light twice a day. Once, when food and water are brought to them, and once when their latrine pot is taken away."

The idea of having been sent here, of having to be down here, for having shot Sabina, scared me. "I truly hope that you are right, and your father does not send me here," I said, fairly sure that my voice broke just a bit.

The prince put his arm around my shoulder. "I assure you, he will not. Were my father to be of a mind to lock you up at all, you would be in one of the tower cells. These," he said, with a glance around the cell we stood in, "are for the worst of our criminals, and you are not one of them. My father will not have you in a cell though, I give you my word."

He removed his arm from me, and turned. "Come, there is more."

11

When we reached the end of the row of cells, the prince again entered one. This time, he closed the gate behind us. No, this one was not a gate. It was a door, as large and solid looking as the one at the top of the staircase. He shone the light on the wall to our left, and I saw something that looked metal. He walked over to it, and I followed. It was a small disc, no more than two inches in diameter. The image on it was one that I did not recognize. A sun, with a man's face in the center of it. The eyes had a look of horror, and the mouth was open in a silent scream. The prince pushed the disc.

A slow, steady rumble started, and then a section of the wall, about the size of a normal door, sank back. When it stopped moving, the rumble began again, and it slid to the left, opening the way.

"Gods," I said in amazement.

The prince smiled. "I told you the dungeons were my favorite place," he said, disappearing into the doorway.

I followed quickly. I could see little from the light of the torch, but the prince turned and found a matching disc on the wall next to the door. When he pressed it, the wall slid back into place. He turned and led us further into...well, into whatever we were in. I could only see a small

amount of our surroundings, and I had no way to
tell the size of the room. After walking only a few
feet, he stopped and reached out a hand across my
chest to keep me from going any further, which was
good because I hadn't noticed the stairs going down
in front of me. There were only a few, and I could
see the bottom maybe six feet down. He touched
the torch to a small basin of liquid. Soon, the fire
spread. And, spread. It raced down a small channel
in the wall, and far off into the distance, before
turning and racing the other way, and then back up
to us again. Within a matter of seconds, we were
surrounded by light.

I had no words to describe my amazement. I
just stared. And, when I had finally gotten over the
trough of flame that ran around the room, I started
to notice other things. The sheer size was the first
thing that caught my attention. The room was
massive. It must have stretched for at least half of
the castle, if not more. Hundreds of feet off into the
distance, the far wall could be seen illuminated by
the thin line of fire running across it's middle. The
floor was a checkerboard of black basalt tile, and
red marble. Columns of red marble stretched from
floor to ceiling, which as I followed them up with
my eyes, was at least thirty feet above our head.
The ceiling was painted with images of demons and
devils on one side, angels and gods on the other. In
the center were images of men, some fighting on the

side of the gods, some on the side of the devils. Lightning arced throughout the entire scene.

On the walls were great alabaster statues. The faces of men, frozen in screams like the medallion that the prince had pushed to open our way here. Each face bore different features however, and it seemed as though some were barely human. Demons, and gargoyles, stood watch high above us, eyes of the same red marble seeming to watch our movements.

There were bookcases on one wall, full of scrolls and books, writings that had gone unread for many years, probably many lifetimes. On the other wall, great shelves held all manner of things. Utensils of some sort, candles, strange things that I had no idea what purpose they served.

In the middle of the room, square tables stretched down either side, chairs arranged four to a table. In the very center of the room, was a massive round table, hollow in the center like a ring. Chairs lined the outside of it, forming a perfect circle. In the heart of the circle, was a massive statue, reaching halfway up to the ceiling. The same screaming man's face carved into it, but four times, one facing each wall. No matter where you stood, that face would be visible.

"What is this place," I stammered, not looking at the prince. I was unable to tear my eyes from the four faced statue.

"I do not know," the prince admitted. "No one seems to know it even exists. After I first stumbled upon it, I asked around. Not pointedly 'do you know what the room in the dungeon with the creepy carvings is for', but casually. None of the meisters, nor my father, seemed to know anything about it. I thought perhaps they were just feigning ignorance, but I kept coming here, and they never seemed to catch me or deter me."

I finally took my eyes from the statue, and looked at him. "What about Leofrick? Does he not wonder where you are?"

The prince seemed to think on that for a minute. "No, I don't think so. I'm not down here for very long typically. And, there is another exit, one that only royalty and a handful of guards know about. So he may just assume I left through that if ever he comes down and doesn't see me," he paused, "but I will have to keep that in mind."

I began walking down the steps. The prince still carried the torch. "Do we need that yet," I asked, raising an eyebrow quizzically.

He smiled, the mischievous smile that seemed to lead to trouble with him. "Yes, for there is one more thing you must yet see."

He sped up, and I followed him, our footsteps echoing through the vast hall. He led right to the round table in the center of the room. On the floor, coming straight out from the center of each face, was another trough of liquid. He turned to me, and looked me directly in the eyes as he lit the fire. With a 'whoosh' the eye's and the mouth burned with fire, giving reason to their silent screams. All four faces lit to life, and the room was suddenly bathed in the heat and bright light of the flames.

"Incredible, is it not?"

I looked around, and nodded. I failed to find words in that moment. I didn't know if the room was scary, or just thrilling. Either way, it truly was one of the most incredible things I had ever seen.

I began walking the length of the room. The details on the statues, and the images on the ceiling, were now even more amazing in the full light. The amount of detailed work that went into this room must have taken decades.

"How long do you think this has been lost," I asked, gesturing around the room in amazement.

"I would guess at least a few generations. If my father doesn't know, then likely his father did not either. And the meisters, some of whom are almost half again my fathers age, also seem to know nothing of this place."

I walked to the shelves that held the hundreds of books and scrolls. "Have you read them," I asked, running a finger across the dust covered shelf in front of me.

"I've looked at a few," the prince answered. "They are strange. Some of them seem to be history books, though no history that I recognize. The others," his voice trailed off.

"The others what?"

"The others," the prince sighed, "I'm not sure what to make of. Fanciful tales, stories of men and battles, stories of exploring the stars, stories of wagons that drive themselves, and things that fly in the sky carrying people."

"Like...dragons?"

The prince chuckled, but saw my apparent embarrassment, and quickly became serious again. "No, like," he searched for a way to explain it to me, "like transports. Like large, metal, winged, flying wagons."

It was my turn to laugh. "Flying wagons," I asked, incredulously. "Fanciful, indeed."

I crossed the room, and began looking at the items on the other wall. Now, even more varying in the full light.

There were weapons. Daggers, swords, and...guns. Guns of all different sizes. At least twenty of them, some long, some like the one I had used in the cave. I touched one of them, and pulled back sharply.

"You knew of these," I asked the prince, pointing to the gun.

He nodded. "I had seen these, though I'm not sure how they work. I pulled the triggers on them, the same as you did in the cave, but nothing happened."

I looked back at the guns, and picked up one of the smaller ones. Keeping it pointed away from me, I examined it. There was a lever and a button on one side of it. I flipped the lever, and nothing happened. I pushed the button, and something fell from the bottom of the gun and hit the ground with a clatter that echoed in the room.

I set the gun down, and bent to pick up the piece that had fallen. The prince walked over to me, and we examined it together. "Those must be the things that shot out of it," he said.

In the piece of metal, were small round tipped projectiles. Why would they have round tips? I picked up the weapon, and slid the piece back in. It stopped with a definitive 'click'.

I put it back on the shelf, and looked at some of the other things there. Next to the weapons there were odd, almost egg shaped, things with pins running through one end. "Should we take the pin out?"

"I think not," the prince said. "We don't know what they do. What if it shoots like the gun?"

A fair point. I returned it to the shelf. There were odd metal rectangles. I picked one up, and while one side was metal, the other was black glass. It had buttons on either side, and a small opening on the bottom. I held it up, and raised an eyebrow at

the prince. He shrugged. "I don't know what most
of it is."

I set it back down. The prince walked over
and sat at one of the desks. I took a seat across
from him. "How long have you been coming
here?"

"A few years," he answered. "I discovered
it by chance, and when I asked about the history of
the dungeons, and if there were secret passages, and
similar questions, no one said anything that would
indicate this place. So, I considered it my special
room. And I come down here as often as I can."

"Have you brought no one else here," I
asked.

He shook his head. "I don't trust anyone
else enough to bring them. I believe that if this
place were discovered, I would be forced to stop
coming here. And, honestly," he paused
thoughtfully, "I'm not sure that if I told someone
that there was a hidden room in the dungeon, with
strange images, and giant faces that have flame in
them, and items that no one has ever seen in our
kingdom, they would believe me. It would be taken
as my imagination."

He was likely right. It wasn't very princely
to be making up fanciful stories, even if he was still
considered to be a child by some. "Can I come
back," I asked, a bit sheepishly.

The prince smiled a large, happy smile. "Yes, of course. This is now our place. I don't have sole ownership of it anymore. In fact, I name you General of the Room of Faces."

"The Room of Faces," I repeated.

"Well, I don't know what else to call it," he laughed.

I stood and kneeled. Half being silly, and half proud that he had given me permission to come here. "I will protect it as best I can, Your Highness."

He stood and pushed me over. "It's Tomren," he laughed, extending a hand to pick me up. "Don't make me regret making you my general."

I laughed back, getting on my feet and looking around. "How long do we have before we must go back?"

The prince shrugged. "I don't know. It will be a few hours before either of us are missed, I suppose. Leofrick won't think anything of it if we do not come back out the door, he is well used to me using the other way."

I had forgotten about the other way he had mentioned. "I want to see the other way too," I admitted.

"You will," he said. "It will let us out in a hallway very near to our chambers."

I nodded, happy that I'd have even more things to see and explore with the prince. "Can I read the books," I asked.

The prince cocked his head to one side. "You are the General of the Room of Faces, I should think you are allowed to explore it freely," he said with a smile.

I just smiled back, and went to the shelves. I picked up a book, leather bound and fastened with a cloth tassel. As I read, it was some sort of history of our kingdom, though I wasn't familiar with the names in it, the prince stood.

"I'll be right back," he said.

"You are leaving me here," I asked, looking around the room, not sure if I was thrilled or slightly creeped out.

The prince laughed. "Are you scared of the face's screams?"

I thought at first that I should have reddened, but I did not. His chiding made me smile. "No, I am not. I just, I don't know, it's just that this is your place."

"Yes, but, they have no latrine here," he said, gesturing around, "and I must make use of one. Come," he said, "I'll show you the other exit."

He led me to the far corner of the room. There was a sconce for a torch, and on it was the same face as adorned so much of the rest of the room. He pulled it towards us, and just like in the dungeon, the stone wall slid back and away.

When it had opened, he walked to the other side, and pointed at a medallion matching the one we had pressed to get in from the dungeons. "Simply press to open. The stairs," he said, glancing at the stone staircase, "lead to a small room. Inside the room is a small hole, through which you can see the entire hallway by where your fathers men train. If the hall is empty, simply press the medallion and the door will open. I'll return soon."

I nodded, and went back into the room as the door slid into place, blending back perfectly with the wall. I turned to go back to the books, but then, I thought again about the guns. I walked over and picked up the same one again. Pointing it away from myself, and towards the wall with the books on it, I pulled the trigger the way I had in the cave. Nothing happened. I put it back. Mayhaps the books would have some instructions on how to use it.

Glancing down the shelf I saw something that caught my eye. It was a cylinder, much like the flameless torch that I had used in the cave. I picked it up, and unlike the one from the cave, it was made of metal. It was also much heavier than the one from the cave. I turned it around, and noticed a small black button near the end. I pushed it, and the tip lit up bright. I shone it around the room, and the light reached even the farthest corners of the ceiling from where I stood. I pushed the button again, and it extinguished.

Taking the flameless torch, I went to the door that the prince had left through, and next to the sconce, I placed it on the ground. It seemed that if there were no torch, this would work just as well when we returned.

No sooner had I set down the flameless torch, the door began sliding open with a small rumble. The prince jumped back a little when he saw me right there.

"Gods, were you just standing there waiting? Afraid of the rest of the room, were you?"

I laughed. "No, look what I found," I said, picking up the cylinder. I showed him how to make it light, and he looked at it for a moment. "I thought it would be good to have here, next to the door."

"Agreed. But," he said quickly, "we must go. Supper will be soon, and we will be expected to eat."

I nodded and started to go up the stairs. "Wait," the prince said, turning around.

On the opposite side of the door from the sconce, was a lever. He pulled it, and suddenly with the sound of metal and stone scraping echoing through the room, the flames were extinguished.

The only light now was a torch at the top of the staircase, dimly shining through the doorway.

"How," I asked.

"I'll show you next time," he said with a glint of excitement in his eye, "for now though, let us go."

12

We left the hidden room, and made our way back to our chambers. The prince stopped at his door, and turned to me. "Thank you," he said, his warm smile making me redden just a bit, and I had to look away.

"For what," I asked after a moment, returning my gaze to him.

"For being my friend. It has been rather lonely growing up here," he said, gesturing around us, "but, you have given me friendship. I have someone to share the things that I enjoy with."

"I will always be your friend," I smiled back at him, "but, you know I will also be leaving this place before long. Gods," the reminder that there was still to be some sort of penance stealing my smile, "I had almost forgotten that I still was in some trouble."

The prince hugged me, resting his walking stick on the wall. I didn't really know how to react, being hugged by royalty had not been something that had occured in my life before. After a second, I hugged him back.

"You will be fine," he said, releasing me, "and, you will be my guest going forward. I shall make sure that we have time together, even once you have left the castle."

Something inside of me stirred, though I couldn't quite place what it was. "That is good to know, and it quells some of my worry," I said with an honest smile.

"Good," he said, giving me another quick embrace before turning back, grabbing his walking stick, and entering his chamber. "Until tomorrow, sleep well, Rorthan."

I entered my own chambers and sat in the large chair. I put my head back, and closed my eyes. The past week had been a whirlwind, and it wasn't over yet. Concern took over once again, and I began to think about what was to happen to me. I tried to trust in the words of the prince, not only was the king a fair one, he also seemed to be genuinely understanding of what had happened. But he also had to do something about what I had done. Before I had a chance to really sink into my thoughts, however, there was a knock at the door.

"Come in," I said, turning to see the door.

A chamber maid entered. "Is there anything you require, sir?"

She wasn't much older than me, if at all. Pretty by all accounts. Her long, blonde hair was pinned up. Her oval face, despite a blemish or two from the pimples of youth that plagued everyone our age, was framed by a curl of her hair on either side. Bright, blue eyes lit her face, and when she smiled, even if it was a dutiful smile, her dimples were clear. "No, thank you."

She nodded, and turned to go. "Actually," I said, and she turned back to me, "could you draw me a bath?"

"Of course, sir," she said with a bow of her head, and went about readying the bath for me.

Gods, I'm no 'sir' and I didn't like the way a servant girl bowing to me made me feel. The prince had grown up like this, and yet he was as kind as anyone I had ever met. A bit ornery at times, sure, but kind and caring just the same. Stories of mean royals, ones who considered themself to be above their people, were abundant from neighboring kingdoms. The prince of the Celts was often said to have those who dared to make eye contact with him flogged. And, here I was, a general's son, yes, but common just the same, and the prince had been kind to me since day one. And he had hugged me twice before we parted for the day. The thought of that made me redden a bit, and my heart raced just a touch.

"It is ready," the maid said after a few minutes, returning from the bathroom. "Will you require anything else?"

"No, that will be all. Thank you."

She bowed her head again, and left.

I removed my clothes, and stepped into the hot water. This was one of the things I would miss about the castle. The large tubs in which one could soak their entire body. After the events of the last week, my aches and pains were eased by a long bath. I would sit in this hot water until it became lukewarm, and mayhaps even longer. I had almost fallen asleep in the water. After my head dipped, and my nose touched the water, I got out and dried myself on the fine cloth that was next to the tub.

I went back into the bedroom, and slid under the blankets. I had relaxed enough that concern over the future did not stop me from falling asleep, despite the sun not being fully down yet.

***

There was a soft knock on the door. So soft, in fact, that the first time I thought I had imagined it. After the second knock, I got up and put on the silk pants from the night clothes that had been given me for the duration of my stay at the castle. The room was dark, except for the moon light filtering through the window. I walked to the door and opened it.

"Let me in," the prince whispered, and I stepped aside. When he had entered, I closed the door back quietly.

"What's wrong," I asked, tone hushed, though not a whisper.

"Nothing," he answered, sitting on the edge of the bed. I lit a small candle, and placed it on the

112

table beside the bed. His hair was messy, and he wore night clothes that were finer than any clothing that I had owned in my life.

"I spoke to my father," he said, a smile on his face. "Come, sit," he said, gesturing to the bed beside him.

I sat nervously, both concerned for what was to come, and suddenly aware that I had no shirt on.

"What is to come of me," I asked, looking him in the eye.

"You are to stay here," he said.

I looked down, tears biting at the corners of my eyes. "The dungeons then."

"What," the prince asked, his tone a bit startled. "No," he said, lifting my chin gently until our eyes met again. My heart raced, faster than it had even when we were in the cave. "No, of course not. Do you think I would come here to tell you that?"

I blinked and his hand moved from my chin to my tears, wiping them away gently.

"What then," I asked, confused. My mind was foggy, a combination of just being awakened, and the prince's hand on my face.

"You are to stay here, as our guest. You are to train," he said, his smile warm, "as my guard and protector."

"Guard and protector," I asked, confused.

"Father said that you have already shown that you have the heart," he said, his hand dropping from my face, "and that when you are old enough, you shall be my personal guard."

"But, what of my father," I asked.

"He will still see you, you are not a prisoner, and I would assume much of your training will come from him and his men. He is the general, after all."

I nodded. "So, we can still have adventures," I asked, a small smile returning to my face.

"Yes," he said, "of course. You are to be my guard, but you are already my General of the Room of Faces, and my best friend," he said, returning his hand to my cheek.

"I-", whatever I was going to say was cut off when the prince put his lips to mine. The feeling of his beard sent a chill down my spine, and his lips tasted of honeyed tea. I shrank back, unsure how to react.

"I'm sorry," he started. But, I leaned forward and kissed him. This time, without hesitation. Our lips met, and parted. His tongue and mine, probing each other's mouth eagerly, each twisting and moving around the other. Gently, he reached up and cupped my face with his hands, and I pressed harder against him, heat rising now.

One of my hands reached behind his head
and my fingers twined into his curls, my other hand
moving down his face, to his neck, to his chest, to
his stomach.

Suddenly, there was a knock at the door. I
sat up straight in bed, sweat covering me, hot and
aroused by the dream. The sun was orange filtering
in through the window.

"Come," I said, my voice breathy and
cracking just a bit.

The meister entered the room. "Good
evening, sir," he said. "I have brought you your tea,
bread, and a bit of cheese. I've been told that
you've been eating fine, but a small bite to eat will
help the tea settle."

I nodded, still sitting in bed. "You can leave
it on the table."

The meister bowed his head. "The tea will
taste better, and soothe faster, if you drink it while it
is still hot. I shall return at first light.". The man
turned and left, closing the door behind him.

I sat there for just a minute. What in the
name of the gods was that dream? I had never had a
dream like that before, and though the prince was
attractive, he was a prince. He was required to one
day marry a princess, or a lady at the very least. He
was a *he*. Gods. It was just a dream. Just a dream.
Just a dream.

But, as I repeated the words over and over in my mind, I could still feel his lips on mine, his tongue gently but eagerly probing my mouth. Just a dream. Just a dream. Just a dream.

13

The tea and food did nothing to relax me. I couldn't sleep, the dream playing over and over in my head. When I closed my eyes, it was only that much more vivid. Finally, I rose and put on some clothes. I released the latch on the door, and it groaned just a little as it opened. I glanced into the hall, trying to think of something that I could claim to need if a guard were in the hallway. But there was no guard. I slipped quietly back to the hidden door, and pressed the disc to reveal it. As it rumbled open I flinched. The sound wasn't particularly loud during the day with the hustle and bustle of the castle, but it was painfully noisy in the silence of night. I looked around again to make sure no one was coming. As soon as the sound stopped, I slipped in and pressed the disc on the inside. As it closed, I carefully made my way down the stairs and to the light that I had left by the door. I pushed the button, and it flicked to life.

I shone the light around the room for a bit. It was definitely even creepier with only the light of the cylinder to reveal it. I headed to the books. I picked up a scroll, but it was written in a language that I did not understand. After a few such scrolls, I found one in english. I took the scroll to the nearest table, and began reading.

*"In the fourteenth year of our Lord, Blacwin
came to us. He was a pale man, with a curious
sounding voice. He spoke our language, but in a
dialect that was different from our own. He claimed
to be from a time after our own. He told us fanciful
tales of horseless buggies, wagons that fly through
the sky like birds, connecting our whole earth from
corner to corner. There may be some truth to his
words, for he had things unlike any that the council
had ever seen. He had a device that with the flick of
his thumb caused a flame to spark. He had metals
such as we had never seen, and something he called
'plastic' that was common on many of his
belongings. On his neck, he wore a torc with a
screaming man on either end of it. His ring bore
the same signet."*

A screaming man? I shone the light back to
the center of the room, and looked at the four faces
that sat there. What was the significance of this
image? I stared at it for a moment, and noticed that
where the mouth and eye openings had been, were
now solid granite. As curious as I was, I returned to
the scroll.

*"While he may have been only a trickster,
perhaps a gleeman from another land, he spent two
days with the council of elders. Blacwin claimed to
need men to help him stop evil from traveling across
the times. He called his clan the 'Brotherhood of
Time'. None of us went with him, and after two*

Plastic? The flying wagons that Tomren had spoken of? Horseless carriages? Different *times*?

I rolled the scroll back up, and returned it to the shelf. I did not grab another. Instead, I walked to the round table, sat, and shone the light on the screaming man that stared at me. If one could indeed go through the ages, and that would explain many of the things I'd seen in the last fortnight, what purpose would it serve? It would explain the guns and other odd things in this room. I looked at the flameless torch. Had this come from a future time? One where man was far more advanced than we were? It made sense, yet the idea of it seemed to be truly preposterous. My mind wanted to try to make sense of it, but sleep was slowly finding its way to my eyes. I folded my arms on the table in front of me, and laid my head on them. Mayhaps just a moment more of thought, and I would get up

and return to my chambers to sleep for what was
left of the night.

***

I awoke to pure darkness. Panic began to set
in as I reached for the flameless torch, and found
nothing. I stood quickly, knocking back the chair I
was in with a loud crash. I felt frantically around
the table in front of me, and again found nothing.
There was absolutely no light. I tried to remember
where I had been sitting, and began to slowly
shuffle, hands outstretched moving back and forth
in front of me, toward what I hoped would be the
wall with the exit. Would I even be able to find the
sconce to open the door in this darkness? I pushed
the thought down, and continued shuffling.

"Where are you going, young Rorthan," a
voice boomed in the darkness, stopping my
movement where I stood. It was familiar, though I
could not place it.

"Who's there," I asked, wishing that my
voice was not weak and full of fear, even to my own
ears.

"How did you come by this place," the voice
asked, ignoring my question. Before I could
answer, another question rang out. "Who else
knows of this room?"

"It's just me, I am the only one."

I heard nothing, and began shuffling forward again. Hands grabbed my arms, strong hands. "I highly doubt the truth in that, General of the Room of Faces."

I raised my knee, and heard a grunt as the hands released me. I ran forward, well, walked with my hands in front of me as quickly as I dared in the darkness, and found the wall. Frantically searching for the sconce.

The room filled with light, as the flame again was lit around it. I spun, and saw a man walking towards me from the other side of the room.

"You have no need to fear me, young Rorthan. I will do you no harm, in this time or any other."

"This time or any other," I repeated. "What does that mean?"

"I think you have an idea of what it means. You have read some of our history, and even seen some of the things that do not belong here in your time. The gun that you used to protect your prince, the flashlight that you had when I found you here."

"Flashlight," I said, realizing immediately that he meant the flameless torch. "From when then?"

"The future, many, many lifetimes from now," he said, still walking towards me.

I tried to take an instinctive step backwards, but only hit the wall.

"Why are you here? What do you want with me," I asked, panic quickly becoming stronger.

"I am here because of you, mostly. And, I want what is best for you," he answered, coming close enough for me to see him clearly. Like his voice, his face was familiar, though I could not remember from where.

"Me?"

He nodded. "Yes, you. You are important to me, as was your mother before you."

My mother? He knew my mother? Something stirred inside my mind, breaking through the panic. "Arthur," I said, half question, half statement.

He cocked his head. "You remember my name. So, you should then remember, that I mean you no harm. I did, afterall, stop you from ending your life all of those years ago."

"You slapped me," I said, a bit sharper than I probably felt, "that much I remember."

He laughed, a genuine laugh, with a smile that touched his eyes. "Yes, I did. You needed a good slap. Perhaps, you still do, though I suspect you are doing well for yourself. You've made friends of the prince, and you are here," he said, gesturing around the room.

"What is this place," I asked, panic dissipating just a little.

"This is just a room. My home away from home, you could say. I suspect that before your prince found it, it had not had visitors other than myself in hundreds of years. It has been long forgotten, as has the order it once was home to."

"The Brotherhood of Time," I asked, but I already knew that it had to be.

Arthur nodded. "This place once was filled with scribes, elders, and warriors. All of us were born in different times, but united in this place." He looked around, eyes not seeing, as if remembering what once was. "Yet, now, it is hidden from those who once met here, and forgotten by all who were not of the Brotherhood. Kings, Queens, Sultans, even Presidents, all came to this place. Some to learn, some to seek power."

"Presidents," I asked, unfamiliar with the term.

"Kings of a fashion, chosen by their people to lead. They do not exist, and will not, for thousands of years. Yet, here they stood, in this hall. This is a place without time. Accessible to all who know how to find it."

"Yet, no one else can find it anymore," I asked, fear forgotten, curiosity full.

"Yes, I am the only one who still comes to this place. I was forced to hide it from the Brotherhood."

"Why? I thought you were part of the Brotherhood?"

"I was, and am, and will be again, and will never be," he said, reaching beside me to where the sconce was.

"That makes no sense."

"Indeed it does not, but so it is." He touched his ring, exactly like the description of the one worn by the man Blacwin in the scroll, to the medallion. It glowed brightly for just a second, as if it had just been pulled from a smith's fire. When he pulled the sconce, the door rumbled aside, but it slid the opposite way, backing into where the stairs were.

Arthur gestured into the opening, pale light coming from somewhere inside. "Would you like to see more? To know more?"

Of course I do, I thought. But, I did not speak it. I simply followed him into the room.

14

Arthur led me into the room. I had no idea what I was looking at. There was a table in the middle, and some chairs, and a long shelf that doubled as a desk ran around three of the walls. But the other things in the room, I had no idea what were. I felt dizzy, whether from the strange lights, the stranger items, or just the whole experience I did not know.

"Sit," Arthur said, pulling me out a chair. It was made of a material that I did not recognize, with small wheels on five feet that spread out from a single pole under the seat. I did as he ordered.

"I wish that I could be more discreet, and ease you into all of this much slower. But, I suspect that teaching you will still take years, and we don't have extra time to waste," he said, as walked to some sort of cupboard on one of the walls. From it he pulled a bottle. "Water," he said, removing the lid and offering it to me. "And that," he said, pointing to the cupboard, "is a refrigerator."

I drank it quickly. Only after it was gone did I realize that it was cold. Not cool, but cold. Almost ice. And, the bottle, what was it made of? It felt strange in my hand, and when I squeezed it, it made an odd crackling noise.

"Plastic," Arthur said, taking the bottle back. "As I said, you have much to learn. And, it will be overwhelming. I hope and pray that you are able to handle it," he said as he sat down in an identical chair and faced me.

"Why are you showing me all of this?"

"Because, I believe that you need to know. I would have probably tried to tell you eventually, if nothing else than out of respect for your mother, but with you finding the gun in the cave, and finding our church, I think I have run out of time to decide. A funny thing, time. I can travel across it, but I still never have enough of it."

"My mother? Church? What church?"

Arthur sighed. "The 'Room of Faces' as your prince has named it. It was our church. A room that could be accessed by all of us, regardless of where we originated in the stream of time. It was our belief that man should not have the power to travel time, that only God should be able to do such things. We served in hopes of stopping those who would use this power for evil."

"Evil? There are others?"

"Yes, there are those who would use the ability to travel to other times for terrible purposes. We tried to stop it, but it did not always work. We were few, and those who would do harm were crafty. There is much history to teach you, and I will. But, it will take time, and you must be patient.

You must trust me, even if only a little at first, and allow me to show you."

"Okay," I said, thinking out loud as I formed the decision in my head, "I will allow you to teach me, and I will trust that you will show me why any of this should matter to me."

"Good-"

Before Arthur could finish, I cut him off. "But, you will tell me of my connection to this, my mothers connection to all of this, before anything else. Only then will I agree to any of this."

The man nodded. "That is fair. Do you know what your mother looked like? Have you seen her likeness?"

"My father has an old painting, he says it is of her."

Arthur rolled his chair to a section of the desk and opened a drawer. He pulled out a piece of paper, and rolled back. "Her?"

I took the paper. It was a picture. But, not one like anything that I had ever seen. It was as if my mother was actually in the paper. She looked a little bit younger than the painting that my father had, and she wore very strange clothes. They hugged her body close, and her shape was clear. Her dark hair hung from under some sort of billed hat that she wore. The hat had an image of a beaver on it. Her eyes were full of life, and her smile reached them easily. She stood there, with Arthur on one side of her, and...my father, also younger, and also in strange clothes...on her other side.

"That...that is my father," I stammered.

"And your mother. And, me. Your mother and I were friends. Your father and I, well, we knew one another. We were not friends, though at times we were brothers."

"What is this painting?"

Arthur chuckled. "Consider this an early lesson. This is no painting. It is a photograph. You will learn how it is taken in time. Would you like to know more about your mother now though?" I didn't take my eyes from the picture, 'photograph' I said in my head trying to link the word to the item, and simply nodded.

"Very well. Your mother was one of my oldest friends. We attended college, higher learning, together. We studied science. And we were damn good at it," a smile that seemed to be nostalgic, happy, and sad all at the same time was on his face when I looked up from the photograph.

"My mother attended higher learning? She was a meister," I asked, surprised even though nothing should be surprising now. But, higher learning was for men. And I had never met a female meister.

"Yes, we call it college. It is open to both men and women. In the time I came from, men and women have the same abilities and rights. They may be whatever they want to be. She did have a 'Masters Degree', we don't have meisters but the word means the same. She was the smartest person I knew. At least as far as book smarts go."

He rolled over to the cupboard again, no, to the refrigerator, and opened it. "More water," he asked.

I nodded, and he brought me another bottle, while himself grabbing a brown glass bottle. "Ale," he said, raising the bottle. "Not for you yet, my boy."

He took a drink from his bottle, and continued. "We were studying time. How it flowed, whether we could bend it, maybe even break what were long accepted as the rules of time. 'Time only flows forward, and you cannot ever go back' was what was believed, and really still is by almost everyone in my time."

"So, my mother was," I paused to gather my thought. "My mother was from the future?"

"She was from my time, yes," he said. "She was born in the year 1975."

"1975," I echoed, amazed more than shocked. "That is almost a thousand years from now."

"That it is. And now the year there is 2025. I can go there at will, and in fact, spend most of my time there."

"So, why not go back to your time in...college," I said, feeling out the word, hoping I had it right, "and stop her from dying?"

Arthur cocked his head. "An insightful thought," he said, taking another drink from his bottle, and sighing heavily. "It shows that you not only have some understanding of the idea of time travel, but you also are caring enough to think of your mother. But if I did that, you would not exist."

I hadn't thought of that. "But she would," I countered, "and she was your friend, not me."

He nodded. "That she was. And, you are so much more than a friend, though one day I hope you will consider me as such. But," he paused for a moment, "I cannot go back to 1975. Nor can I return to 1990, or 2000, or even 2024. Think of it as a stream. While I am here, in this time, the stream continues there, in that time. If I leave, and am here for a day, or a month, or a year, then a day, or a month, or a year passes there as well. I can return to the stream, but only at its current point."

"I think I understand. But, how do you find your way back to that time? And is that the only time that you can travel to?"

"There are beacons. The oldest one that we have found is from almost one thousand years before now," he said, gesturing around him. "And the farthest one ahead is the one I am from. It seems that they have been placed about every 250 years, so I can go to many different streams, but not close in between them."

I must have stared dumbly at him, because he smiled. "It's a lot to understand, and your mother and I devoted our lives to learning about it. We were testing all kinds of theories when we were approached by the Brotherhood of Time. They told a convincing story, and we eventually joined. But," he said, taking another drink from his bottle, "that is another part of the story. The fact is, even if I wanted to go back and change what happened to your mother, I could not. It is not possible. At least, not in any way that is known right now."

I lowered my head back to the picture. "She was beautiful," I said.

"She was," he said, and I thought I noticed a bit of pain in his voice. "You look very much like her, and from what I've seen, you have her heart and mind as well."

I smiled. "I wish I had met her. Had heard her voice. Felt her touch."

"You did," Arthur said, "even if you can't remember it. She held you, she talked to you, sang to you, loved you dearly in what time she had with you."

I felt a tear prick at my eye as I looked at the picture.

"Would you like to hear her," Arthur asked.

"How?"

"That picture that you hold, it was taken with a device called a camera. It captures an image, a split second in time. But," he said, rolling his chair to the desk, and pushing buttons on a black board, "there are also cameras that capture more than just a split second. They capture the movement and sound of moments, even hours. The person may leave this life, but what is captured will remain forever. You can't hold a conversation with them, of course, but whatever they said and did in those moments, are forever captured. The still photograph that you hold is called a 'picture', but the moving ones are called 'video'."

"And you have this of my mother?"

"I do," he said, the...window?...that he was looking at changed as he was pushing the buttons on the board.

"What is that," I said, pointing at the thing.

"I'm sorry," he said, turning to look at me. "Of course. That is a monitor. A screen, if you prefer, it will be a better choice as time goes on to just call it a screen. It will show the recordings of your mother."

Again, none of it made sense to me. But, if what he said was true, and right now I had no reason to doubt him, I would accept it and not ask more questions at the moment.

"I have watched these all many times over. I will make sure that you are able to see them all.

There are some from before your mother was pregnant, some while, and even a couple that were taken after you were born. Those are hard for me to watch, but you should see them. The one I will show you is from that time. Your mother is weak, and does not look like she does in the picture. But, she made it for you. Specifically for this moment, were it to come." Arthur paused for a moment, and then added, "she did not name you 'Rorthan'. That was your fathers doing. He knew damn well that she had a name for you, one that she wanted you to be called. And he chose not to honor that wish."

He turned back to the board, pressed a button, and the screen was filled with my mother's face, a triangle across the middle of the screen. He was right. She did not look as I saw in the picture. She was deathly pale, her eyes sunken in, and her skin was gaunt. She was holding a baby, me I could only assume. Her eyes were facing the screen however. He pushed a button, and her image began to move, her voice filling the room.

"Sebastian," she said. My name was Sebastian?

"I will never get to see you grow, and I am sorry that I have failed you in that. But, I will always be with you. I have left you videos like this one, writings and letters, and you have my blood running through your veins. Don't ever forget that every moment of your existence, whether while you were in my belly, or now, I have loved you. Giving you life is the greatest thing that I have ever done. You have a purpose, and I know you will find that. Whether your purpose is simply to exist, find happiness, and live, or whether you will do so much more, I will be proud of you forever. Do not let anyone ever stop you from doing what you want, loving your life, and being proud. Your father and I will be forever proud of you, I love you Sebastian!"

The screen stopped, and went back to my mothers face from the beginning, the triangle returning.

"Sebastian," I asked.

"That is what your mother wanted, yes. It was her father's name, and she wanted you to bear it. But I suppose that doesn't matter now."

"It does," I said. "I will ask to be called that, perhaps the king will grant me that small favor."

Tears in my eyes, I looked to Arthur. He also had tears flowing freely. "Can I see it again?"

Without a word, he pushed a button, and my mothers voice again filled the room. This time, I sobbed openly.

15

I watched many more videos that night, I saw my mother at all different points in her life. There were videos of her as a young child, dancing or playing, celebrating her year day and winter solstice, her 'birthday' and 'Christmas' as I would learn to call them. There were videos of her when she was an adult, at what appeared to be a school of higher learning, college as Arthur had called it. She was often with Arthur in these videos of the adult Eleanor. One person that never appeared in the videos was my father. There were so many things in the videos that I did not understand, though at least some of the times it seemed as though she was riding in one of the horseless buggies that I had read of.

I had lost all sense of the hour, and I assume Arthur had as well. Finally, with a yawn, I stood. "I need to get back to my chambers," I said. "It may already be past light, and I may have already been missed."

Arthur rose from his chair as well. "Of course, I'm sorry, I hadn't thought about that. I was lost in the moment."

"I was as well, I will find an excuse if I'm questioned."

He nodded. "Please, do not tell anyone, even your prince, of this room, or me."

"Very well, for now," I said, "but, when can I come back here?"

Arthur thought for a moment. "Can you meet me in the church in two nights time?"

"I will find a way," I said, determined to speak to him again, and see my mothers face again.

"Good," he said, leading me out of the room, and back into the church. "Remember, I do not want your prince to know of me or my room, at least not as of yet."

"You have my word," I said, "I will not speak of it, at the very least until I see you again."

He touched his ring to the sconce before pulling it, and the door slid back into a solid wall. Pulling it again, this time not with his ring, but instead with his other hand, it slid to the right and revealed the staircase.

"I wish you well, until we meet again, Sebastian," he said, with a smile.

I smiled back, happy to be reminded that I did, indeed, have a name. "Thank you, and the same to you."

I turned and walked up the staircase, hearing the door close behind me. After checking to make sure the hall was empty, which of course it wasn't so I had to stand in the small room watching for a few minutes, I opened the hidden door and returned to the castle. Daylight filled the castle, my best guess was that it was mid morning. I must be missed by now. Anxiety crept up, and I walked just a little bit faster.

I slipped quietly back into my chambers, and closed the door. When I turned, the prince sat on one of the chairs inside.

"Your Highness," I said, more of a yelp than I would have liked.

"Where have you been," he practically hissed. "I've been here for an hour at least. My father has requested your presence this afternoon."

"I went to our room when I couldn't sleep," I said quickly. "Gods, my presence? It's time for me to learn my fate I suppose."

"The room? Without me," the prince asked, though his slight smile and chiding tone made me believe he was not offended.

"Yes, I read some of the writings there. What has your father told you," I asked, taking a seat in the chair across from the prince. He looked handsome this morning, his sandy hair perfectly falling to the white coat that he wore. Golden buttons ran from under his chin, to the end of his coat, which went just past his waste. His black pants bore a winding scrollwork pattern of gold threads, and contrasted his coat perfectly.

The prince waved his hand dismissively. "He hasn't told me, but I assure you, it will be fine. What did you learn in the books?"

"I will show you later, but I think that it has something to do with traveling time. The whole room I mean, I think it was like a base or something for men that could traverse different times."

"Traverse time," the prince said, questioningly, "surely, such a thing isn't possible."

This gave me an irrational shot of anger. If it wasn't true, then the videos that I had watched of my mother weren't real, and that made me want to strike the prince for saying it. "It is," I said sharply. "Think of the things we saw in the cave. The flashlight, the gun-"

"Flashlight," the prince asked, spiking my anger even more.

"Yes, the bloody flashlight, that's what the flameless torch is called."

The prince nodded, dropping his eyes. I just snapped at the prince, and he did not admonish me, he simply backed down. Why? "I'm sorry, I have not been sleeping well, and I am anxious over what is to come."

The prince raised his eyes, and their blue shined brightly in the sun that filtered through the window. He reached across and took one of my hands, cupping it in his. "My father will do you no harm. He knows that I care for you, and he knows

138

that you saved my life. I assure you, you will be treated well."

I felt a rush when he took my hands, and another when he said that he cared for me. 'Be still', I silently told my beating heart. Outloud, I just nodded.

The prince smiled, and stood, releasing my hands. "Now then," he said heading towards the wardrobe, "let us get you presentable for an audience with the king."

***

Less than an hour later, Tomren and I were walking down the hall to the throne room. The prince had brought me a fine outfit to wear. A modest coat of white like his, with silver buttons. The pants were not black, but a dark gray. I felt odd wearing such fine clothes, and my anxiety at the coming meeting was so that I didn't speak while we walked.

"Here we are," the prince said, approaching the throne room. A guard stood on either side of the doors.

One of the guards turned and opened the doors, and ushered us in. The doors closed firmly behind, and I turned with a start. Two guards stood on either side of the doors on the inside as well.

The prince put a hand on my arm, and turned me back towards the throne. As we walked,

I took in the room as best I could. This was my first time in the throne room. The walls were adorned with armor, and paintings of knights. The ground was white marble, with black marble columns supporting the ceiling above. There were seats on either side of the room, though they were thankfully empty today.

As we walked I saw my father standing to one side, with Sabina. They wore the matching uniforms of the King's Men, a deep red coat and pants with black buttons. Their swords sheathed in silver scabbards. My father glared at me as we approached, but Sabina gave me a small smile. Why would she smile at me? I had almost killed her. The smile seemed genuine, and caring, but maybe it was a smile because she knew of some horrible punishment that I was about to receive.

When we reached the throne the king was sitting straight on his throne, and the prince went to stand beside his father. I bent my knee, and bowed my head.

"Stand, young Rorthan," the king said. He wore basic, at least basic for a king, clothes, and no crown, his hair cleanly pulled into a top knot. He smiled at me as I stood, his blue eyes touched by his smile. He had some crows feet, and despite being king, he clearly had seen his share of sun and battle. His skin was tanned and leathery, his hands wrinkled with age. But, he was still muscular, and I thought for a second that the prince would have this look when he got older, still handsome, but clearly having lived plenty of life and seen plenty of things.

"Young Rorthan," the king began, "I want to again thank you for saving my son's life in the cave, and I do appreciate that you fought for his life when you thought him to be in danger." I bowed my head slightly, unsure whether I was supposed to say a thank you or not. "We are here, however," the king continued, and I winced knowing why we were here, "because despite your attempt to save my son's life, you shot Sabina." He gestured a hand at the woman, who bowed her head much the same as I had.

Her hair was short cut, like a mans, but fiery red. Her skin pale, with freckles, but perfectly smooth. Her green eyes were bright. The only blemish was a small scar that ran along her jaw bone from her left ear to her chin.

"What do you believe would be a fair punishment, young Rorthan," the king asked. I was taken back by this. Why would he ask me? How would I know what was fair?

"Your Majesty," I said, voice quavering, "I attempted to kill one of your soldiers. Our law demands that, as a traitor, I be executed for this crime." Tears bit at the corners of my eyes at having voiced out loud what I had been thinking the entire time since it happened. It was the law, and the king surely had to follow it. At least I had been given the opportunity to spend my last days with the prince. And, gods, I had got to hear my mother speak.

The king nodded. "It is indeed the law. However," he said, looking me in the eyes, compassion showing in his face, "circumstances must be considered when passing judgement on such serious matters. I have a duty to all of my people, even those that have committed a crime."

The king turned toward my father and Sabina. "Sabina," he said, "what would you have me do with the boy?"

"Your Majesty," she said, with another bow of her head. "While the boy is right, the law does say that he should be executed as a traitor," she looked at me now, "surely you are right. The circumstances must be considered. He was injured, the prince was injured, and he was fleeing from men of the Brotherhood. Shooting me, while certainly unfortunate, is understandable. The boy was protecting the prince. That is my job, my duty, and I would have done the same." She smiled at me. "And, I will be fine. I am nearly healed already. As far as I can see, there was no harm done."

The king nodded. My father snorted. Sabina turned to him, but looked away quickly when she saw the disgust on his face.

"General," the king asked, "what would you do with the boy?"

"The law is the law, Your Majesty."

Sabina inhaled sharply, nearly a gasp. The king blinked, seemingly taken off guard. "You would have me execute the boy," the king asked, still seemingly stunned.

"The law is the law, Your Majesty," was all my father said. He did not look towards me, nor did he make eye contact with the king. He simply stared forward.

The king studied him. "And, this," he said, pointing to me, "is your son."

My father looked at me. "He is a disgrace. And," he said, looking away from me, "he is no son of mine." This was the second time since the cave that I had seen my father, and the second time that he had denounced me in front of the king.

"I warned you last time," the king said evenly, "that you should control your tongue."

My father reddened. "Apologies, Your Majesty," my father said weakly, "but, he is an embarrassment to my name, and he dishonors my house."

"The only dishonor," the king said, standing from his throne, "upon your house is your own behavior."

"Your Majesty-" my father started to say, but he was cut off by the king.

"Hold your tongue, Rorthan," the king snapped. "The only dishonor upon your house is your own behavior," he repeated. "I have known and trusted you for many years. My son," he said, looking to the prince, "was saved by yours. You should be proud that your boy saved my boy's life, as you have saved mine more than once. Our sons have formed a bond, one that started with the idea of a silly adventure in the woods, and ended with them escaping from the Brotherhood."

The king paused for a moment, looking to my father, and then to me. "Their bond was solidified when your son took the life of a man who wanted to kidnap my son. I have kept an eye on them for the last sennight, watching when I can, relying on others to keep me informed when I couldn't watch with my own eyes," the king smiled warmly at me. "It would seem that my son has made a true and honest friend, one that will protect him in any way that he can. I am grateful for that."

The king turned and went back to his throne, sitting down once more. "Young Rorthan," he said, looking me in the eye, "what you have done for my son is greatly appreciated. I owe you a debt that I will not forget. However, as for the crimes that you have been accused of, I find you guilty. You have admitted them, and there is no doubt that you did them. But," he said mildly, "I do not believe that they were intentional, nor do I believe that you deserve any severe punishment for them. You will return home this night with your father. When you have fully recovered from your injuries, you shall come back and spend one night in the dungeon. From sundown, until sunrise, you will be in a cell."

I bowed my head, relief rushing over me.

"Furthermore," the king continued, "you will spend every other night, for the next year, cleaning the kitchens in the castle. This is your punishment."

I glanced over to my father, his expression unreadable. "Thank you, Your Majesty," I said, my voice trembling with relief and gratitude.

The king came down from his throne, and put his hand on my shoulder. "Thank you, young Rorthan. I look forward to seeing you again." With that, the king and the prince left the throne room.

My father began to leave, but was stopped at the door by one of the guards. "The king has ordered that you are to return home for the day, General," the man said. "He requests your presence at first light tomorrow. Further, young Rorthan is to spend the afternoon packing his belongings, and he will be escorted to your home before sundown."

The guard stepped aside, and my father stormed through the door. I returned to my chambers. Such relief washed over me that as soon as the door was closed, I began weeping.

16

I didn't have much to pack really. The clothes that I had been wearing were not my own, and the only thing I had of my own was what I now wore. Gone were the nice clothes that had been loaned to me, and in their place I wore the roughspun tunic and pants that my father had brought from home at some point. I looked at my reflection in the looking glass. Two days ago I had requested a looking glass, and now I regretted that decision. I was saddened just a bit to see myself. Not my face, it had remained the same. But, me. The boy that had been a guest at the castle, the boy that had almost been able to forget that he did not belong here. The boy who had worn the finest clothes, and slept in a bed that was bigger and softer than anything he could imagine. The boy that, despite all of that, was still just a general's son, and a common boy. It was time to return to that, and there was some small amount of comfort in that normality. A knock at the door interrupted my thoughts, but I didn't look away. "Enter," I said.

"Sir, are you ready," a woman's voice asked, and I turned, surprised. I had expected a meister, or a servant, or maybe even the prince, but I had not expected Sabina.

"Sabina, ma'am," I stammered out, "I...I am ready, yes."

Sabina smiled, "Good. We must leave soon."

"We," I asked, surprised again. Was this a trick of some kind? Had her words in the throne room been just to catch me off guard, when she really intended to do me harm?

"Yes, I will be accompanying you to your home," she answered, her smile not fading.

"Oh, of course, I'm sorry, I just had not expected you."

"I suppose not, but I offered," she said. Oh boy, she was going to kill me, or at least beat me, on the road back to my home.

"Offered," I asked.

"Yes. I wanted to talk with you. I wanted you to know that I meant what I said. I have no hard feelings towards you. In fact, I not only respect what you did to protect our prince, but I also believe that I would have done the same. Or, at least I hope that I would have. But, you showed bravery and honor, both by what you did, and by admitting to your mistake and being willing to pay for it."

"Well, I had hoped not to be executed," I admitted, somewhat quietly.

She laughed, an honest, gentle laugh. "No, I suppose not. And, I'm glad that the king was understanding."

"My bloody father wasn't," I said, without thinking. She was one of his soldiers, and if she told him what I had said, he would likely punish me.

"No," she admitted, waving her hand dismissively. "May I," she asked, nodding at one of the chairs.

"Of course, my apologies."

"Thank you," she said as she sat. "Your father is a proud man, and you hurt that pride. Even if many, even most I dare say, will never know of the things that happened in the cave, his image in front of his men and his king was tarnished. Or at least to him it was. Truthfully, I think all of us agree that what you did was admirable," she smiled again as she said that.

"I shot you," I said, "and yet, you think that it was admirable. You don't want to get payback for that?"

She laughed again. "Oh, gods no. It was just a small wound, and I am fine now. I have a scar, and I can say that I had been shot. Most of us can't say that we have been shot by a gun. Most in our time," she stopped, seemingly choosing her words carefully.

"Most in our time have never even seen a gun, let alone been shot by one," I finished.

She looked surprised. "Yes. How much did they tell you," she asked, raising an eyebrow.

I shook my head. "Not much. And, the king said I must not speak of the gun, under pain of death, though I assume that it's okay to discuss it with you since you are aware, more than I, of its existence. As for the 'time'", I continued, taking a deep breath, "I have pieced together enough to know that the gun and the flas...flameless torch," I caught myself, hoping that she didn't notice, "are not from our time. And, through conversations, I've guessed that they must come from the future."

She nodded. "How very astute of you. Indeed, the gun and flashlight," she put slight emphasis on the last word, smiling at me, "are not something that will exist for many, many lifetimes. Thus, the promise of execution that comes with that knowledge, should you tell anyone."

"Indeed," was all I could think to say. She must have realised that I knew more than I was letting on, and it dawned on me that had I just said 'flashlight' without stumbling and correcting myself, she would have likely not even noticed.

"We are in a very quiet, and yet very dangerous, battle. Your father has felt the weight of that battle for many years, and it has worn him down, I'm afraid."

"The Brotherhood," I asked.

"Yes, The Brotherhood of Time. They are religious nutters that believe any who use the power to traverse time are abominations and must be destroyed. The irony, of course," she sighed, "is that they use that very power."

"Hypocrites," I said, a bit under my breath.

"Some, yes. And in my experience most religious people are hypocrites," she admitted. "But, some of the Brotherhood are so devoted that they follow their bible and end up sacrificing themselves when they believe they have done enough for God. Do you know what they do to people who travel through time?"

I shook my head. "No, I only know that the one man was told to kill me and take the prince."

"They would have simply shot you, because you are not a 'witch' as they call those who travel time. They use scripture to defend what they do. They say that in the Book of Revelation it says witches are to be cast into a "lake of fire and sulphur". They use this to excuse the fact that they burn alive those who travel time. And, some, when they believe that they have served their purpose to God, set themselves ablaze and burn."

"That is," I paused, looking for the right word, "disgusting."

Sabina nodded. "It is. And, thankfully, you did not have to experience any of that. But, what you did to defend the prince, that was heroic and the right thing to do. Therefore, I do not blame you, nor hold ill will towards you.”

She stood, and smoothed out the front of her coat. She looked at me, and stuck out one of her hands. “Friends,” she asked, with a smile.

I took her hand and shook it. “Friends,” I said, hoping that my voice was more certain than my mind. I still wasn’t convinced that this woman did not mean me harm.

“Do you need a hand with your bags?”

I shook my head. “No, it is just one small tuck. Thank you.”

“Very well,” she said, turning toward the door. “I will meet you in the stables.”

***

When I got to the stables, Sabina was there waiting. We mounted our horses, and left the castle. The trip wasn’t a long one, and I could make it on foot in under an hour. On horse, it was over after maybe a quarter of an hour, which was probably for the best. We rode in silence, and in my mind I wrestled with leaving the castle, and the fact that the prince did not come say goodbye to me. It was odd that he hadn’t come to see me, but I suppose I would see him again when I came to the castle next. He was my friend, but he was also busy.

151

When we arrived at my house I climbed down from my horse. There was a crash and yelling inside the house, and Sabina jumped down quickly, drawing her sword.

"It's fine," I said, stopping her. "My father has likely been drinking, and he is probably in a sour mood still."

She returned her sword, but kept her hand on it, looking at the door of the house. "Is this normal?"

I shrugged. "There are days where I know it will come, the anniversary of the day my mother died, for one. Others, I am caught off guard. But, I suppose it's normal enough."

She looked at me, putting her hand on my shoulder. "I'm sorry, that is not a good way to live. Are you going to be okay?"

I tried to smile, hoping that it actually appeared on my face. "I will be fine. He will likely tell me that he wishes I had died instead of my mother, and things of such nature, but I've heard them all before."

Sabina looked as though tears were forming, and she pulled me into a rough hug. "I'm sorry, you do not deserve that." She released me, and looked at me. "Be well, young Rorthan, and I will see you soon at the castle, I'm sure."

I nodded, and thanked her. She mounted her horse once more, and took the reins of the other horse in her hands and went back towards the castle.

I stood there for a moment, unsure if I wanted to go into the house. In the last few weeks I had fired a gun, and faced off with the Brotherhood of Time, I can surely handle my drunk father. I steeled myself, and opened the front door. It seemed to me that all of our belongings were on the floor. Broken vases, cups, plates, and other things littered the house. My father stood there, a goblet of wine in his hand.

"Oh, the bastard returns," he slurred, raising his cup towards me.

"Father-", I started to speak, but he pointed a gun at me.

"You shot me, you bastard, you shot Sabina," he said, waving the gun around, "you disgrace my name, and the king barely chastises you."

"The king-"

"The king is a gods damned fool. Your mother should be here, you bastard, and you should be dead instead. I have no use for a soft, bitch of a boy like you. No son of mine would be weak like you. And you think I don't see your desire to bed the prince?"

"You think I don't know that," I screamed. "I know that mother did not deserve-"

"Shut your mouth, bastard," he yelled back. "You do not get to speak of her." He dropped the gun, and when he bent over to pick it up, he stumbled and fell over. The wine had obviously been flowing for a while.

I ran over and picked up the gun, but he grabbed my leg as I tried to back up again. I fell, and he stood up over me. "I'll fix the mistake," he said, "you don't deserve the life you have."

As he bent down, I squeezed the trigger on the gun. Nothing happened. He slapped it out of my hand, and grabbed me by the shirt, picking me up and throwing me to the other side of the room. The room spun as my head hit the wall.

He picked up the gun, and slid the top of it back. The top snapped back into place. "You don't even know how to use one of these, do you, bastard?"

I tried to stand up, and crumpled back down. He pointed the gun at me, and I heard it crack. The wood beside my head splintered, and I tried to scamper away. He stepped closer to me, and grabbed my shirt again, putting the end of the gun to my neck. It burned, and I could hear my skin sizzle like bacon. He smiled, watching me try to fight him off, screaming in pain. He lifted me up, stumbling as he did, and hit me across the head with the gun. I saw bright spots, and I felt warm blood trickling down my head.

He threw me back against the wall, and pointed the gun at me again. "Hold still, bastard," he said.

"Fuck you," I said evenly, using every ounce of strength to speak and use words that I would never think of using. "I'm not a bastard, my name is Sebastian," I yelled at him, straightening my back as much as I could.

The look on his face was as though I had just slapped him. "How dare you use that name. You shouldn't even know that name," he roared, pointing the gun towards me again.

I scampered to the side, as the crack came again, this time it was three shots in very quick succession. One of them hit my shoulder, and I cried out.

"You have no name, bastard. I made sure not to name you. Your whore mother, and that man that she fucked, can welcome you in hell," he started, and then his hand lowered and he began to cry. "I loved your mother, how could she do that to me? How dare she treat me as some lesser man because she thought she was special? Just because her world was full of things I hadn't seen, did not make me a fool. I am no fool. I knew that she didn't love me, but I loved her. I treated her like my queen, and she took another man into her bed. And you came out from between her legs, killing her.

Maybe she deserved it for what she did, bastard, but you deserved it even moreso."

He raised the gun again, and wiped his tears with his free hand. "And now, I'll fix that." But before he could fire the gun, the door crashed in. He spun, and screamed in pain, and I saw his hand and the gun drop to the floor.

Sabina rushed to my side. "Rorthan," she said, putting her hand over my shoulder. "Oh, Rorthan. What did he do to you?"

"My name is Sebastian," I said, before my eyes closed, the last of my strength leaving me. "Rorthan is his name. My mother named me Sebastian." And then the world fell silent.

<h1 style="text-align:center">17</h1>

I woke up in the room that had been my chambers for the last week. At first, I didn't think anything of it. I had forgotten going home, and what my father had done. I sat up in bed, and instantly regretted it. My body screamed at me in protest, and the room spun, dropping me back to my pillow.

"Easy," the prince said, appearing at my side.

I turned my head slowly. "Tomren," I asked.

The prince smiled. He had been sitting in one of the chairs, and when I awoke he was quickly beside me. He reached down, and put my hand in his. "Yes," he said with a smile.

"It hurts," I said, closing my eyes.

"What does? Should I fetch the meister," he asked.

I shook my head. "No. I'm okay. It just hurts. All of it. My body, and my heart."

The prince squeezed my hand. "What happened, why did he do this," the prince asked, and I could have sworn that his voice had a tremble in it.

"He was drunk, and he was angry that your father did not punish me more harshly. But," I said, pausing, trying to decide if I wanted to tell him all of what my father said.

"But, what?"

"But, he kept saying terrible things to me. I don't know why. He said terrible things, Tomren. He kept calling me a 'bastard' over and over. And, not like just cursing me, he said that I was not his son. He said that my mother laid with another man, and that is why she died after she had me, but that it should have been me. He said that he was going to fix that mistake, and he was going to kill me. He had a gun, and he shot me, and he was about to kill me when Sabina came in. He was going to kill me, and he's not my father. Who is my father, if not him? Who am I," as I asked the last question, my body gave in to my heart, and I began sobbing. I couldn't stop. I was breathing in short, tight gasps, and I was crying so fiercely that no sound came out.

"I'm sorry," the prince said, hugging my face tight to his chest. "We will figure it out. We will get you answers, and we will see your...the general, punished. But," he said, stroking my hair, "you have to breathe. Calm yourself, or you will pass out again."

"I...can't...help...it," I said, in between shallow breaths and sobs.

The prince backed my head away from his chest, and put his head next to mine. "Breath with me," he said, "inhale when I do, exhale when I do."

He took long, dramatic breaths. At first I couldn't, but after a moment, my breathing leveled. We were breathing in unison, and my sobbing had calmed down as well. He pulled his face from mine. He wasn't far, and his cerulean eyes drew me in, calming me. I leaned forward and kissed him.

It wasn't the passionate, tongue filled kiss that I had dreamt of. But, I kissed him, and he...kissed back. Just a moment of our lips touching.

"I'm sorry," I said, pulling back just a little.

"Why?"

"Well, because, I don't know, I mean, you're the prince, and I'm just me, and you're a boy and I'm a boy, and I don't think your father would approve of this, and-"

The prince took my hand in his again, kissed my forehead, and smiled in a way I had never seen him smile before. "I fancy you, Rorthan. My father is not here, and who or what I am is irrelevant."

This should have been a magical moment, but he called me Rorthan. Almost without thinking, I said calmly, "My name is not Rorthan. That was my father's...the general's name. Call me Sebastian."

Tomren raised an eyebrow. "Sebastian?"

I smiled. "Yes, it was the name my mother gave me. Oh, gods, my mother. What time is it? How long have I been here," I asked, my smile fading and my hands pulling out of his. I stood, though wobbly, and the prince steadied me.

"It is night," he said, gesturing to the window. "You were brought here by Sabina last night. What is wrong?"

"The church, I need to get to the church," I said, quickly.

"What church? It's too late for church, we can go to the chapel tomorrow."

I held my head. "No, damn it, no," I snapped and he shrank back just a little. "I'm sorry, I mean The Room of Faces," I said gently, feeling silly saying it.

"The room is a church?"

I nodded, "Yes, and please, I need to get there now."

"No, you need to rest. Lay back down, and I'll get the meister to make you some tea. We can go tomorrow," he said, taking my arm and trying to guide me back to bed.

"No," I said, sharper than I would have liked, and shrugged my arm free. "Please, Tomren, I'm going with or without you, but in my condition I would appreciate your help. Please."

The prince cocked his head to the side. "You're determined?"

"Yes," I said, nodding furiously. That probably wasn't best for my head. I sat down on the bed as another wave of dizziness crashed over me.

"Okay," he said. Then he smiled, the same warm smile he had earlier.

"What," I asked as I stood.

"You keep," he started, and his smile somehow seemed to get even bigger, "you keep calling me 'Tomren'."

I smiled back. "Well, we did kiss, and I think that means I get to call you by your name. At least, when we are alone."

"Indeed, Sebastian."

I smiled as he helped me to the door. I loved the way my name sounded on his beautiful lips. "Okay, let's go. Quiet, you aren't supposed to be out of bed."

I nodded, and we made our way to the door.

At the top of the staircase, Tomren stopped and lit the torch with his flint. We made our way to the bottom, and he pushed the medallion to open the door. It slid away, and he helped me inside.

"Stand here for a second," he said, entering the church. Moments later, the flame ran around the room, and he was back to help me enter the room. He sat me down at the closest desk, and pulled another chair next to me. "What now," he asked, clearly curious about my sudden urge to come here. "And why did you call this place a 'church'?"

"Because it is," Arthur's voice boomed from behind us. "Why did you bring him?"

The prince stood, and spun. He drew a dagger from his waist. I didn't even realize he had a weapon. I jumped up as quickly as I could in my condition, and stood in front of him.

"Sebastian, get behind me," he said. I was surprised to hear him use my name so freely and quickly.

"You told him your name," Arthur asked.

"I did. I trust him."

"I trust no one," Arthur retorted.

"You trusted me," I said. "And I trust him." I reached out and grabbed Tomren's hand.

"Very well," Arthur sighed. "It's too late now to pretend that I don't exist, and I will be able to answer his questions easier than you. Hell, you probably have your own. But," he said with an amused smile, "could you ask him to put his little knife away?"

"I'm right bloody here," the prince said, stepping beside me, though I noticed, not letting go of my hand. He put his dagger back in his waste.

"Indeed you are, Your Highness," Arthur said, bowing his head with genuine respect. As he walked toward us, he seemed to notice for the first time that I was injured. "What happened?"

"My father," I started, but was quickly crying again.

"Rorthan did this to you," he asked in a growl, his face turning dark in the fire light.

"He did, and he is in the custody of my father now. And," Tomren said, looking to me, "it cost him a hand."

I had forgotten somehow that Sabina had cut it off when she rescued me. My knees buckled.

"Quickly," Arthur said, "bring him here." He turned and closed the stone door, reopening it in the other direction. The lights inside glowed bright.

Tomren helped me in, and sat me down in one of the rolling chairs. "What is this place," he asked, looking around in wonder.

Arthur sat. "Sit, young prince," he said, gesturing to a chair. "I will tell you, but first, I need to know what happened to Sebastian."

I looked up, and started to tear up. Quickly, Tomren grabbed my hand, which caused Arthur to raise an eyebrow. When Arthur said nothing, Tomren recounted what had happened, telling both what I had told him, and what he had heard from Sabina. It would seem that she had a bad feeling after she left, and when she came back she heard a gunshot. She looked in one of our windows, and as soon as she saw what was happening she burst in.

"I see. And, he was captured?"

I nodded, and Tomren answered. "He was. He sits in the dungeon now, and will be brought before my father in the morning."

"I hope that your father deals with him appropriately," Arthur sighed. "I would prefer not to have to get involved. Now then," he said standing and walking over to the refrigerator. He grabbed three waters, and handed Tomren and I both one. "You want to know who I am, and what this place is?"

"Yes," Tomren said, before turning to me and adding, "and why my best friend did not tell me of it."

"Well," Arthur said, sitting back down in his chair, "I suppose because I asked him not to. I do not trust people, young prince. And though I have observed you, and the goings on in the kingdom, and I believe you and your father to both be fair, I must be cautious still. But, here you are, and answers you will have."

For the next few hours, Arthur explained to Tomren many of the same things he explained to me. He showed him videos, though thankfully he did not show any of the ones with my mother in them.

Eventually, I began to doze off, and Arthur stopped. "Prince Tomren, I believe it is time for you to take your friend here back to his bed chambers."

I sat up straight. "I'm fine," I said, as firmly as I could, "continue."

Tomren stood. "He's right. You need rest, and before long the meister may be checking in. We need to return." He turned to Arthur. "Can we come back?"

Arthur smiled. "Yes. I will return here every evening. When he is well," he said, gesturing towards me, "come and see me. I will know if you have come, and I will tell you more then."

We both thanked him, and made our way back to my chamber. Once there, Tomren laid me back in the bed. "Rest," he said, "I will return in the morning." He kissed my forehead, and then left. Thankfully no meister came to my room that night. Despite all that had occurred, I fell into a deep and restful sleep.

18

The next morning, I was awakened by a knock at the door. The meister brought in food, a wonderful plate of sausage, oats, and fruit. He also brought tea, and some herbal concoction that he applied to my shoulder. I winced as he rubbed it into my skin, though he did so as gently as he could.

"This will help the wound to heal. It should also help with the pain," he said. The meister grabbed the cup of tea, and handed it to me. "Drink half, eat the food, and then finish the tea."

I tasted the tea. It wasn't terrible, but it certainly wasn't something I would choose to drink on a normal day. I must have made a face, because the meister laughed.

"It may not be pleasant, but it is helpful. Today will be my last day serving you," the meister said, "tomorrow, Meister Mowbray will be taking over."

I swallowed the bite of the sausage that I had been chewing. "Why?"

"The king wishes it so," he said, rising. "It has been an honor assisting you these last weeks, and I hope to get to speak with you again."

I stood as well, though somewhat slower than he had. "Thank you for all you have done."

He nodded. "You are welcome, young Rorthan."

I winced as he said that, but he had already turned and was leaving. Gods, how do you suddenly have people start calling you by a new name? Gods be damned if I wouldn't figure a way. Young Rorthan died at the general's hands. My name was Sebastian.

I finished the food, bathed, and sat down in a chair by the window. I could see the forest in the distance, and it hit me just how much had changed in such a little time. I became friends, or whatever we were, with the prince. I had saved him, or so they say, and my father...no not my father, the general, hated me for it. He tried to kill me. The man who had raised me. The man who had called himself my father, whom I had called father, tried to kill me. Sabina had saved me thankfully, but he wanted me dead. Because, apparently, saving the prince isn't enough to make him proud. What did that make me? If I really was a bastard, then I had no mother and no father now. Or, at least no father whom I knew. Where would I go? What would I do to survive? Gods, would I be sent to an orphanage? If that happened, I would lose my right to access the castle, and I wouldn't be able to go to the church. I wouldn't get to see Arthur, or the videos of my mother.

I wouldn't see the prince. This thought gave me pause, and all else left my mind. Tears filled my eyes. The thought of not seeing the prince, of losing my friend, made my heart beat fast and loud in my ears. I hadn't known the prince for that long, but we had become close, we had even kissed, and I had no one else in my life. I could not lose him too.

The door must have opened, though I was too busy wallowing in my own pity to hear it.

"What is wrong," the prince asked, at my side suddenly. He placed a hand on my shoulder.

I just looked up at him. How could I tell him that he was all I had left now? And, even if I had that much courage, I wouldn't be able to get the words out. I was crying now, but I would be sobbing and unable to speak if I tried to convey that message to him.

"You are safe here," he said, "no one will hurt you ever again."

I snorted. "You don't know that. And, I can't stay here forever. I'll end up in an orphanage somewhere, and-".

"No," the prince said quietly, kneeling down beside me. He wiped my tears away. "I will not let that happen. I will make sure you have a home. There are Lords and Ladies in the kingdom that would care for you lovingly. I will make sure that you are not left to an orphanage, you have my word."

I turned toward him, and buried my head in his chest. "Why would you do that for me? Why are you being nice to me at all," I asked through my sobs.

He ran his fingers through my hair. "I am your friend. You saved my life. You," he said, pulling my head back to look in my eyes, "are my General of The Room of Faces."

I laughed a small, pitiful laugh, but a laugh nonetheless. "I don't want to be a general of anything," I said. "General's be damned."

He pulled me back into a hug. "Fine. You are my best friend. I will protect you always. Now," he said, releasing me and standing, "My father wants to see you. He would like us to join him in his dining hall."

"I don't know if I can do it right now. I'm," I gestured from my head to my toes, "a mess. I can barely stop crying for a moment."

The prince smiled, that perfect smile, and wiped my tears. "Be strong. I will be there. Please, we must go. I'll be strong with you."

I wanted to ask him again why he was being nice to me. Why did he care at all what happened to me? We had only been friends for such a short time. But, I just got up, went to the basin in front of my looking glass, splashed water on my face, and turned.

"Okay, let's go," I said, determined.

Tomren laughed. "Perhaps we will find you some different clothes first."

***

We were ushered into the dining hall. It wasn't very large in comparison to the hall where they held feasts. It was more of just a dining room. The table sat eight people, and only the king was sitting at the moment. He was at the head of the table, and there was a guard on either side of him. The king stood when we entered, placing his napkin on the table in front of him.

"Please, come in. Sit, eat," he said, gesturing to the seats beside him.

"Thank you, Your Majesty," I said, bowing my head before sitting.

"Are you hungry," he asked after we had all sat down.

"No, thank you," I shook my head, "the meister brought me tea and breakfast first thing this morning."

The king nodded. "Of course."

"Well, I'm fairly sure I could eat an entire pig, and at least a dozen eggs," the prince said with a smile. The three of us chuckled lightly, but it felt good to laugh.

"Young Rorthan," the king began.

"He prefers not to be called that," the prince interjected. "The general has disowned him, and he was never given a proper name."

The king looked at me. "The fact that you were never given a forename was unfortunate, and I always assumed it was just grief. And once enough time had passed, I suppose it just seemed odd then to give you a name. I have heard about the things that your fa...the general," he corrected himself, "said to you. I am sorry."

I shrugged. "Thank you. I am still trying to understand. But," I said, raising my eyes to his, "I was given a name, he just never used it. My mother wanted me to be called Sebastian."

There was a look on his face that only lasted a second. Recognition? Surprise? Knowing? It was gone as quick as it came.

"Very well. Sebastian," the king said as he stood from his chair, "I am King Osbert Hammond." He extended his hand towards me. I shook his hand, and he sat back down.

"I want to thank you again, for what you have done for my son. You not only saved his life, you also have given him friendship that has been lacking in it," he said, looking to his son. The prince smiled at me. "As a father, it makes me happy to see him enjoying his time with a boy his age."

"The prince is a good person, you have done well raising him," I said, unsure what to really say to such a compliment from the king.

"Thank you," he said, earnestly. "Have you thought about what you will do, now that...well, now that things are how they are?"

I felt the tears sting my eyes. I blinked furiously, trying to push them back. "I have, and I honestly don't know. I have no family, Sire, and I am still not old enough to live on my own."

"Which is why," the prince cut in, saving me, "I had hoped that maybe he could be sent to a Lord. Lord Alured, perhaps? He and his wife have no children, and yet I know they had always desired them."

The king looked at his son, perhaps with a bit of pride. "A fair idea, and certainly one that I shall look into. For now-" the king was cut off by the door opening.

Two guards led in Sabina, and...the general. His feet were shackled, and his left hand was tied to the stump on the right. Irons would not stay on, I supposed. Sabina walked in front of him, head held high.

The guards pushed the general to his knees at the foot of the table. The king stood. Unsure what to do, I stood as well, and though I don't think I had to, the prince followed my lead.

"Leave us," the king said. The guards and Sabina turned to go. "Sabina, stay with us," the king stopped her.

She turned back and stood behind the general.

"Rorthan," the king sighed. "You, Rorthan, were my most trusted general. You advised me wisely for many years. We suffered loss together. We basked in victory together. You know things that very few people in this kingdom know. You have been an advisor, a leader, and a friend. And yet, here we are. Your loyalty was tested, and it failed."

"Your Majesty-" the general started.

"You will not speak," the king said, his voice firm and steady. "You will remain silent, or you will find yourself unable to speak. Unless I ask you a question, you will not utter a word. Do you understand?"

The general nodded. "Good," the king continued. He looked at me. "That young man saved my son's life, and you clearly did not agree with my decree on what would happen to him for the...misunderstanding that occurred while he was saving my son. This tested your loyalty to me. My most trusted general showed that he could not be trusted."

The general opened his mouth, and quickly closed it.

"You have done so much good for this kingdom in your life. And, yet, you decided that you knew better than the king, and so you cost the kingdom its most trusted general. Twice in the past fortnight, I have warned you to bite your tongue when you said that he," he said, pointing to me, "was not your son. Did I not?"

This made my breath catch in my chest. He had. The general had said that I was 'no son' of his, and the king had told him to watch what he said. Had the king known that I was not his son, that I was a bastard?

"You did, Sire."

The king nodded. "And, yet, you chose to not only tell the boy that you are not his father, you chose to beat him, shoot him, and try to kill him, did you not?"

Tears again pricked at my eyes. Hearing it said out loud by the king brought every moment rushing back. How could he do that to me? Because I'm not his son, I realized. He merely tolerated my existence.

"Your Majesty, I was drunk. My pride was wounded."

"That does not answer my question. Did you do the things you are accused of," the king asked.

The general held his head high. "I did."

"You defied a direct order from your king, and you thought you knew better of what the boy deserved, did you not?"

"I do know better, he is my son."

This took the room by surprise, and my breath caught in a gasp. How dare he say that now.

The king stood, and walked towards the general. "But, he is not, is he? He is Sebastian, the son of your late wife, yes. But, he is not your son. And you made sure that he knew that, did you not?"

The general looked at the king, but didn't answer him. "And how does he know that name? Have you thought of that, o' wise king," sarcasm dripped from that last part. "Have you thought about the fact that two of the three people who knew that name are in this room, and the other is banished under pain of death? I bloody well did not tell him. Did you?"

The king slapped the general. "Watch yourself. You have already committed treasonous acts, and you are dreadfully close to meeting the headsman, Rorthan."

The general's back straightened. "Oh, so you do not want him to know about-".

His words were cut short by a blood chilling scream from his mouth. The king had kicked the stub where his hand once was.

"One more word," the king said, grabbing him by the shirt, "and I will have your tongue."

The general pulled his arm close to his body and rocked back and forth.

"Sabina," the king said, walking over to her. "You have served me loyally, and you saved Sebastian's life. You did not hesitate to do what was right, even when that meant standing up to your commander." He reached in the pocket of his coat. When he pulled his hand out, it held the pendant of a general.

"Sabina Ayers," he said, pinning the pendant to her shirt, "you are hereby to be known as General Ayers. You will lead the members of the King's Men, and you are to train Sebastian," he said, gesturing to me, "and welcome him into the fold when he is ready."

Rorthan snorted, a look of disgust on his face, but to his credit he said nothing. The king glared at him.

"You, Rorthan. You are hereby sentenced to live the remainder of your natural days in the dungeon. You will not leave the cell. You will see no light, from the time the door locks behind you, until the day you breathe your last breath. Food will be brought to you, and there will be no schedule to when it is brought. It may be daily, it may be that a whole pile of slop is brought to you and you will not be brought food again for days or even weeks. The guard that is to bring your food and empty your chamber pot will wear night goggles, they will show you no light and speak no words. You will go mad. But, still, until you die, you will not know the touch of another, nor the sound of their voice, nor the look of their face."

I had no idea what these 'night goggles' were, but the look on the former general's face was one of pure and unbridled fear. I had never seen that look on his face in my life.

"As for young Sebastian," the king said, turning to me and offering a smile, "he will be my ward. I will have him taught the finest of lessons under the greatest of tutors. He will train with General Sabina. He will wear only the finest clothes, and eat only the finest of foods."

The king paused, and looked at Rorthan before turning back to me. "Sebastian, you have endured many things for someone so young in years. Because you have been a friend to my son, because you have guarded him with your life, I will treat you as a son. You will live with us here, in the castle. You will have all of the honors and freedoms that he does. The only thing that he has that you will not, is a claim to the throne. I will allow you to choose a new surname. And when the time comes, I will grant you land, and title, and wife. Stand, Sebastian," he said, walking toward me.

I stood, unsure of what to think of what he just said. Raised as a prince? Given title when I am of age? To live at the castle? Gods, to get to be by the prince every day?

"Sebastian, I am sorry for the trials that you have faced," he began, and when I bowed my head, he stopped. "You will learn the proper etiquette for a prince. For though you will not have the title of prince, you will be treated as one. You need not bow every time that I speak to you. I cannot ever expect that you will view me as a father, but I will always hope that you view me as a, well, maybe like the awesome uncle that happens to also be the king."

I nodded. "Thank you, Your Majesty."

The king smiled, and it reached all the way to his eyes. "Gods, this is what I mean, boy." He put a hand on my shoulder. "It is okay. We will teach you," he said, glancing at Tomren.

He turned back to Sabina, and his smile faded to a firm facade. "General Ayers, take the prisoner to the dungeon. When he has been secured, return to me please. We have much to discuss."

Sabina bowed her head, and reached down, pulling Rorthan roughly to his feet.

"As for you," the king said to his former general, "I hope that the faces of those that you knew, and this moment here, in this hall, haunt you for the rest of your days. I hope that the coming madness is slow to take you, and you have years to think on all that you have done, and all that you have lost." The king turned, and walked out of the hall.

I looked to the prince, he had already come to my side of the table, and took my arm and led me out of the hall. I glanced back to see Rorthan being led away. That was the last time I would see his face. I imagined that the pure fear on it resembled that which had been on my own face as I prepared for him to end my life. And I smiled at him.

19

By the time we had returned to my chambers I was exhausted, both body and mind. My body was still recovering from the damage that Rorthan had caused, and my mind was racing with so many emotions I wasn't sure I could process them all. I was just exhausted. Tomren started to guide me to the chair by the window, but I stopped him.

"Please, just put me into bed. I need to rest."

Tomren had just helped me get settled, and sat down beside me on the bed, when there was a knock on the door. "Come," I called. The king entered and I struggled to sit up. The king held up a hand to stop me.

"Please, rest," he said, "I will call Beltoch to ensure that you are comfortable. How are you?"

Tomren helped me prop myself up. "Thank you," I said to him with a smile. I turned to face the king. "I am well, thank you for everything that you have done for me."

The king waved his hand dismissively. "You are very welcome, Sebastian. But, please, know that I meant everything that I said this morning. You have been dealt a poor lot in life. I am happy that I am in a position to help you, even if only a little."

"A little," I repeated, in disbelief. "You have helped me heal twice now. You have offered me more than I could ever have imagined, hoped for, or deserved. You have helped me much more than a little, Your Majesty."

The king smiled. "What do you call my son?"

I looked toward Tomren. Was this a trick question of some kind? I didn't really know he was getting at. "As of late, I call him Tomren, Sire."

He looked at his son. I now realized that not only had the prince remained by my side, his hand rested on mine. The king's eyes came back to mine. "Good. He calls me father. I am not your father, nor are we related by blood. I have, however, known you for your entire life, though I have not been close with you. I knew your mother, and she did everything that she could to help my dear Chelsey when she was at the end of her time here. I will always be grateful for that, and with all you have done for my boy, I am grateful to you. So," he sighed, smiling after, "when we are alone, in these settings, you may call me Osbert. I will be your king until I die, then my dear son will be your king. But I want you to think of us as much more than just the rulers of the kingdom."

I nodded. "Thank you, Osbert," I stretched out the name a bit, feeling it out. It felt strange, and almost wrong to call the king by his name. But, he is the one who asked me to, and so I would do as he asked.

He smiled. "You'll get used to it," he gave me a wink. "Now, then, I do have one other matter that I must discuss with you."

I sat up a little taller, my body aching with the effort. Tomren squeezed my hand gently.

"Your name, 'Sebastian'," he started, "how did you learn of this name?"

Rorthan had said that Arthur was banished, and if he returned he would be executed. I could not tell of him, and risk harm coming to him. He had not only given me no reason to wish him ill, he was my only link to my mother. "My...the Gener...Rorthan," I sputtered, trying to make my words make sense, and trying to figure out a lie in my head. My head pounded, my heart blasting my ears with a loud thump, thump.

The king held up a hand. "I know that you have been through much, Sebastian, and I am a patient man. But, please do not lie to me. Know that I have knowledge of many, many things. Some of them I have reason to believe that the two of you," he said with a glance toward Tomren, before returning his gaze to me, "are aware of. More than you should be. And that doesn't upset me, but please, be honest."

I looked down, and began picking at my fingernails. "I," I started, but stopped. I looked up at the king. I owed him much, and I owed Arthur little, despite him being my only link to the videos of my mother. "I met Arthur when I was eight. Rorthan had been drunk, and he said things, things that hurt me, things like why did I have to survive and my mother die."

The king brought a chair to the side of my bed. "I am sorry that you had to endure that. I had no idea he had said these things to you."

I shook my head. "He didn't. He had gotten drunk, he always did so on the anniversary of her death." I laughed mirthlessly. "The irony that every year day I have, soon after I am reminded of the fact that I killed my mother. People normally look forward to their year day. Mayhaps one day I will, but I have never done so yet."

The king frowned at me. "I am sorry to hear that. It is not fair to you, none of it, least of all to have your father put you through that every year."

"But he's not, is he?"

The king shook his head, and looked away. "No, Sebastian, he is not. I do not know who your father is, not for sure. I do suspect that I know, but it also does not matter. Rorthan loved your mother very much, and he stood by her and agreed to give you his name and raise you as his own. I do think he loved you in a way, as best he could."

"Do not make excuses for him," I snapped. The king sat back sharply in his chair as if I had struck him. That made me pause, my mind registering how I had just spoken to the king. But, it did not stop me. Anger rose inside, and I felt my face darken. "He was a grown man, and he treated me like rubbish. And," I said, my eyes looking directly at the king's own, "it may not matter to you who my true father is, but it damn well matters to me. I do not have anyone to call family." I looked away, the last few words breaking and trembling, my anger with them.

The king sat forward again. This time he put his hand on my arm. "You have Tomren, and you have me. And, while I will never fill the role of father for you, I will always look after you, and I will do my best to give you a good life. You have my word on that."

I didn't look at him. I couldn't. It was all I could do to keep myself from crying, and I did not want the king to see that.

"It will take time," the king said, sitting back again, "but you will press on. You have great strength, and you have shown it already in your short life. But," he sighed, "back to Arthur."

I nodded. I had forgotten that he had wanted to know about him. "Right. After I had heard Rorthan say those things, I left. I ran to the cliffs, and I sat there. I grieved, and I wept, and I yelled into the night, but my screams were swallowed by the wind. I had thought I was alone. I did not want to return to the house. I thought that I wanted to die. I sat on the edge, and let myself slip."

Tomren's breath caught, and he gripped my hand a little tighter. "A strong hand grabbed my shirt," I continued, "and pulled me back. He set me straight, he told me that my mother had loved me, and that he was once her friend. He said he once had a bond with my father."

"And, he told you the name that your mother had given you," the king asked.

"No," I said, shaking my head. "He simply pulled me back from the edge, and gave me a moment to think about whether I truly wanted to fall or not. I turned back to look at the sea below, and there was a flash of lightning, and when I looked back toward him, he was gone."

The king nodded. "But, you saw him again."

It wasn't a question. "Not long ago. He told me...things."

The king sat there for a moment, seeming to think that over. "I'm sure he did. Probably more than I would like for him to have told you. Where did you see him?"

I hated to lie to the king. I truly did. I hoped that Tomren would not expose my lie, but I did it anyway. "In the market. He was just there, and we spoke, and then he was gone." The prince didn't flinch, nor did he say anything to contradict me. I squeezed his hand this time.

"He tends to do that," the king said. "Do you think that he will find you again?"

I shrugged. "I don't know. Mayhaps."

"He was banished from this kingdom. I thought him to be something that evidence in the years since says he may not have been. I was younger, had just learned of, well, you know, time and such," he said, waving his hand in the air, "and I was scared of him and the Brotherhood."

It surprised me that the king seemed to be almost at a loss for words. "But, he does not belong to the Brotherhood," I said.

The king's eyes narrowed a bit, and he nodded. "I suspected as much as time went on. But, it does not change that he was banished. If you see him again, I would ask that you tell him I would like to meet with him. Tell him what I have told you, that I do not believe him to be the man I feared he was. But," he said firmly, "I do have questions that need answered. And, if he will answer them to my satisfaction, I will allow him to have freedom in my kingdom again."

I thought about that for a minute. "And, if I do see him, and I do tell him this, and I do convince him to speak with you, how does he know you will not just capture him?"

The king smiled. "He didn't tell you everything I see. I cannot capture him. I suppose I could kill him outright, but I do hope that he knows that I am not that man, and," he said, his face becoming serious, "I hope you do as well. No harm will come to him, at least not while we are meeting."

I just nodded.

The king stood, and placed a hand on my shoulder. "I will send Beltoch in to make sure you are comfortable for the remainder of the day. Rest," he said, looking to Tomren, "we will leave you for now. Tomorrow we will break our fast together. In fact, I would like it to become our habit, to at least share first meal together. This is your home now."

I smiled. "Thank you, Your...Osbert."

The king and the prince left the room. The reality of how alone I truly was came rushing back to me in that empty room. The king seemed to be a good man, and he seemed to genuinely care for my well being. And Tomren certainly was my friend. But, I was in a castle, with the man I knew as my father in a dark hole in the dungeon, and at most I had three people that cared about me in the whole of the world.

20

At first meal the following day, I listened more than I participated. The king seemed to discuss the basic comings and goings of the kingdom with Tomren. He asked for his input on several matters, and he even included me occasionally. He asked how I was feeling, and I told him that I was in much less pain today, more uncomfortable than anything. The food was good, but I barely had tasted it. All I could think about as they went about their morning routine was how strange and different this all was. A month earlier, I was just the general's son. I was nothing special, I had never talked to the prince, let alone the king. I had wished that I could get the education that the prince got. I had dreamed of what it would be like to eat in the castle, to live in the castle. And, now here I was. Having breakfast with the king, no, having breakfast with Osbert and Tomren. The generosity was incredible, but it still felt...odd. No matter how I tried, it didn't feel right.

"Just give it time," the king said, as if reading my mind.

"I'm sorry?"

"You look like you are trying to figure everything out, trying to adjust to everything at once. Much has happened to you, and you will need time to adjust.”

I nodded. “It is a lot,” I admitted.

The king looked at me for a moment. “In the future,” he said so casually it was impressive, “there are people, doc...meisters, who are called ‘therapists’. They talk to you, meisters for your mind, if you will. They have done wonderful things to help me to deal with my challenges, and I believe that they have helped Tomren as well.” Tomren nodded at that. The king continued, “Would you like to speak with one? I truly believe that you will find it to be enlightening.”

I pushed the food around on my plate for a moment. What could talking do? Would it make my mother come back? Would I suddenly be loved by the only family that I ever knew? “I don’t know, maybe,” I shrugged.

“Think on it. The offer is open to you at any time. Simply let one of us know, and I will see it done.”

“May I go out today? For a walk I mean,” I asked, quickly adding, “I would like to have some fresh air.”

The king nodded. “Of course, you are free to come and go as you please. However,” he said, placing his fork down, and looking at me, “it is known to some now, and will be widely known by day’s end, that you are my ward. There are those that would harm you simply for that reason. I ask that if you leave the castle, you take a guard with you."

His reasoning made sense, and it was a fair enough request, though it still made me bristle. "If I must," I answered, not rudely.

"I would feel better. Tomren has obligations until late afternoon, but I'm sure he would be willing to accompany you on a walk then."

Tomren smiled and nodded. "Of course, I would enjoy that."

I smiled back. "Thank you."

They went back to discussing matters that I knew little of, though I was determined that soon I would learn. Just not today. Not yet.

When the meal ended, I returned to my chambers, and sat by the window. My thoughts were dark, and I felt hopelessness wash over me again. No one wanted me. My mother didn't want me enough to live. My father didn't want me enough to even make himself known to me. The general didn't want me enough to treat me as a child should be treated, let alone as the son I was called for many years. Sure, the king and the prince wanted me to stay with them, although I couldn't help but wonder if that was just from some sense of duty for having saved Tomren's life. But it would be of no matter to them if I were gone. Perhaps, it would be for the best if I left. Surely they would look for me for a while, but they would soon move on with their lives.

I stood and packed a tuck, just what little was mine, plus a torch and flint. I stood and walked to the door, turning and looking at what had been my room for the last few weeks. It hadn't been long, but it had been comfortable and I had been cared for. My shoulder still ached where I had been shot, and I still had bruises. But, I would manage on my own. I left the room, and was going to leave the castle, when I decided to go to the church first. I could certainly use the flashlight, and maybe even the gun. There was one scullery maid that was in the hall walking briskly with a pile of dishes, but she was soon gone. I walked to the hidden door, and opened it. As soon as it opened, I disappeared into it and closed it again.

At the bottom of the steps, I found the flashlight, and turned it on. It seemed dimmer. I shined it around the room and the light did not reach the far corners as it once had. That didn't seem very encouraging, but it wasn't going to stop me either. I went over to the wall with the guns on it, and grabbed the one I had looked at before. I slid the top back as I had seen Rorthan do, and when I released it, it snapped back with a distinct click. I slipped it into my tuck. I thought about taking some of the other things, but I didn't know what any of them did really, and I didn't need the extra weight.

I went back to the door, and left. The hall was empty, and I returned to the castle, walking towards the main doors. If the king had mentioned to any of the guards that I wasn't to leave without one of them though, I would be stopped. I decided to go back to the gardens where I had met Tomren.

The smell of the herbs brought back that first meeting, and I felt just a little bit sad that I was leaving like this. I cared for Tomren, and he seemed to care about me as well, but the last thing I needed was to lose another person that I cared about.

I walked to the edge of the castle grounds, to the place where Tomren and I had snuck out the first time. And, I slipped away into the forest.

***

I walked in the direction of the cave, or at least I thought I did. I'm not sure what exactly I had wanted to do once I got there, but I figured I would go see it once more before I left. As I walked, it was like something was pulling me to it. I could almost feel the cave. I got gooseflesh when I realized that I was feeling it, sensing it. The feeling pushed my feet faster, and before long I saw it. There was one guard, and he seemed to be pacing. No, not pacing, he was patrolling, walking a small path around the area in front of the cave. He disappeared for a couple of moments, and was

192

back. Then he did it all over again. Once he was out of sight, I moved quickly, or as quickly as I could with the tuck and the aches starting to return after walking through the woods. I made it in though, and I didn't hear any sounds of pursuit.

I walked as far as I could before it was too dark to see in front of me. I got the flashlight out of my tuck, and turned it on. I found my way back to the place where we had met the men that wanted to kill me and take the prince. There were still large chunks of the spires on the ground, the one that had stabbed Tomren through the shoulder still bore his dried blood. I shone the light in the direction that the one man had walked off in after giving the order to kill me. Slowly and carefully I began walking. That same feeling that had drawn me to the cave was strong here, mayhaps even stronger. I stopped when I reached the far wall. There was nothing further. The feeling in my head urged me to keep going still.

I turned back, and as I turned, the flashlight caught something metal in the stone. I found it after a second of searching. It was one of the discs that bore the face of the Brotherhood. I pushed it, and the stone moved, sliding back and then to the right. I shone the light down the hall that had opened in front of me. There was something metal at the end of it.

As I started to walk towards it, the object began glowing. It was about half as tall as I, and as big around as the trunk of a tree. It shone as if it was all metal, a solid black cylinder with a pure white light coming out of its top. It thrummed deeply.

"Don't touch it," Arthur's voice called from behind me.

I whirled, almost falling. "What are you doing here," I practically squeaked. I cleared my throat for good measure. "You followed me?"

"I did," Arthur admitted. "And you are lucky that I did."

I turned back to the object, it glowed brighter the closer I got to it. "What is it?"

"It is one of the beacons that I told you about. How did you know where to find it," he asked almost excitedly.

I raised an eyebrow. "I don't know, I guess I just found it."

Arthur shook his head. "You didn't feel drawn to it?"

I took a step back from him, and closer to the beacon. It glowed even brighter. "Mayhaps," I said.

"Do not touch it," he repeated. "You did feel it. I know you did. And the fact that it is reacting to you tells me that I am correct."

"The king banished you," I blurted out.

Arthur seemed surprised by my sudden change of subject. "He did," Arthur admitted. "He thought that I was one of them, one of that disgusting Brotherhood. And, at one time I was. But, when I learned of their true actions, the depravity that ate at their core, I left them behind."

"He wants to talk to you," I said.

Arthur cocked his head. "Why," he asked. "What did you tell him," he added quickly.

"My name."

Arthur nodded. "Of course. Three people alive today knew of that name. Rorthan certainly wouldn't have told you. The king knew that he himself was not the one to tell you. So, that left me. Did you tell him where we met?"

"No, I told him about the cliffs when I was younger. I told him that this time I met you in the market not long ago. That you appeared and disappeared just as quickly. He said that he believes he was wrong about you, he has found evidence since your being banished that says as much. And that he wants to meet with you."

Arthur seemed to think about this, but said nothing. He just looked at me, and then behind my back to the thing that was glowing, and back to me.

I turned to it, but didn't get closer. "What does it do? Why is it glowing like that?"

Arthur closed the space between us, and put a firm hand on my good shoulder. "It is glowing like that because you are near it. And you have a power that you do not know how to control."

I snapped my head to look at him. "Are you saying that I'm doing this," I asked incredulously, waving my hand towards it. As I did, the hum intensified, and I noticed the wind. It had been there, growing. But, I hadn't noticed it until now because I had been too mesmerized by the beacon. But, now it went from a breeze to a gentle wind.

"Yes, and you have no idea how to control it," Arthur said, his voice rising slightly to be heard above the rushing of the air.

As much as I didn't want to admit it to him, I could feel it. It could feel the thrum of it in my head, and I could feel the power in it growing. And, I had felt it, or sensed it, as I walked. Even from a distance I knew it was there, though I had never seen it.

"Then show me," I said, pulling away from him, and taking a step closer.

The wind was whipping now, and there was a metallic taste to the air.

"Stop," Arthur yelled above the wind, "and I will. Come back to the castle with me."

There was something about the way that it was pulling me in. I didn't want to stop. I got closer, and reached out to it. I stopped short of touching it when my hair stood up on my head. No, my hair stood on all of my body, my arms fluffing up. There were what looked like small lightning bolts that went from the beacon to my fingertips. They did not hurt, but tingled. Every part of me tingled now, and the wind was stiff. The glow from the beacon was a beam of bright, pure white light that went to the ceiling, and seemed to go through the ceiling. The thrumming was so strong I could feel my insides vibrating.

I pulled away suddenly. I stepped back, and the wind slowed, and the vibrations calmed. I turned to Arthur, his eyes were wide, but he didn't seem to be afraid. I was now though. "The wind and the vibration, that is how it felt when the Brotherhood appeared and wanted to take Tomren that day."

Arthur nodded. "Yes. I can teach you. I can show you how to control what is in you."

I didn't know what was in me, I didn't know what was even happening with the thing he called a beacon. "What is in me? What is happening?"

"The power to not only use the beacons as any of us who know how can, but the power to sense them. To feel them, and control them. You can feel time calling to you, and you can choose to answer it, or you can ignore it. But, you must know what you are doing if you choose to answer it. Or I promise, you will find yourself in a very strange place, and you will lack the knowledge of how to come back here, back to your prince. Even worse, you may find yourself in the hands of the Brotherhood, and they will not be kind to you."

"I have nothing here," I said. "What is in me," I repeated.

Arthur looked at me. "Power, dear Sebastian. Power. A power that no one else wields in this time, or any other. The power to end the disgusting acts of the Brotherhood."

"I did not even know the Brotherhood existed a moon ago. Hell, I didn't know any of this existed. They have never done me any harm."

"No? Did they not try to take your friend? Did one of their Brothers not order you killed? Do you not think that they will try to take Tomren again? You have the power to change that. But you have to commit to staying and learning."

What if they did try to take Tomren again? What would they do to him? Gods, I just wanted to be free of this all. I just wanted to leave, and live a quiet life somewhere.

"Will you meet with the king," I asked.

Arthur eyed me for a minute. "How do I know he won't kill me?"

"He gave his word," I said quickly. "He said he would not try to capture you, and he would not harm you while you meet with him."

"Very well," he said after a brief time. "But, you must not tell him of the church, nor of what happened here today. The prince either."

Tomren was the one who showed me the church, so that made no difference. But how could I not tell him about today? "Fine," I said after a second.

"You begin training with me first thing tomorrow. You will come to the church. Then you can tell me when the king wants to meet with me."

"On the morrow then. After breaking my fast with the king, I will come see you."

"Good," Arthur said, with a small smile. "Let us leave this place."

21

The king was not at supper that evening, Tomren and I were informed that he had important business to attend to.

"Does the king often miss supper," I asked as we began eating.

Tomren shrugged. "Sometimes. He always has breakfast with me, well now with us I suppose," he said, looking up from his plate and smiling. "But, supper is never a sure thing."

"I had hoped to see him. I saw Arthur today, and he agreed to meet with your father."

Tomren put his fork down, and cocked his head. "I had wondered where you were today. I didn't see you all afternoon. Where did you see him? I went to the church, but it seemed empty, though I suppose I cannot get into his room so I have no way to know."

I shook my head. "No, I went for a walk, around the woods where we had first gone, and he found me there."

"You went without a guard? Or me?"

I felt my skin redden. Gods, he always finds a way to change my color. "I had much to think on, and I wanted to be alone for a bit." It wasn't entirely untrue, but I still felt bad not being honest with him. He nodded and began eating again.

"Just be careful going out like that. The woods can be dangerous, as we found out. I would hate for anything to happen to you." He smiled warmly, all the way to his eyes. "I've become very fond of you."

I felt my collar warm again, and I looked down. "I'm sorry. I guess I didn't really plan it out. But," I said, a bit more cheerfully, "maybe after supper we can go for a walk?"

"I would like that."

The rest of the meal was eaten in comfortable silence, both of us in our own thoughts. When the servants came and removed the dishes, we went outside.

We walked through the castle grounds, Tomren telling me the history of this part or that. Occasionally he would tell me of a memory that he had in a particular place.

In one such place, he stopped and looked around for a moment. We were in the far corner of the grounds. There was a bench set just into the edge of the wood. The sky was brilliant hues of orange, pink, and red. The sun was behind the castle, turning it into a silhouette. A few clouds dotted the fiery sky, and it looked absolutely magical.

"This may be my favorite place and time of day here," Tomren said.

"It is beautiful," I said with an honest wonder in my voice.

"It is. And," the prince said, his eyes not leaving the sky, "it is the only place where I have an actual memory of my mother. Well, at least I think I do."

I took my eyes from the sunset, and looked at him. He looked happy, and sad. Content, and dissatisfied. It was as if part of him was missing. And, in truth, I suppose it was. I understood the feeling of not having a mother, and longing for that bond in my life. I put my hand on his. "Tell me."

He didn't look at me, and for a moment, he didn't say anything. With a sigh, he finally started speaking. "I was little. My father tells me that it's not a real memory, that I've just created it. But, I remember her here. We sat on this bench, and we watched the sunset. She was already sick, the black bile. The meisters all said that black bile did not kill. That she would be fine, and they tried many different things. I think she knew better though. She sat here, and told me that I was the most perfect child that she could have hoped for."

He laughed bitterly. "She told me that she was proud of me, and she was sorry that she would not be here to see me grow into a king. She said she was sorry that she wouldn't be here to comfort me for my first heartbreak, or to give me advice about girls. She held me tight, and told me to always remember that she loved me, and that she would be here in this place when I needed to talk."

His fingers laced into mine. "I'm not crazy."

I squeezed his hand gently. "I never would say that you are."

My heart beat faster when he squeezed back. "I know," he said. "Those therapists that my father spoke of. They say that I made it up. That it's all in my head, that it's what I want to imagine of her. But, I remember it."

"I'm sure it happened. And," I said, turning to him, "I'm sure that she would be proud of who you are."

"Would she," he asked. "I don't know. Would she truly be proud of me? I do my duty, sure. But, I am also impulsive. Rebellious, even. And, it's my duty to marry whomever my father deems best for the kingdom. But," he said, turning to me now, "here I am. I don't want a queen. I'm falling for someone that I can never have. It is not acceptable for me to care for a man the way I care for you, and I can never be with you."

I was shocked by his words. "I...we…I don't know," I said, trying to arrange my thoughts. "Wouldn't your mother want you to be yourself?

"Maybe," he said, laying his head on my shoulder. "But, she did not love my father. Not at first. Her heart belonged to another. Both of my parents were very open about this fact. I think most of the kingdom knew. But, duty required that they marry. And, so they did. She grew to love him, of course, and he her. But, she didn't choose that life. And I don't get to choose mine."

His cerulean eyes glistened in the fading sunset. "You don't have to do anything yet. You have years yet before you will be betrothed. And, who knows what the future holds?"

"Well," he said, his mood a bit lighter, "I mean, Arthur for one. I suppose we could too, if we went there." The idea gave me a thrill. Running off to the future, just the two of us. No one to tell us who to be, where to go, how to live. "Maybe one day we will. But for now we have this moment."

Tomren lifted his mouth to mine. His lips touched my own gently, and I turned to him. There was no hesitation this time. I put my hand on his cheek, and his hand wrapped around to the back of my head, fingers lacing into my hair. His lips parted, and our tongues touched. Slowly, gently, our tongues danced in the sunset. Passion rose, and he pulled me closer, tighter somehow. Our kiss became deeper, and he turned himself onto my lap, straddling me. His lips went to my neck, and he sucked it with deep passion. He kissed gently around the still healing burn from Rorthan's gun, the slight pain only serving to heighten my senses. I buried my own lips into his neck, he smelled of sandalwood and teak. I kissed gently on his skin, and a moan escaped his lips.

I ran my hand inside of his shirt, passion in full control of me now. I felt his muscles, running my hand down to his stomach. It was firm, and his muscles felt like a washboard. He brought his lips back to mine, and his hands began exploring my own body. I knew that what they found was not as perfect as what mine had, but it did not slow him. His hands went lower, and suddenly he held me in his hand.

He pulled his face back just slightly, and smiled. "I've thought about this so many times since we met," he admitted.

The sun was down now, the moon rising, and the sky nearly dark. He slipped off of me, and undid my trousers. I put my fingers in his hair as he took me in his mouth. Nothing else mattered in that moment. It was just Sebastian and Tomren, one in the early night. I felt my release, and I brought him up to kiss him again, turning him around onto the bench. I removed his garments the same as he had mine. I had no idea what I was doing, but he had felt so perfect that I tried to do the same. He moaned my name, and this only furthered my confidence. I put all of my passion into pleasing him, and by the time we were done and dressed, the moon was bright.

"I love you," he whispered into my ear, his breath on my neck making me stiffen again.

"And I, you," I said breathily. I knew in that moment that whatever happened, my world would never be the same.

We walked back to the castle, our fingers intertwined. As we got closer, he let my hand go. He did so gently, regretfully, but it still hurt. "I'm sorry," he said.

I knew what he meant, and I shook my head. "I understand. Duty, expectations."

"It leaves little room for love," he admitted. "But, what we have, I will cherish it, enjoy it, and nurture it. I don't want to ever lose you from my life. You are a part of me now. You have a part of my soul, Sebastian."

I looked at him in the moonlight. "We have time. Wherever we find ourselves, and whatever happens, you will have my heart for as long as it beats."

We entered the castle a few minutes later, nothing more needing to be said. When we got to Tomren's bed chamber, he turned to me. "Goodnight, Sebastian," he said. The tingle I felt when I thought about how he had moaned that name, my name, only a short time earlier, was only heightened when he kissed me again. He took a quick glance around the hall, and then pulled me in.

A quick, passionate kiss, and he was gone. His bed chamber door closing behind him.

I went to my own chamber, closed the door, and sat by the window for a moment. The sky was fully dark, and the moonlight lit the castle grounds perfectly. A slight breeze blew into my window. It had been a perfect evening.

22

"Would you like me to have someone draw you a bath," Beltoch asked. He had come to my chamber shortly after I returned from the evening with Tomren. After making sure that I drank my tea, he had applied a poultice to my shoulder. He said that it would be only a couple of more days before it would no longer be needed.

"Please, that would be good."

"Very well. Do remember not to get the dressing wet," he said as he left.

A moment later, a servant girl came in and began preparing the bath for me. Once it was done, I took off my clothes and stepped in. The water was hot, and it made the aches begin to melt away.

I set my head back and thought about the evening I had just had. I had not expected it, and it had definitely been the best night of my life. I knew that Tomren was right. He would be expected to marry, maybe even as soon as his next year day. But that didn't mean that we couldn't enjoy our time now. And even when he was married, if we were discreet, mayhaps we could continue to see each other. Royalty often has mistresses, and though this was slightly different, with discretion perhaps it could work.

But would I really be satisfied being his secret love? Sneaking embraces, kisses, and...oh yes, and *that*, when we could. Part of me wanted that, but part of me longed for the relationship to be known. I wanted to not have to hide our love as if it was shameful. I wanted to walk through the castle grounds and not have Tomren drop my hand when we got close enough for someone to see. Was he ashamed because I was a boy, or was he ashamed because I was the son of a disgraced general? Was it that he couldn't be with someone that had no monies, no land, and no title? Or was it that he couldn't be with someone who had a cock? Was it his father's scorn that worried him? Was he afraid of the murmurs of the castle staff?

In the end, did it really matter why? Maybe I should have left when I wanted to. I still could, I supposed, but he would still be in danger. Not that I could really protect him, who am I? I had done it once, sure, but I was acting off of pure instinct. Would I be able to do so again, knowing what I was facing?

The only way that I could be sure would be to train with Arthur. More determined than ever, and unable to sleep, I got out of bed and dressed quickly. I slipped silently into the church, and lit the flashlight.

"Arthur," I called out. "Are you here?"

There was no answer, except my own echo. I took the flint and torch, and lit it. Turning off the flashlight, I walked to the faces in the center of the room. I lit them, and they blazed bright. The light cast shadows across the room, the carvings looked intimidating in the orange glow.

I sat at the round table, and looked at the face before me. A silent screaming man. The symbol of a Brotherhood that wanted to take Tomren, though whether to question him, kill him, or bargain him, I did not know. None of those options would do. I rested my head on my hands, and wondered what the future would hold, if either of us would even survive long enough to have it matter if he would one day be betrothed to a woman.

"Hello, Sebastian," Arthur said from somewhere behind me.

His voice suddenly breaking the silence caused me to jump. "Gods, did you have to scare me," I squeaked.

"I'm sorry, it was not my intention to scare you. What did King Hammond have to say?"

"I didn't see him, he was not at supper. I will talk with him tomorrow morning."

"If the king didn't send you with word, why are you here again today? Training was to begin tomorrow," he said as he walked toward me.

"I couldn't sleep," I said, resting my head back onto my hands. "I have many things on my mind, and I had hoped that coming here would provide me with some sort of rest."

Arthur nodded thoughtfully. "And has it?"

"I don't think so. I know what I need to do, but even if I do it, even if I train and make it so that I can protect Tomren, I still…" I trailed off before I said 'cannot have him'.

"You still can not be with the boy the way you, and if I am seeing things right he wants to as well?"

My head snapped up, my eyes meeting his. "I'm sure that I do not know what you mean," I said sharply, though I doubt that my blush added any weight to those words.

"It is okay, I do not feel about that matter as many do. In my time, it is much more acceptable to love whom you will, regardless of whether it is a man or a woman. Though the stigma still does exist," he admitted, "it is not the same as it is here."

"He will be promised to a woman, a queen or a lord's daughter, no doubt. And I will be just me. The king may still make an arrangement for my own mariage, me being his ward now," I said, returning my head to my hands.

"You are his ward," Arthur asked, seeming surprised at first. "That makes sense, you and Tomren have become close, though I doubt the king knows how close. And he would want what is best for Tomren. He has always been a caring man, firm yes, but caring. He would of course take care of you after Rorthan's betrayal."

"But he would never let me love his son as I do."

"No," Arthur sighed, "it is not the way of things here."

I looked at him again. "No, it is not. But, if what you say is true, it is not the way of things *now*."

"What you are suggesting is a dangerous thing," he warned. "The world in which I come from is much different, and it would take years of training for both of you to prepare yourselves."

"But, it could be done?"

Arthur thought for a moment. "Yes, in theory. But, you forget that the Brotherhood is at least interested in Tomren. They will try again to get him, and they are twice as strong in the future as they are now. And, in the future, you would need an identity. You couldn't be yourself, you would have to have papers showing who you are, where you were born. You would need money. It would take much work."

"But, it could be done," I repeated, this time as a statement.

"Yes, it could."

"Then how do we start?"

"Do you remember how I made the door reveal my room, instead of the staircase to leave the church," Arthur asked.

I nodded. "The sconce, you touched it with the ring, and the ring glowed bright."

"Yes. Come."

I followed him to the door. He pulled the sconce, and the door closed, blending back into the wall.

"You, Sebastian, do not need my ring. Do you remember the way that the beacon felt? How it pulled you towards it?"

"Yes, but I didn't have any control over it. It just was. And, until you told me, I did not even realize that it was happening."

"You will learn control. This will be a first step. Do you feel the sconce? It won't be as strong of a feeling as the beacon was. It will be a weaker pull by far, but can you feel it?"

I felt nothing, except mayhaps dumb for trying to 'feel' a door. "No," I said, with an exasperated sigh.

"If you are frustrated already, then we will have no hope of training you. The training will be much more difficult than this, but it will take time and you must be patient. Unless, your prince is not worth it to you?"

I shot him what I hoped was a fierce look. "I don't feel anything."

"Pull the sconce," he said.

I did, and the door slid out, revealing the staircase.

Arthur took my hand. "Feel it," he said, holding my hand just in front of the metal.

There was something there. A slight tingle in my hand, and a prick of sensation in my mind. "I feel...something," I admitted.

"Good. Pull it again, but do it while feeling the 'something', hold on to that feeling when you pull it."

I reached out, and slowly put my hand to the sconce. As it got close, I felt the tip of my finger tingle. I pulled back and dropped my hand to my side.

"What is wrong," Arthur asked.

"It just feels strange."

"And it will, until you learn to feel it, accept it, and embrace it. Now pull it."

Slowly I brought my hand back up to the sconce. It felt like a small spark when I finally touched it. I held on to that spark, and pulled. The door slid across the hallway, revealing Arthur's room. "I did it!"

"Yes, you did. Now go inside, and I will try to explain how you did it," he said. "And why you should not get too excited about it yet."

Well, I had been excited, I just used some power that I have in me. Magic? And it worked, and I did it.

As we sat down in the rolling chairs, I snapped. "Why shouldn't I get excited? I just used my magic!"

Arthur roared with laughter. It filled the room, and it made me hot and red with anger. "I...I'm sorry...I...don't mean to, I mean, I'm not laughing at you," he said between gasps.

I just glared at him, as he walked over to the refrigerator and got out a bottle for each of us.

"It's not magic, dear boy. It's science. Magic is not real. Most people even in this time do not believe in it anymore. Did you truly believe that you had magic?"

"I don't know," I admitted sheepishly. "But if not magic, what?"

Arthur sat back in his chair and studied me for a second. "I'm sorry, I truly didn't mean to laugh. I just had no idea that you would think it magic. I am to blame for that," he said with a gentle smile. "When the birds leave for the winter, and come back in the spring, do you know where they go?"

"Somewhere warmer," I shrugged.

"Yes, but they have to know how to get there. They have to be guided by something. That 'something' is a mineral in their brain called 'magnetite'. It is present in all animals, and in the year 1992 scientists in my time discovered it in the brain's of humans. It is what the animals use, we believe, to navigate across the planet. The way that the magnet in a compass points to the north, the animals use the magnetic field of the earth to navigate."

"So we have the ability to navigate," I asked, an eyebrow raised. I couldn't imagine what this had to do with the door, or the beacon, or time.

"No, not most of us. We don't have much in our brains. But, your mother and I studied how it was connected to the beacons that the Brotherhood used. We had seen a bird one day, fly towards a beacon, and the beacon lit up. This struck us as odd, since we had never seen the beacon do that on it's own. It needed power, electricity, the same thing that makes your flashlight, and these screens," he said, gesturing around him, "and almost everything we use in the future, work. But as the bird touched the beacon, it was gone in a flash of light. We knew what happened to it, but we didn't know why."

"And it was this 'magnetite'? But, if we all have it in our brains, what makes me different?"

"You have more of it," Arthur said. "Much more. When your mother decided that she wanted to have a child, we made sure that you would have more."

"How," I asked. "How could you 'make sure' of anything about me?"

Arthur took a sip of his bottle. "Science. I can't even begin to explain how to you right now. It's more than most people in my time would understand, and there is no way to explain it to you yet. One day, you may have learned and seen enough to understand, but for now, know that your mother and I wanted to help the Brotherhood, so we made sure that you had high amounts of magnetite."

"How would that help the Brotherhood," I asked, ignoring the fact that they had wanted to help the very people that now were my enemies.

"In order to use the beacons, and many of the other tools we use, we must have a key. Not a key as you think of it, but a special magnetite item. Mine," he said, looking at his hand, "is my ring. Others use bracelets, or arm cuffs, or torcs. But we all must have the key. You do not need a key."

"So I can travel time?"

"Anyone can if they have a key, but you *are* the key. You can use what is in you, in your mind. If we could have figured out how to make that work on a large scale, we would have made it so any of the brothers could move freely without their key."

"How can I use this 'magnetite' to travel time?"

"I don't know," Arthur admitted. "Your mother was going to watch you, help you learn.

She would have figured out how to teach you the power. I will do what I can to teach you. The power must be controlled before you can do anything. Had you touched the beacon in the cave, you would have ended up in another time, that much I know. But when, I do not know. You would have disappeared, and I would have had to check dozens of times to try to find you. And had I not been there, you would have been gone, and we would have never known where you went. You must learn control."

"How do you know what time you are going to," I asked.

"The beacons all have their own magnetic alignments. We can select which ones we want to go to, using our computers," he said, gesturing to the screens. "But, you will have to learn how to tell them apart by feel. And that will take time."

"What if I pick the wrong beacon, how will I know what to do?"

Arthur paused and thought about this for a moment. "The door felt different from the beacon in the cave, yes?"

I nodded, but didn't say anything. "Then you must learn how the beacon for this time feels. More specifically, this room. I have a beacon here. One that your mother and I created, one that only we know of. It saves me from having to go to the cave."

"What does it feel like to go to a different time?"

"Disorienting. Like being bounced up and down, until you finally land. It is over quickly, but it will be difficult for you to adjust to until you have experienced it a few times. Think of it as skipping a rock on a lake. The rock comes down, touches the water, and bounces back up again, only to return to the water before continuing on. You will skip times, whether forward or backward, and you will settle in that time for just an instant, before carrying on to the time you end up in. The further you go, the longer it takes, and the more disorienting it is."

There was only one way to get used to it then. "When can I do it?"

"When I say you are ready, and not a moment sooner. Promise me that you will not try to do it without me."

I had no desire to get lost in time. "You have my word."

"Good," Arthur smiled. "Now, return to your bed. Sleep, if you can, and come see me in the morning."

23

I laid awake in bed that night, trying desperately to feel anything. I thought I could feel the beacon in the cave, but it may have just been exhaustion. When I finally fell asleep, I didn't dream.

I awoke to a knock on the door. "Come in," I said, sitting up.

Beltoch brought in a cart with his poultice, clean wraps, and tea. "How did you sleep," he asked as he approached the bed.

"Well enough," I answered.

"Let me see that shoulder," he said, removing the wrap.

It wasn't as tender as it had been, and it really didn't hurt anymore. It was just uncomfortable. "How does it look," I asked, hoping to be free of this routine soon.

"It looks well, young master. I say only one or two more days perhaps, and you will have no more need of my medicines."

I smiled. "Thank you for all you have done for it, I feel much better."

"You're welcome," the meister said with a slight bow of his head. "Is your neck okay?"

"My neck," I asked, confused. My neck was never an issue.

"Yes, there appears to be a bruise on it. Unless, of course, you have a young maiden that you have been sneaking off to see?"

I touched where Tomren's mouth had suckled the night before. I turned red, and the meister lowered his eyes.

"Of course, young master. I meant no offense. I was young once too, and I should've thought of that before saying anything. Such activities do not come to mind first thing as they did back then though."

"No offense taken," I smiled. I would need to find a way to hide it. "Do you perhaps have a salve that could get rid of the mark," I asked.

Beltoch chuckled lightly before clearing his throat. "I do not, I'm afraid. It will just take time to fade."

Well, hopefully the king would not notice. I didn't really want to answer questions about what girl I had seen. "Thank you anyway, Meister Beltoch."

The man nodded. He finished dressing my shoulder. "I will see you again tomorrow. I bid you a good day, young master."

And with that I was alone again. I dressed and walked to the dining hall. Morning meal went the way I had come to believe most had before my presence. The king and his son discussed matters of the kingdom, and at times I believe that they forgot I was even there.

"Arthur has agreed to meet with you," I said when a pause in their discussion came. "He said that he would seek me out again for a time and a place."

The king sipped his tea, and placed the cup down. "Very good. Ask him to meet me here. He may come to the main gate, and he will be brought before me. He knows that he can leave me at any time, and that I am unable to stop him."

"I will," was all I said.

As soon as the meal had ended, I made my way back to the church. I pulled the sconce to open the door to Arthur's room. I clung to the feeling in my mind, and it worked on the first attempt. Arthur was sitting there, looking at his screen. On it was my mother.

"You loved her," I said more than asked.

He spun around in his chair as if he hadn't heard me enter. "Yes, very much. I knew her for many years. We grew close."

I suspected that it was more than that, but I didn't press it further. "The king said that you can come to the castle gate at any time and he will give you an audience. He reminds that you can leave at any time, though I suspect he means that even if he wanted to stop you he could not."

Arthur nodded, and smiled wryly. "That is exactly what he means. He does not know that I am here, in his own castle. That is unless you or your prince have told him. But, he knows that I can go to any time that I want, and that I will do so if I feel cornered. I've done it twice to him, before I gave up on trying to reason with him."

"Why now? Why do you think that he can be reasoned with now," I asked, sitting down in one of the chairs.

Arthur shrugged. "I don't know. I've been watching, observing how he has ruled, what decisions he has made. He has proven to be a fair and just king, and he has shown no desire to exploit his knowledge of time travel for his own gain. He has matured, I suppose."

"How long have you been watching?"

"Many years. I've been paying attention to this time for nearly two decades. For whatever reason, the Brotherhood was very interested in this time. So, your mother and I came here often. That is how she met your father. I've spent more of the last twenty years here than I have in my own time, really."

I got up, and went to the refrigerator to get a bottle of water. As I reached out to open the door, I stopped with my hand extended in mid air. I felt something. I felt the pull of something, behind the wall. I started scanning the wall, first with my eyes, and after a moment with my hand. I ran my hand over the wall to the right of the refrigerator, and stopped. The tingle touched my finger tip.

"You should not be able to feel that," Arthur said suddenly. I turned to look at him, but I did not remove my hand from the wall. "What is it?"

He rose and walked over to where I stood. "My beacon. The room it is in is shielded, or at least it should be. I have no doubt that the Brotherhood have hunted for it, but they have not found it yet."

"Shielded," I repeated, curious.

"Yes. Your mother actually helped with that. As we realized that the Brotherhood was not what we thought, we began trying to figure out how to stop them. We wanted to begin with this time, to protect you and her. She intended to stay here, you know. To live out her days in peace here. In the months leading up to your birth, we realized who we were dealing with. And so we tried to plan our escape. Your mother not only created a beacon that was much more powerful than the others, but she found a way to keep it from being discovered."

"How is it different? How is it shielded? She was going to stay?" Questions began flowing out, and I had to force my mouth to stop moving.

"Yes, she was. She wanted to raise you here, in this time. And, how the beacon is shielded I honestly don't know for sure. Your mother was better at these things. I do know that whatever she did, I have tried and failed to copy," he sat down with a sigh. "And, it is different because it is smaller, but more powerful and yet somehow it uses less energy. When you were in the cave, what was it like when the Brotherhood came?"

I thought for a moment, still standing by the spot in the wall where my hand had felt the hidden entrance. "It was chaotic. Like a huge thunderstorm, but with no rain. There was lightning and thunder, and the cave rumbled and shook. But, it was over just as suddenly as it had begun."

Arthur nodded. "That is the typical way of it. We call it the 'Storm of Time'. But," he pointed to the wall, or what was behind the wall, "your mother made a beacon where none of that occurs. The only effect of the time travel is a bright flash of lightning."

I looked back to the wall. I reached out and felt the spot again. I saw no evidence of a button, but in my mind I pressed one anyway. And suddenly the door opened. It slid silently and quickly away, revealing a small chamber. It was plain, with just a small screen and what I assumed was the beacon. The beacon began pulsing with light as I got closer to it.

"Do not touch it," Arthur reminded me from the doorway.. "But, feel it with your mind. Learn how this beacon feels. If you ever get lost, return to not only this time, but this beacon. It will be the safest, and the most protected."

I could feel the difference between this place, the buttons to open the doors, and the beacon in the cave. "I think I feel it."

"Good, now, please return."

I turned back, left the room, and touched the wall. The door slid silently back into place. What other mysteries were hidden in the walls here?

"I want to show you something," Arthur said, sitting back down in his chair.

I walked over to him, and slid a chair beside his own. I sat there, and watched as he touched a board on the table in front of him. It had letters and numbers on it.

The screen above our heads changed, and the picture of my mother was gone. In its place were things I did not recognize. Arthur reached into his pocket, and removed a very small rectangle from it. "This is called a thumb drive," he said.

"What is it for," I asked, though in my mind there were at least a dozen other questions. What do the buttons do? What are all of the small images on the screen? Where did my mother go? When do I get to learn how to use the screen?

"It stores information. The screen is connected to a computer, the computer is what has the videos and pictures of your mother on them. This thumb drive can be plugged in, like so," he said as he bent over in his seat, to the small box on a ledge under the table. I had not noticed it before.

He put the thing in, and a tone sounded from the screen. Writing appeared on screen 'External storage discovered'. He slid his finger across a small pad, and the arrow on the screen moved. When the arrow was on the words, he tapped the pad. A new box opened on the screen, and he moved the arrow over to something that said 'Eleanor1' and tapped the pad again. My mother's face appeared on screen.

"Keep this with you," he said, pulling the thumb drive from the computer. "Do you remember what I just did after I plugged it in?"

I nodded. "I believe so.

"Let's find out," he said, handing the thumb drive to me.

I copied what I had seen him do, and after getting it wrong the first time, I managed to do what he had done.

"Good. If something happens to me, plug this in and open the file that says 'SebastianMessage'. Do not do so unless I have died, or disappeared for more than a fortnight."

"What does it do," I asked.

"It is a message, but one you do not need unless I am gone. Do you understand?"

Not really, none of it made sense, but I understood enough I supposed. "Yes, don't do...whatever that is that we just did, unless something were to happen to you."

"Good," he said. "Now, see if you can find any other hidden places in this room with your magnetic sense."

I tried, but failed to find any other secrets in the room. "The more you feel, the more you use it, the easier it will become. It will sharpen, as a stone sharpens a blade when run across it," Arthur said reassuringly. "Keep trying."

And I did just that.

24

The next morning as the king, Tomren, and I ate first meal, a guard came in and said something in the king's ear.

"Ah, very good. Have him join us," the king said, setting down his fork and wiping his mouth.

A moment later, Arthur was led in. He bowed his head to the king, to the prince, and then to me. It was odd to see him act in such a manner. "Your Majesty, Your Highness, Sebastian," he said in order as he bowed.

"Sit, please, eat with us," the king said, gesturing at a seat. "You may leave us," he said to the guards.

Arthur sat down on my side of the table, one chair away from me.

"Thank you, Sire."

"It has been a long time, Arthur. We did not part ways on very good terms," the king started, "but I believe that I may have been lacking all of the information I needed. Do you still belong to the Brotherhood of Time?"

Arthur grabbed a sausage, and shook his head. "I do not. I learned a great many things since we last met, and I already had my doubts about them at our last meeting. It has been many years since I have been in contact with them." He took a bite of the sausage before continuing.

"I have reason to believe that they are still looking for me, however. And, it is apparent that they still have at least some interest in the prince," he said, pointing the sausage at Tomren.

"So it would seem," the king acknowledged. "Why do they want you?"

"Oh, I feel it's less me that they want, and more of what I know. And, truly, I think they want Sebastian more than anything, though they do not realize that it is him they seek."

The king sat back, as if pondering this. "The research that you were doing before. The mag...magnetatte-"

"Magnetite," Arthur offered, not rudely.

"Yes. You did indeed complete your research?"

Arthur looked to me. "We at least succeeded in creating increased levels, yes."

"The boy," the king asked, before correcting himself, "Sebastian, I mean."

Arthur nodded. "But, I think the Brotherhood believes it to be another. They knew what we were going to attempt, and who better to give the power to than a prince," he said, raising an eyebrow in the direction of Tomren.

"That makes sense. Of course Eleanor would want to try it on her own child. And of course, the Brotherhood would assume that power would go to royalty. I will be more cautious with both boys from now on," the king said.

"I think that would be wise," Arthur agreed, taking another bite of the sausage.

"Who else knows about Sebastian," the king asked, going back to his own meal. It was as if they were two old friends, or at least acquaintances, catching up.

"No one as far as I know. Even Rorthan did not know. I believe that the Brotherhood has already decided that it is your son, and I think unless and until they discover that it is not, they will not bother to look elsewhere."

"How long would it take if they were to capture him," the king said, looking at his son, "to realize that he was not the one?"

"Less than a day. A few hours, maybe a little more. They would run tests, and that wouldn't take long."

"And then, they would kill him." It wasn't a question.

I swallowed hard and Tomren's eyes went big, but to his credit he did not speak.

"I would suspect, yes," Arthur admitted. "Though it is possible they would attempt to ransom him for something."

"But, they have no way of getting here except through the beacon, correct," the king asked, poking lazily at his eggs.

"None, Your Majesty."

But, what about the beacon in the chamber of the church? Arthur thought it to be shielded but what if they knew of it? I was going to ask this, but thought the better of it. I would ask Arthur when we were alone.

"Good," the king said, putting down his fork. "Then I shall add guards to the cave, and I will make sure that no one comes through. What of you, Arthur? What do you want? Why did you agree to meet with me?" The questions were not asked rudely, but I still sensed an edge to them.

If Arthur did as well, he did not show it. "I wanted to warn you that they may be after the prince. But," he said, wiping his mouth and then his hands on a rag, "I also would like to teach Sebastian how to control what he has in him."

"Would you take him from here, or would you train him in this time," the king asked.

"I would begin his training here. We would remain here for six moons, maybe a bit more. And then, we would go to my time and spend the same there. If all went well, he would be ready to perhaps help to close the doors to time. If he could cut off the Brotherhood's ability to travel, your son would be safe."

"Can we not just destroy the beacon now," the king asked with a shrug. "That would eliminate any need of Sebastian or Tomren being in danger."

"It would," Arthur agreed, "but it doesn't guarantee that they wouldn't come for them still. We need to close off all beacons. And, ideally, we need to destroy the beacon here last. Once the last beacon is destroyed, we will be stuck in that time. I'm sure Sebastian would prefer to live out his days in this time."

I looked at Tomren. I wanted to spend my days where he was. If that was in this time, or any other, it wouldn't matter to me. I still nodded in agreement, because the fact was we needed to make Tomren safe, and this was the best plan we had.

"Very well. What would you need from me," the king asked.

"Respectfully, Your Majesty, simply that you stay out of his training, and allow me access to Sebastian without hindrance. I will give you updates as we go, if it would please you, but he and I must be allowed to come and go freely, and without eyes monitoring what we are doing and where we are."

"Agreed, but I want-"

Whatever King Hammond was going to say was cut off by the doors bursting open.

"Sire," Sabina said breathlessly, "Rorthan has escaped."

Before the King could respond, or before I even truly processed what she said, four things happened simultaneously. There was a sharp crack. Not the loud sound that I had come to associate with a gun, it was quieter, as if fired from a far distance. But, it was a shot just the same. One of the windows in the dining room shattered. The king, Tomren, and I all dove from our seats to the marble floor. Arthur's head slumped, and a cloud of red mist came from behind it. His body slid down to the floor beside me, and his lifeless eyes stared straight ahead, a hole leaking blood from his temple. In an instant, Sabina drew her sword, and looked around the room for the source of the sound.

Guards rushed in and surrounded the king and his son. Sabina was by my side quickly, lifting me. "We need to get somewhere more secure," she said, pulling me. I stayed where I was, slumping down.

I heard her words, but I couldn't remove my eyes from Arthur's. Tomren and the king were already being rushed away by his guards. "We need to go," Sabina said again, and lifted me more firmly, and half dragged, half ushered me out of the dining hall.

Sabina led me back to my chambers, closing the door behind us.

"Tomren," I said.

"Safe, I'm sure. Are you hurt," she asked, looking me over.

I don't think I answered. I didn't feel like I was hurt. But nothing felt real. Like this was all some dream that I was watching, or one of the videos that Arthur had shown me. Arthur. I must have said his name out loud, because Sabina shook her head.

"He is gone," was all she said.

Where did he go? My mind wasn't working right, and then everything was fuzzy. And then, everything was black.

25

I woke up to the smell of something awful. I was in my chambers, and Beltoch was holding a bowl of something under my nose that made me want to retch. I took in several sharp breaths, and sat up.

"What happened," I asked as I rubbed my head. I had a splitting headache.

Beltoch put the bowl down, and handed me a cup of cool water. "You fainted. Drink this, and then you and Sabina can speak. I will leave a pot of tea that I want you to drink in the next hour."

As he left the room, Sabina followed, thanking him and securing the door behind him. "Rorthan escaped," she said.

"How," was the only thing that came into my mind when she said that. I could almost remember hearing that in the dining hall before...before Arthur was killed. "Did he kill Arthur," I added.

"We don't know how, but he clearly had help. It is possible that he is working with the Brotherhood of Time, and that we have a spy in our midst. As far as Arthur's murderer is concerned, we do not know for sure, but it does indeed look most likely that Rorthan shot him."

"But why now? Why would the Brotherhood kill him now, and why not kill the king or the prince or even myself, as well?"

Sabina held up her palms. "I don't know. I don't have answers to those questions. I suspect they would have killed any one of you had they had more time, but we reacted quickly. Arthur was likely their main target. He has hid himself from the king, and everyone, for years. They've likely been waiting for him to show himself again so that they could kill him."

"He was supposed to train me though. The king gave him permission to train me on the beacons. I was to learn about the future, I was to go to the future. I don't know what to do without him here to show me how to use," I started to say 'my powers'. But, I saw Sabina stiffen just slightly and her hand shifted calmly, slowly to the hilt of her sword. Something wasn't right. "How to use the beacon," I finished.

Sabina relaxed slightly, her hand moving away from her sword. Why would she reach for her sword?

"Is everything alright," I asked her.

"No, not really," she said. "Rorthan has escaped, we don't know who helped him or how he got away, and he shot Arthur. A killer escaped from the dungeons, and took shots into the royal dining hall. Perhaps he was even trying to kill the king but missed."

"Mayhaps," I said. "I'm tired, Sabina. I'm going to drink my tea, and try to sleep."

Sabina walked over to the door, and turned. "Be careful, Sebastian. If Rorthan is dumb enough to still be near, your will not be safe. I will be sure to post guards outside of your door. Be safe."

After she left, I went over to the window and sat down. The image of Arthur's lifeless eyes, and the hole in his temple, came rushing back. I began to weep quietly. There was so much to learn from him, and now he was gone. If the Brotherhood was after him, then they were likely still after Tomren. Only three of us now knew that Tomren was not the one with the powers. He was in danger, and it was because of me. I always seemed to bring him danger and bad tidings.

There was a soft knock on the door. Wiping my tears, I started to get up to answer it, but the door opened, and Tomren walked in, closing it back. I returned to my seat.

"I'm sorry, I know that he was your friend," Tomren said, crossing the room swiftly and coming to my side. He wiped my tears away, and gave my forehead a gentle but lingering kiss. "How are you holding up?"

I looked into his ocean eyes, and began to weep yet again. "I don't know what to do now. I keep bringing danger, sorrow, and death to those around me. And, without Arthur, I have no one to teach me."

Tomren wrapped me in his strong arms, my head resting gently on his stomach. "You bring me happiness and love. The things that are occurring are not your fault, you are not the cause of the things happening in our kingdom. You are good, and you have brightened my life in ways that I could have only dreamed of."

I turned my face into him, and wrapped my arms around him, pulling him to me tightly. I sat like that and wept. Tomren rubbed my head, and said nothing.

Finally, I pulled back and looked up at him again. "I need to get to the church."

Tomren released me, and sat on the edge of the bed. "I don't know that we can. My father has assigned guards to watch us until your father has been found. He worries that we may be in danger. If,"

"He is not my father," I snapped. "I'm sorry, that was far harsher than I should have been," I quickly apologized.

The prince looked abashed, diverting his eyes to his feet for a brief time. "No, you are right. I'm sorry, it is just habit, but that does not make it okay." He looked back up at me. "But, until

Rorthan is found, I fear that my father will keep us under guard day and night."

I stood and walked over to him, taking his hand in mine. "I'm sorry," I repeated. "I am stressed, and it has been a long day. Gods, it has been a long couple of months," I said, sitting on the bed next to him.

"It has," the prince acknowledged. He looked at the tray on my table. "Have you drank the tea that Beltoch left for you?"

I shook my head. "I have not. I don't feel like drinking tea right now."

Tomren stood. "Nonetheless, you should," he said, walking over and pouring a cup.

He walked back over, and handed it to me. I drank it, and handed the cup back. "Pleased?"

Tomren set the cup down, and smiled at me. "Yes, but more so if you rest now."

"I will, if you stay."

Tomren looked at me for a moment. "Then lie down," he said, walking back to the bed.

As I laid down, he sat on the chair by the window. "No," I said, "I want to feel you."

Tomren stood, and lay down on his back beside me on the bed. I rolled into him, putting my head on his chest. He wrapped his arm around me and rubbed my hair again. I was soon asleep.

****

When I woke again, though the prince was no longer holding me, he was still beside me, snoring softly. I slipped out of the bed, and over to the window. I reached into the table next to my chair and retrieved the thumb drive that Arthur had given me. I had to get to the church and find out what it contained. He told me that if anything happened to him, I must watch the video. He must have known that he was in some sort of danger, but could he have ever known that he would be dead not even a day later? Tears began to prick my eyes again. I wiped them away furiously, pushing the sadness down. I needed to be strong now, and figure out how to make Arthur's death, and my mothers, to not have been for nothing. I could mourn later.

I walked quietly to the door, and opened it. A guard turned and asked if everything was okay.

"Yes, I was just trying to go for a walk. The prince must have been exhausted because he fell asleep, and I didn't want to disturb him so I thought I would clear my mind."

The guard glanced into the room and saw the prince sleeping on my bed, but thankfully did not question it. I'm not sure what excuse I would have been able to come up with as to why he had been sleeping in my bed other than the rather weak one I had already given. "Of course, but you are to be accompanied by a guard at the order of the king," he said looking back to me.

My heart sank, there was no way that I could go to the church with a guard. "But, if you accompany me, there will be no one here to guard the prince," I said with a gesture toward Tomren's sleeping form. "I will be just fine, I'll be back before long. I'm not leaving the castle, and surely whatever danger there was is now mitigated by the high alert of you brave lot."

The guard glanced at Tomren again. "The king has given strict orders, I'm sorry. If you wish not to disturb Prince Tomren, I'm afraid you will have to stay until another guard passes, and then someone can accompany you."

Gods. I needed to be alone, and I needed to go now. I tried to imagine what would happen if I just took off running, but I doubted that I would get away, and that would likely just anger the king. "What if I find the first guard that I can, and I have him accompany me," I asked after a moment.

The guard sighed. "Very well, but if you are caught, you had better not tell them that I let you leave. Do not place blame on me, I don't want the punishment."

I agreed, and slipped down the hall. There was no way to enter the secret passage to the church, so I would have to go to the dungeons. And that meant another guard, and another attempt to talk them into allowing me to be alone. I tried to come up with convincing arguments as I made my way to the dungeons, but I couldn't stop thinking about what I needed to do once in the church. What would be in the message that Arthur had left for me? My pulse was racing as it had this morning, despite there being no danger to cause it to be heightened.

When I finally got to the dungeons, I was relieved to see that Leofrick was on duty.

"Hello Sebastian," he said when he saw me. I had not seen him since taking the name Sebastian, but I supposed that the news traveled freely through the castle guard. "Where is your guard?"

"I snuck out," I said with a shrug.

Leofrick frowned. "I will have to find out who was supposed to be guarding you. They will be rebuked. What are you doing here?"

I need to go to the church, and its entrance is hidden in the last cell. I have to go so that I can play a video message from Arthur. Mind letting me pass? "I, uh, well, I wanted to, uh-"

"I understand," Leofrick cut me off, and put a hand on my shoulder.

"You do," I asked, rather confused.

"Yes, we all have learned that he was not your real father, but I'm sure it still stings what happened. There is nothing left in his cell from his escape, but you can see for yourself if you'd like.

There is no one else down there, so if you want to be alone you can. I'll have words with the commander about your guard not doing their job and being with you."

Gods, he just saved me from having to make up an excuse. I gave a small, grateful smile. "Thank you, I couldn't find the words. I suppose I'm rather embarrassed."

Leofrick squeezed my shoulder, before stepping aside. "No need to be embarrassed. What happened was not your fault, and we are all rather fond of you for standing up as you did. We've all heard how you fought back, and we all respect that from someone so young."

"Thank you," I said again as I walked past him and into the doorway. I turned back before adding, "Please, don't mention me slipping away from my guard. I'm to blame, and I wouldn't want him in trouble for my mischief. And, I don't think the king would be happy with me either."

Leofrick thought for a second. "Very well, but next time, I will not be understanding. I admire your bravery, but there is danger to be sure."

I nodded and turned back, grabbing a torch and heading down the stairs into the dungeons.

26

I made my way to the last cell, and opened the door into the church, making my way to Arthur's room. I entered and made sure the door closed behind me. I sat in his chair, and it felt strange to see the room from that perspective. Suddenly, alone in the secret room, all of my emotions came bursting to the surface and I wept. I sat there sobbing loudly, uncontrolled, with no one to hear or try to comfort me. After several moments I collected myself. I now not only needed to find the Brotherhood and stop them to protect Tomren, I felt the need to avenge Arthur. Rorthan could have escaped and fled, he could have disappeared and lived his life as a fugitive. It wouldn't have been difficult for him to restart elsewhere. He certainly had skills that would make him valuable to all sorts of rabble. Yet, he woke up and chose violence. And in that moment, I decided that that choice would cost him his life, and the price would be collected by my hands.

Turning the chair toward the screens, I turned on the computer and entered the password as Arthur had shown me. I plugged in the thumb drive, and selected the file. The screen filled with Arthur's face.

"Hello, Sebastian," his voice said through the speakers. "If you are watching this video, then things have taken a poor turn. I have recorded numerous videos in the event that something were to happen to me. It was my hope that you would never view them, but if you are watching this, then I have given you no real training. For that I am sorry."

He sat back in his chair, exposing more of himself and relaxing the tone of the video just a bit. "Do you remember when I told you that when you travel time, you should imagine yourself as a rock skipping on the water?"

"Yes," I said out loud, feeling sheepish when I realized that the video was not expecting a response.

"The beacons are placed every two hundred and fifty years. So, everytime that you feel yourself anchor, when you feel yourself touch the water so to speak, that will be two hundred and fifty years in the direction that you are traveling. The beacon's all need to have a time imputed into them where the traveler wants to go. I believe, though I have no way to test this theory now if you are watching this, that you do not need to follow the input. You will simply need to feel the time and seize it when you get where you want to go. For instance, when you activate the beacon, and you choose to go forward, when you use your built in magnetic senses, you will, I believe, feel the up and down pull of the beacons."

I wasn't sure how much sense I could make of it, but what he said seemed logical enough. I would feel the beacon pulling me to it, and I would be able to choose whether to land there, or bounce to the next beacon. But, how would I choose? How would I know how to tell if he was right, without risking myself going to some unknown time? I could end up anywhere, and I would have no one with me to help me find my way back. I could just disappear and leave those in this time wondering where I went.

"The time that I want you to travel to on your first trip is my time," Arthur's image continued, snapping me out of my concern. "I want you to feel forward. I can't tell you how to do that, you will have to just do it and hope that your power comes with some measure of intuition. I can, however, help you a bit I think. My time is one thousand years ahead of yours. So, if I'm correct about your power, you should feel the up and down of four beacons. On the fourth, anchor yourself. If you do, I believe that you will be in my time. I am sorry that I won't be there to help you, and all I can say is trust your ability. Feel it, and make it do as you want."

Feel it? Sure, that sounds easy enough, I learned a little bit about how to feel the pulsing

when I discovered his hidden beacon. But, make it
do as I want? How? I can't do this on my own.
This was insanity.

"When you arrive in 2025, you will be in a
world beyond your imagination. The things you
have seen, the guns, the screens, the flashlight, these
are just the very tip of the mountain. You must
have someone to teach you. There is a friend, his
name is Marcus el-Kilahl, he knows everything I
do. He will teach you, but you must get to him. His
address is 2126 Carraway Drive, Ely. Write that
address down."

I took a piece of paper from the desk, and
wrote down the 'address'. What in the ruddy hell is
an address?

"I have left a phone for you at the beacon in
2025. Turn the phone on like this," he said,
demonstrating how to activate the screen he held in
his hand. "When it is on there will be another
video, it is the only thing on the main screen, touch
it like this," again, he showed the screen and he
touched a symbol on it. It began playing a video of
himself, and he quickly turned the screen back off.

"That video will give you directions on how
to use the screen, and how to get to Marcus. I've
also left you new clothes in the beacon room, as you
cannot go dressed as a member of the royal family.
I know that this is a lot for you to try to do at once,
and I wish with all of my heart that I could be there

to help you, but this appears to be the best I can do.
I will try to guide you through these videos as best I
can. But you will need to trust your ability, and
your smarts. You are a very smart young man, and I
trust your intuition. You must trust yourself too.
You have done amazingly well with all you have
seen and learned so far, but this jump to the future
will truly test your mind. Do not let it overwhelm
you, focus on only the task at hand, and get yourself
to Marcus. He will help you in my stead. Good
luck, Sebastian. Do not wait long before going. If
something has happened to me, then you also must
be in danger."

The last line that Arthur said echoed in my
head. Something did happen to him, and the man
who killed him had already wanted to kill me
before. I needed to go quickly. But, I could not just
leave Tomren. I had to tell him, or at least say
goodbye to him, before I went.

The thought of Tomren saddened me. I had
come to love him in a way I never knew possible.
And now I had to leave him. I would find a way to
protect both him and myself, and I would come
back. But, by then he could find another lover. Or
his father could betroth him to a princess and I
could come back to him being married. I wanted
him to be safe, and I could make that happen or I
would try to my last breath. But I also wanted him.
And the thought of losing him, but making sure he

lived brought both a tear to my eye, and a smile to my face.

***

I managed to get back to my room without being seen by any guards. The same guard as before stood watch outside my door, and he said nothing as I slipped back into the room. Tomren still slept on my bed, though he had now pulled the blankets up and was very peaceful looking. I walked over and kissed him lightly on his cheek. He stirred, but when he did not wake, I went over to the desk and took out a piece of parchment and dipped the quill in ink.

"*Tomren,*

You have all of my love. Please know that, and know that the time I have had with you has been the best months of my life. I have to go, I need to stop the Brotherhood from threatening you anymore. I'm going to go to Arthur's time. He left me instructions, and I must follow them to protect you. I hope that I am successful, and I will return when I can. I am terrified, but also determined. But I'm not just terrified of facing the Brotherhood. I will have help with that task. I am scared that you will forget me when I am gone. That I will have become just a summer tryst, and that when I return I will find you married and in love with a beautiful princess. If so, know that I am

250

happy for you, and that I wish you nothing but the best. You have shown me kindness unlike anyone else in my life ever has. You have shown me friendship. You have shown me passion more amazing than anything I could have ever dreamed of. Most importantly, you have shown me love. You have shown me what it is like to be loved, and what it is like to love another. And that love is why I must go. I will give all of me to protect you.

All of my love,

       Sebastian"

I folded the letter, and placed it on the pillow next to him. I kissed his face one more time, tears blurring my eyes. Doubt crept in for just a moment. The desire to climb beside him in the bed and hold him and just forget about all of it flashed in my mind. But, that could never be. We could never be. I could, however, make sure that he lived a long and happy life.

I slipped quietly back out of the door, closing it behind me. The guard sighed and eyed me warily.

"Would you please get Meister Mowbray, I don't feel well."

The guard looked at me for a moment. "I cannot leave this post. I will tell the next guard I see to fetch the Meister."

"Please, I don-" my words cut off as I pretended a dizzy spell, and reached out to him, grabbing hold of him to keep from falling.

He supported me easily, and helped me back into the room. Eyeing the sleeping prince, he quietly set me down. "I shall return quickly," he whispered before silently leaving and closing the door. I waited a moment, and got up. I cracked the door open to see an empty hallway, and hastily made my way to the hidden door at the end of it. I was in, and the door closed behind me, before the guard or the meister returned.

I made my way down the steps, and into the church. I didn't bother to turn on the flashlight as I closed the door to the church, opening it to Arthur's room. The bluish glow of the lights illuminated my way. I quickly closed the door again, making my way to the beacon room. Inside, I found the clothes that he had said would be there. The trousers were a strange material, blue in some spots, almost white in others. And tight, they were very tight in areas that I didn't think they should be. The shirt had no buttons and an image of a man holding a sword of light to the stars, and a princess next to him holding a strange looking gun. There was a golden man, and some sort of domed thing on his other side. A black mask was large behind them, with words about some galaxy long ago. None of it looked like anything from "long ago", but rather from the

future. I guess this is how people dressed in 2025.
There were strange shoes, with a rounded check
mark. They were actually the most comfortable
part of the outfit. There was also a plain silver link
necklace. I don't know why Arthur had left jewelry
for me, but maybe this was what people wore in the
future.

After I changed and approached the beacon,
it pulsed, and came to life. I could feel it, feel the
tingle of its power, of *my* power. I slowly reached
out my hand. Small bolts of light, like tiny
lightning bolts, flashed between my hand and the
beacon. They did not hurt, but the tingle intensified
to an almost painful point.

I looked behind me, doubt making me pause
for only a moment. I touched the beacon, lunged
forward in my mind, and felt myself seem to rise as
the room went white in bright light. The light
dimmed, and I could see the earth changing rapidly
below me. The trees growing, dying, and new trees
coming to life. The castle aging, and for an instant I
thought it was burning, but the flames flashed so
quickly I couldn't be sure. Suddenly, I felt myself
coming back down. This had to be the first beacon.
As I started to feel the ground beneath me again, I
pushed back and was rising once more. The earth
again changing. The castle got even older, and parts
of it crumbled away. The process of falling and
rising repeated three more times, and as I was

coming back down the fourth time, the castle was almost completely gone. There were only small parts of it remaining in the flash that I saw before I was down fully. I fought the urge to rise again, it was as if I was being pulled back up. My eyes again went blind with white light. When I felt the solid earth under me again, I opened my eyes. I was in the beacon room. The only difference between the room I had just left and the one I now stood in, was the pile of decayed fabric where I had left my clothes when I changed. And the phone that was exactly as Arthur had promised. I turned it on, and watched the video. I was in 2025.

27

"Sebastian," the video on the phone began, "I am sorry that you find yourself in this situation. The fact that you are seeing this video means that I am either incapacitated or dead. Either way, you are in a time that you have not been prepared for. The things you have seen only begin to scratch the surface of what you will see the moment that you walk out into the world. Do not allow yourself to become overwhelmed. In this phone is a single contact, Marcus el-Kilahl, however the number may not work. We have to change numbers periodically to hide from the Brotherhood. I gave you the address before you left, so hopefully you still have that written down. If you cannot reach him by phone, you must open the app called 'Pyck uP', and put that address in as your destination. Follow the directions on the app, and a vehicle will take you to him. You must be strong, this world is going to be completely foreign to you. I am sorry that I am not there. Marcus has all of the information you need, as well as other videos from me. The videos are on phones that can only be opened by your hand. He will show you how."

I paused the video. None of this made much sense to me. He had explained how phones work in the future, he had explained that there were vehicles that moved without horses. I had read of some things in the books at the church. But all of this was so much to try to understand. I needed to finish the video and just go out and do it. The more time I sat here thinking on things, the more my courage would fail me.

Hitting play on the screen, Arthur's voice once again filled the room. "Trust him, he is a friend. If it is day time, there may be people outside of the church. While the church remains hidden, the castle itself is little more than ruins. People come around to see it, and learn of its history, so it is possible they will be outside. Do not talk to them. Do not let them see you leave the church. You must protect its location, the Brotherhood continues even in this time, to search for it. Be careful, find Marcus."

The video ended abruptly, and I watched it one more time to make sure I did not miss anything that he had said. When it finished again, I stepped out of his room and into the church. Lights like the ones in Arthur's room flashed to life when I entered it. Other than the lights, it looked the same.

In place of the sconce from my time, there was a familiar medallion bearing the face of the Brotherhood. I pushed the medallion, and the door closed over Arthur's room, and revealed the staircase leading up to the castle. Except, it didn't lead up to the castle. At the top of the stairs, the door remained, but the view outside of it was grass, and trees, and just...nature. No structure, no castle bustle. I looked as best I could to make sure there was no one in sight, and I opened it.

When I stepped out, I was plunged into a new world. What should have been the hallway with my bed chamber was just a small archway around me. It stretched six, maybe seven paces, and then it was just grass. There were trees where once there was an impressive castle. The turrets, and some of the walls remained, but the interior was overgrown with brush. There was no roof, and nothing inside of the walls.

My nose was immediately assaulted by air that smelled acrid. It wasn't the air that I was used to breathing. Despite being cloudless, the sky was hazy, not the clear view that I was expecting. A loud sound above me made me duck down and look up. A tiny winged thing was moving through the sky, higher than I had ever seen anything fly.

"Bruh, it's just a plane. Don't you guys have planes in England," a voice called over. The accent was strange.

I turned to see a man, slightly older than myself, with a wry smile on his face. He had on clothes that were similar to mine, although his pants only came to his knees. Around his neck was a strap with some kind of brick on it. He looked down at it.

"Don't tell me you don't have cameras either," he said.

"I'm not from here," was all I could think to say.

The man cocked his head to the side. "Not a local? You sound like you are. Are you part of the tour then? I think they've started to pack back into the bus, I just wanted to get a few pictures," he said, holding up his camera.

Arthur had told me about cameras, but I only had seen the ones in the phones. "Are you alright man," the stranger asked.

I nodded. "Yes, I think I just need to sit for a minute," I said, lowering myself carefully to the grass.

"Let's get you back to the bus, and get you some water. Where were you sitting on the bus, I don't remember seeing you," he asked, looking concerned.

"I wasn-". My words were cut off by a loud horn sounding three times. "What was that," I asked, tensing.

The man looked at me again. "Dude, it was just the bus letting us know we need to board. Are you sure you're okay?"

"Yes, yes, I'm fine. I wasn't part of your tour though, I'm just exploring on my own."

The man looked at me for a minute. "Are you gonna be alright if I go then? I gotta get back on the bus before it leaves. You want me to call someone or something?"

I shook my head. "No, I'm fine. I've got a phone, I'll call my ride soon."

The man nodded, and extended his hand, helping me up from the ground. "Alright, well good luck man," he said, and then walked off toward where the horn had sounded.

I pulled out my phone. Turning the screen on, I touched the contact for Marcus, and listened. The phone made a strange sound twice, and then a woman's voice told me that the call could not be completed before the phone went silent in my hand. Okay, so that didn't work. I went back to the main screen and opened the "Pyck uP" app. I did what Arthur had said, and the screen told me that I would be picked up in 4 minutes. I walked to the point on the screen's map where I was supposed to be, and waited.

Moment's later, a buggy came up the path. It was strange, unlike any that I had ever seen. No horse, all metal and glass. When it stopped, I just stood there. I didn't know how to get in. The glass nearest to me slid down, and a woman inside with chestnut hair said my name.

"Yes, I'm Sebastian," I responded.

"Excellent. If you want to get in, we can go," she said, expectantly.

I didn't know how to get in though. What in the ruddy hell was I supposed to do? I started to climb through where the glass had slid down.

I got my top half through the window when the driver asked, "What are you doing? Are you high or something?"

High? "No, I'm at the same level you are," I said, very confused.

"Then why don't you use the door like a normal person?"

I took myself back out from the window, and looked at the car. I grabbed the bar on the side of it, and a door opened. I climbed in, relieved that the bar had been a handle. "Sorry, I'm new here," I muttered.

The woman looked at me, half amused, half concerned. "And they don't have cars where you're from?"

"No, this is my first time in one," I said, quiet and embarrassed.

She looked absolutely stunned. "Well, I'm honored to be your first ride."

My face must have reddened, because she chuckled. "Your first car ride," she amended.

I looked at my phone, and it said that we would be at Marcus's house in 17 minutes. Thankfully, the driver didn't speak anymore, and the rest of the drive was in silence.

I was overwhelmed. After only a moment or two, we were in a town, buildings unlike anything I had ever seen lined either side of the streets. There were cars of all shapes, sizes, and colors. People were walking everywhere, crossing the pathway in front of our car when we stopped. We seemed to stop every time there was a red light. And we began moving again when the light switched to green. The movement was faster than I was used to on horse, and I felt my stomach lurching with every stop, and every turn.

I looked to my phone again. 3 minutes until we arrived at Marcus's home.

"Are you visiting family," the woman asked, breaking the silence and snapping my head up from my phone.

"A friend," I answered.

"Well, friends can be as important as family," she said. "Hopefully you enjoy our little town. Will you be staying long?"

Little town? This was bigger than any town I had seen in my whole life. Even the city around the castle wasn't this big. "I'm not sure," I answered. "I'm going to just see how it goes."

The woman nodded, and began prattling on about things I should see while I was visiting. I was relieved when the car came to a stop in front of a white home. 2126 were the numbers on the front. My phone vibrated and thanked me for riding with

'Debra'. I thanked her, and got out of the car, walking up to the home.

The house was three levels tall. Marcus must have been a wealthy man. I approached the door, and knocked on it. No one came to the door. Surely, even if Marcus wasn't home, he must have servants to answer the door in a house this big. I knocked again. Nothing, no answer. I turned the knob on the door, and it opened just a crack. The inside of the house was dark, the windows all covered by drapes that blocked out almost all of the light. I pushed the door open fully, and walked in.

"Hello," I called out. "Marcus?"

The response that I got was the sound of a gun being cocked. My breath caught, and I whirled to see a brown skinned man with short cut dark hair, and a long full beard. The beard had bits of white mixed in with the raven mass. He was maybe thirty five summers by the look of him, although it seemed as though his years had not been easy. And he was aiming an unfamiliar looking gun at me.

"Who are you," he asked, his brown eyes flashing with a mixture of fear and anger.

"My name is Sebastian," I managed to stammer out. "Arthur sent me here, he said to find you."

The man relaxed a bit, but his gun stayed trained on me. "Where is he?"

"He's dead," I said, before I could stop myself.

The man tensed again. "How do you know my name? Why did he send you here? How do I know you're not one of them, one of the Brotherhood?"

So this was Marcus. "I have a message from him on my phone, the phone that he left for me on this side of the beacon," I said, reaching my hand into my pocket.

"Slowly," Marcus barked.

I nodded, and slowly took the phone out. I unlocked the screen, and began playing Arthur's message. Marcus lowered his gun.

"That doesn't mean that you didn't just find the phone. How do I know that you are Sebastian?"

I don't ruddy know. I wanted to say as much. I started to say as much in fact, when I realized that I could prove myself. "The phone, it only unlocks for me. He said he programmed it for me."

Marcus nodded. "Of course," he said, setting the gun down and extending his hand. "Marcus el-Kilahl," he said.

"Sebastian," I said, shaking his hand.

"Come, follow me. Let's get you somewhere more secure, and get you some food and drink, and you can tell me how my friend died."

28

Marcus led me to the second level of the house and opened a door. "You can use this room for sleeping, it also has a bathroom attached so you can shower and such."

The room was not as big as the one in the castle, but it was not small either. "Thank you," I said, walking around the room. The door to the bathroom was open, and I walked in. There was a tub for washing, but it had a curtain that hid most of it, and a strange metal piece coming out of the wall above my head. There was a sink basin, but no water in it. Again, there was a metal piece on the sink. And a toilet like the ones in the castle, but made of some sort of white glass.

My face must have shown my wonder and confusion, because Marcus chuckled softly. "Of course," he said, "you don't have running water in your time."

I raised an eyebrow. "No," I said, even more confused now, "our water flows. How does water run?"

Marcus smirked. "Like this," he said, turning the handle on the sink. Water came out of the metal protrusion.

I ran my hand under the water as it flowed. It was cool and clear. He proceeded to explain how to use all of the amenities, the shower, sink, and toilet. I was dumbfounded. "This is amazing."

Marcus shook his head, his face becoming somber. "Arthur should be here to show you these things. I am not going to always remember that this is new to you. There is so much more to understand, so much more to see, so much more to learn. And I'll have to teach you, and you'll have to learn, while also exploring your ability and figuring out what your next move should be."

I turned the faucet off on the sink, and looked at Marcus again. "I will be grateful for any and all help that you provide, and I will do my best to learn quickly."

Marcus nodded. "Why don't you take a shower, and try to relax for a few minutes. I will go downstairs and make us something to eat. When you are done with your shower, come downstairs, and I'll be in the back of the house in the kitchen. We can get some food in us, and figure out what we do next." I thanked him again, and he smiled. "Welcome to 2025," he said, closing the door behind him.

I turned the water on in the shower, and removed my clothing. The looking glass above the sink was more clear than any that I had ever seen. I looked different in the clarity. I looked tired, exhausted. As I surveyed myself, the reality of my situation began to sink in. I was in a time almost a thousand years more advanced than my own. I left the boy I loved in the past, and had no one in this time except for a man that I had just met. I had no family. I had no clue what to do in this strange world I found myself in. As my head spun, I grabbed onto the sink to steady myself. The heat from the shower had begun to fog the looking glass. I felt like the world was closing in around me. I began breathing faster and faster. My head seemed to spin even more. I grabbed the sink even harder and squeezed my eyes shut, listening to the shower. The running water seemed to help me relax just a bit. Then I noticed that the water sounded different. I opened my eyes again, and saw that the water was coming out of the spout slowly, slower than was natural. For a few seconds, I could see the water falling at what seemed like half of its normal rate. I reached out and touched the water, and it changed paths. Slowly. I watched as it began moving toward the wall of the shower, and gasped. Just as quickly as the change had come, it was gone. The water splashed the wall, and the flow began normal again. What in the gods was that?

I stepped into the shower, and let the hot water run over me. What had just happened? It was as if time had slowed for me. I had never experienced anything like that. Much like everything else in this world, it was something new. Maybe it was something normal in this world. I took the soap that Marcus had left for me and began lathering myself. Everything was so different here. Where do I even start to make sense of things, to figure out what to do? I realized how much I missed Tomren. I thought of our night in the moonlight together. We had talked about coming here together, and here I was alone. We also explored each other that night. I found myself stiffening at the thought, and the soap was slick on my body. I replayed the night over in my head. I began imagining Tomren here with me now. What his body would look like under the running water. What I would do to him as the water ran over our tangled bodies. What he would do to me. I found myself fully aroused, and began rubbing the slick soap over my manhood. I imagined it was Tomren's hand, I imagined his lips on mine. I closed my eyes and pictured him. I thought about where my hands would wander. I imagined getting on my knees before him as the water rushed over his closed eyes, his head back, mouth wide in a moan, as my own mouth slid up and down his manhood. I imagined the taste of him as he grabbed the back of my head gently, and writhed in my mouth. The feeling of his seed exploding into my waiting throat. I exploded in that moment, and moaned loudly. As soon as I was done, I fell to my knees and wept. I was alone, I felt more empty than I ever had, and I missed the man that I loved.

***

I got out of the shower to see that Marcus had left some fresh clothes for me on the bed. I dressed quickly, and went downstairs to the kitchen. "Something smells amazing," I said as I suddenly realized how hungry I was.

"I just ordered some chinese, your timing is perfect."

I looked at the containers on the table. The food in them looked different than any of the foods I was used to, but the smell and my hunger took away any reservation that I may have had.

"Help yourself," Marcus said, waving his hand to a plate and fork on the counter. He paused, and then asked, "you do have forks in your time, right?"

I laughed. It felt good to laugh. "Yes, we have forks. And, even spoons," I said with a smile.

I fixed a plate of food and sat down. It was amazing, flavors unlike anything I had ever tasted. As I shoved the food in my mouth, much faster than was polite, Marcus set a glass of dark liquid down beside me. There were bubbles in the liquid. "Soda," he said, "Cola to be more specific."

I swallowed it down quickly, and was shocked by the bubbles. I coughed, but quickly drank more. It too was amazing. "Well, I think I'm going to like the food here," I said with a smile.

Marcus smiled back. "Hopefully, you'll come to like much more about this time. Arthur has left enough money to last you a lifetime without having to work, so you can enjoy life a little bit. But, we need to focus on keeping you safe. Do you think they know where you went?"

My mood quickly became somber. "I don't know," I said with a shrug. "They aren't after me I don't think. They were after Tomren, they think he is the one with the abilities. So, the idea was I could come here and find them, and hopefully end their madness. I was to train, but after…" I hesitated, my eyes moistening "after Arthur was killed, I came here because that was what he told me to do in the message he left me. I don't know what to do now."

Marcus stepped closer to me, and put a hand on my shoulder. "We will train you. And, there is someone who can help us. For now though, you need to eat and rest for a few days. I'll try to help you through some of the basics of our time. Hopefully, we can make this easier for you."

"Where do we start?"

"Well, I can show you what we've been doing and working on here. I can also try to acclimate you to some of the things that you will see and experience in your everyday life here. It is vastly different, but you have me to help you, and I will make damn sure I do my best. Arthur was one of my best friends, and he believed in me when no one else did."

"Arthur," I repeated his name. "I wish he was here. He said he had left me messages?"

Marcus smacked the table softly. "Shit, that's right! I had forgotten about the messages. When you're done eating we can go get them."

I put my fork down. I had eaten enough for now. "Let's go, I'm full." Marcus took a drink from his soda, and stood. "Follow me."

He led me down to the basement and into what looked like a storage room. I could feel the magnemite in me drawing to something at the other end of the room. Near the far end, he walked up to a bookcase and removed a book. Behind the book was a small, familiar medallion. He stepped aside, and gestured to it. "After you," he said with a smile.

I approached the bookcase and touched the button. There was a distinct 'click' and the bookcase sank backwards a few inches, and then slid to the left. Immediately lights flickered from inside, and revealed a room much like Arthur's room in the church. I stepped inside.

Marcus followed me in, and then turned and touched the medallion on the inside of the room, and the bookcase slid back into place. He walked over to a keyboard, and sat. I took one of several rolling chairs in the room and sat next to him as he started the computer. "The messages that Arthur left for you are all on the phone over there," he said, pointing to a table next to a refrigerator that was identical to Arthurs.

I stood and retrieved the phone. After powering it up, I unlocked the screen with my thumb. There were five video files on the main screen, all numbered one through five. "Have you watched them," I asked Marcus.

"No," he replied, shaking his head. "Though, I was present when he recorded the first four. The fifth one, he told me he was going to record before he left. I do not know what it contains."

I nodded, and turned the screen back off. Even though Marcus knew what was in four of the videos, I wanted to watch them in private. I did not want my emotions to betray me in front of him. "What do you do here," I asked, changing the subject.

"Lately, we copy and preserve history."

"Like, writing down what is already written," I asked, a bit confused by why they would be doing this.

"Sort of, this book," he said, reaching to his left and grabbing a thick, leather bound tome and handing it to me, "is the most detailed record of your time and kingdom that we have. But it keeps changing."

"Changing," I repeated questioningly. "What do you mean? How do you know it is changing?"

Marcus finished logging into the computer, and opened a folder called 'History pics'. He turned to me. "That book has an almost daily log written in it from a meister in your time, Beltoch Mowbray."

I perked up a bit. "I know Beltoch, he helped heal my wounds."

Marcus nodded, and continued. "The book was an incredible find, though I believe that perhaps Arthur nudged Beltoch to begin writing everything down for our benefit. Either way, I noticed one day that something was different. There was a day when Prince Tomren went into the woods, and was killed in an accident in the cave that you two explored on your first adventure. However, as I was reading it yet again, it changed. Tomren no longer died. He was saved. By you," he said, looking at me.

"That's in the book," I asked, eyeing it incredulously.

"It is," Marcus said with a sigh. "It is why Arthur decided to reveal himself to you in the church. When we realized that things were changing, he wanted to act. What you have inside of you was literally changing history, even though you had no knowledge or intention to do so."

"Don't the copies that you make change also?".

Marcus nodded again. "Yes, and I discovered that fact very quickly. However, these," he said, gesturing to the folder of pictures on the screen, "do not change. I do not know what the original history in the book was. But, about six months ago, I photographed the book. Everyday, though I admit that when Arthur did not return home I missed a couple of days, I compare the picture to what is written in the book. They often align. Sometimes, though, they do not. When they don't, we try to figure out why. For instance, today in the photos," he said, opening the picture with the current date on it, "there is nothing of significance. The king is still mourning for the loss of his son, Prince Tomren, and General Rorthan is continuing to search for those responsible for his death. What does the book say?"

I stared blankly at the book in front of me. If I had not been there that day with the prince, he would have gone into the cave, and never come out. The two brotherhood assassins would have killed him. I changed history.

"The book, what does it say about today," Marcus gently asked again.

I opened the book and began turning to the page with today's date. So if the book shows what is currently happening, and the pictures what would have happened had things never changed, then he should have-

"You son of a bitch," I said, my face red with anger. I stood suddenly, and the chair rolled back with a crash. "You knew, you fucking knew that Arthur was going to die. It was in this book, you knew and you didn't stop it."

Marcus rolled his chair back from me just a small distance, but otherwise remained calm. "I did. But, only the day of his death. We agreed to never look past the current day. If we read into the future of your time, we could end up changing things even more. We could try to stop something terrible from happening, only to make things worse. We only look at the current day. And when it is different, we try to figure out why. Never read past the current date, Sebastian."

I closed the couple of feet separating us, and grabbed him by his shirt. "You knew, and you didn't stop it. You let him die. He thought you were his friend. Are you one of them? Are you Brotherhood?"

Marcus, to his credit, still did not flinch or react to my anger. "I could not stop it. I am not able to travel, he never showed me how to use the beacons. I am here as a historian, not a scientist. I was powerless," he said, his voice cracking. "I knew that my friend was going to be murdered, and that you were going to disappear, and I could do nothing at all to prevent it from happening. So, if you would feel better by punching me, by all means, take a swing. Otherwise, please release me."

I let go of his shirt, but did not back away. "You should have been looking into the future for him. You should have been protecting him. You could have stopped all of this," my anger now being put out by the sadness rising in me. It was as if the fire of my rage was being extinguished by the tears that I now felt falling down my cheeks.

Marcus stood and retrieved my chair, and put a hand on my arm, leading me back to it. "Sit," he said. "You may be correct. And I have second guessed that every single moment since it happened. But, Arthur was clear, and our agreement was clear: current day. That is all we were to look at. The past, the current day, but never the future. I gave him my word, and he trusted me. The only thing I can take comfort in is that I did not betray him."

I snorted. "Comfort. Well, at least you can feel good knowing that you didn't betray him by saving his gods damned life."

Marcus looked at the book. "Are you going to continue to blame me for Arthur's death, or are we going to continue on as he wanted us to do?"

He was right, of course. If this was the agreement that he had formed with Arthur, then he did the right thing by following it. I was acting like an arsehole, but I didn't really care. My anger simmered knowing that Arthur's death was preventable. "Fine, the book," I said, opening it again. I turned to the current date, and began reading. I screamed, my heart racing, and stood again flinging the chair back. This time though, there was no crash. The chair slowly rolled backwards. Marcus very, very slowly, began to move toward the book. The expression on his face began to develop into one of concern as he moved toward me. I closed the book, and stepped back, going to the other side of the room. As I passed the still rolling chair, I put a hand on it to stop it. After a few seconds, everything returned to normal.

"What the hell," Marcus said, as he reached for where the book had been on the table, and spun to see me clutching it on the other side of the room. "How did you do that," he asked, his eyes wide, almost fearful.

I shook my head, though I'm not sure if I did so to clear it, or to match my words. "I don't know."

29

Marcus had led me back upstairs to the kitchen and given me some water. "We need to find out what that was, and how you did it."

I sipped the water. "I don't know how I did it, but it's not the first time."

"Arthur didn't say anything about you being able to slow time. That is not something that is anywhere in any of the references to the Brotherhood either. I've never heard of such a thing," Marcus replied incredulously.

"That is probably because Arthur did not know. The first time I did it was this morning when I was taking a shower." I told him how I had slowed the water down, and explained that I did not know how I did it then either.

"And this has never happened before in your life," he asked. "Also, it's not called a 'looking glass' anymore, it is a 'mirror'. The mirror fogged as you were standing in front of it. When you were a child you don't remember anything like this happening?"

I shook my head. "Never. I can't explain it. I panicked both times, the first time because I was overwhelmed with everything and all of a sudden, the water was slow. This time, I was reading the book and Tomren," I jumped up. "Shit, the book. Tomren.'

I sprinted down the stairs and back to the book, as Marcus followed calling for me to slow down. "What...is going...on," he panted.

"The book, it says," I flipped it open to today's date, and turned it to him.

"The search continues for Prince Tomren, though I fear he has either been taken to another time, or he is already dead," Marcus read. "Jesus."

Marcus flipped back a few pages. "It says that after you disappeared, Tomren went for a walk on the castle grounds, and was not seen again. But, it's only been a day, it's possible that he just got lost."

"Not likely," I said. "He has an excellent sense of direction. He wouldn't have left and not come back unless something was wrong. I need to go back. I need to help look for him."

Marcus closed the distance between us, and put a hand on my shoulder. "The king surely has his best men looking for your friend. There is little you could do there. And," he said, taking a step back and looking me in the eyes, "if the Brotherhood did indeed take him, they likely would have brought him here. And your best chance to save him, and stop the Brotherhood for good, is to figure out what is going on with you, and learn to control your powers."

But Tomren is missing. The man that I love, the only reason I'm in this damned time, the only reason that I even care about the Brotherhood, is missing. I couldn't bring myself to think about the fact that he may be dead. I would not think about that. He was missing, and both Beltoch and Marcus were likely correct, he was brought to a different time. More than likely, he would have been brought to this time. But the easiest way to subdue him and make sure that he couldn't be found, would be to take him out of his time completely. "You're right. He is not there anymore. How do we figure out my abilities?"

"I'm not sure. I'm not a scientist. I'm a historian, and I'm simply here for my knowledge in that field. Arthur would know if he-"

"Yet, he is dead, isn't he," I snapped, cutting off Marcus.

"Yes," he said, softly. "He is indeed."

I quickly apologized. "I'm sorry, I know he was your friend too. I am on edge, I'm afraid. Everything is strange and new right now, and I have no one to help or guide me."

"I may not be able to guide you on what to do, but I can certainly work beside you and help you. And, I will try my best to guide you through this new time you find yourself in. But, it is getting late. We should go to bed for the night and try to get some sleep. This will all be here tomorrow."

I was exhausted. "Yes, sleep is a good idea. I hope I can," I said as I walked out of the room and up towards my bedroom. I stopped and turned back. "Thank you for your help, and everything that you have done for me."

"You're welcome," Marcus said with a nod of his head.

***

Sleep was hard to find, and once I managed to get there, the dreams haunted me. After tossing and turning for what felt like days, but when I looked at the clock I saw it was only a couple of hours, I got up and went into the bathroom. Looking into the looking glass, or mirror as Marcus had corrected, I realized that I didn't even recognize myself. At first, I thought maybe it was just because this mirror was so clear, but I soon knew that that wasn't it. I had lost weight. My eyes had dark bags, and looked sunken into my head. Near the base of my neck I still bore the scar from the hot gun barrel that Rorthan had pressed to my skin. The trials that I was going through were taking a toll on me. I turned the shower on, left it cool, and stood under the downpour. I let the cool water run down me, closing my eyes and trying to just relax. What can I even do here? I didn't know where to start. I could see now that I only came here out of a mixture of fear and hope. Fear that the Brotherhood would hurt Tomren, and hope that I could do something here. The fear may have come true with Tomren missing. But the hope? I had no hope left. I had a historian and some videos from a dead man. I didn't even know where to start. I turned off the water, and dried off. I walked back to the bed, and climbed under the sheets without dressing. The phone Arthur had left for me rested on the table next to the bed.

I picked it up and turned it on. When the lock screen came on, I used my thumb and unlocked it. I opened the first video.

"Sebastian," Arthur's voice said. The video was him sitting in what I now knew was the basement of this home. He smiled, though it did not reach his eyes. "I am again sorry that I am not there to personally speak with you. I hope that Marcus has been hospitable," he said, with a slightly bigger smile, and looked away from the camera to someone behind it. I could hear Marcus chuckle. Arthur looked back. "I have left these messages to guide you as best I can. Marcus is a friend, and I trust him fully, but he is not a scientist and what you possess inside of you is as much a mystery to him as it is to you. The fact is, I believe that you can change the future for the better, and eliminate the Brotherhood of Time for good. I also believe, and I wish I was there to confirm and guide you, that now that you have passed through a beacon you may have unlocked further abilities from the magnetite that is inside of you. I don't know fully what those are, but I can imagine you may have already sensed a difference. Take your time exploring them, learn how to use them. You will have to feel them, as you felt the beacon and medallion in my office in the church. Feel them, flex them slowly, and only when alone or with just Marcus. Do not ever, ever try to use them outside of his home, and never in front of anyone else."

The video went on for a few minutes before it ended with Arthur bidding me to be safe. The other three videos were all recorded in the same fashion, and with essentially the same message. I opened the fifth video.

"Sebastian, my boy," Arthur said, almost in a whisper. It was dark, and it looked as though he was outside somewhere. He kept looking around, as if he was afraid that someone else was there. "I don't have much time. I am certain the Brotherhood has found me. I am going to come back to your time, and hopefully you will never see this message. But, if you do, that means I am dead. Trust no one other than Osbert and Tomren. If you must, I believe that you can trust Rorthan. But only if you have no other choice. He is a bitter, jealous, and violent asshole, but he is no friend of the Brotherhood and he loved your mother. Him hurting you was a reflection of that jealousy magnified by the wine. If you have nowhere else to turn, he will help you if you can find him."

I paused the video. Trust Rorthan? Is he mad? Rorthan tried to kill me. I'm only alive because of Sabina. Surely I could trust her. Or Marcus. He didn't mention Marcus. Maybe that's because he figured I would assume as much since he sent me here. I hit play. "There is one more person that you can trust, but I do not want you to have to contact her if you can avoid it. I will leave instructions on how to reach her. Do not trust anyone else, not even Marcus."

I paused the video again. "Not even Marcus"? But Arthur is the one who sent me here. He is the one that told me to trust Marcus. How in the hell can I manage here if I can't trust Marcus? I hit play again. "I've uncovered some things that make me doubt him, but I have no solid proof. It is my hope that it is just suspicion from years of living this life and hiding, but if you are seeing this video then that means that I never got to prove my suspicions one way or another. I want you to find a way to take the book with your time's history. Then, I want you to run."

The rest of the video contained instructions on what to do once I had the book and left this house. He told me not to use the card that he left for me once I flee, but he left instructions on how to go to the bank and take 'cash' out of my account.

He had left me with a card with my picture on it and the name 'Sebastian Moore'. Apparently I needed this 'identification card' to access the money that he had left for me. It also contained the way to contact the "her" that Arthur claimed I could trust but would not tell me who she was. At the end, he told me to watch the video until I was sure I understood my next step, and then explained how to disable the phone. I watched the video three more times before following Arthur's directions and disabling the phone.

Shit. I was alone again, with no one to trust. But, unlike an hour ago, when I didn't know what to do, I had a plan. I had a means of knowing what my next step was. And I would follow Arthur's plan.

30

"How did you sleep," Marcus asked me the next morning as we sat at the table in the kitchen.

He had prepared pancakes, sausage, bacon, and orange juice for us. "After I took a shower, I slept well, thank you."

"Good, I'm glad. I figured after breakfast we should check the book again, and then perhaps we could go out and I could show you some of the city."

I smiled and nodded. "That sounds great," I said. I hoped that my smile hid my distrust.

"Perfect," he said, returning my smile before going back to eating his breakfast.

We finished breakfast in silence. I tried to eat my food as if I were starving, but my stomach was in knots. If he couldn't be trusted, would Marcus be taking me somewhere in the city to harm me? Would there be Brotherhood waiting for us? But, if he was indeed working with them, why was there no Brotherhood here already? They could have been waiting for me when I arrived, or he could have called them the instant I did and they would have been able to come for me. It didn't make sense, and I hoped that Arthur was wrong. But, with no way of knowing, I had to do as Arthur said and leave.

I helped him clear the food and dishes, and we went down to the basement. "Did you watch the videos that Arthur left for you," Marcus asked casually.

I nodded. "I did. I hope that we are able to figure it all out. If I can learn to control my apparent ability, maybe we can get Tomren back and stop the Brotherhood for good."

Marcus smiled gently. "I'm sure we will be able to. What about the last video? Did he give any new directions?"

Yes, he told me not to trust you. That I should take the book and run. "No, it was just another 'I'm sorry I'm not there, if you're watching this I must be dead' video," I said with what I hoped was enough emotion in my voice.

Marcus nodded. "He cared very much for you, I'm sorry that this is how things turned out."

Marcus sat at the computer, and pulled up the day's pictures. I flipped to the date in the book. He read mundane going ons about the kingdom, this subject's complaint, and that subject's petition.

"They are still searching for Tomren, though it sounds as though they are running out of places to look," I said, comparing the book to the pictures.

Marcus closed the pictures. "They will find him," he said reassuringly.

I nodded. "I certainly pray to the gods that they do."

I looked at the book before me. I had to find a way to remove it and myself from the house with it without Marcus seeing. It shouldn't be too difficult since the book is just left here in the basement without being locked away.

I pushed the book further onto the desk and stood. "Will we be going out today," I asked.

Marcus looked at me for a moment, considering. "We could. I could take you shopping, perhaps introduce you to some of the things in the city that you will have to adjust to."

"That sounds excellent. I'm eager to start learning."

"Give me a little bit to shower, and we can go," he said, standing and pushing his chair back under the desk.

***

An hour later, we were walking down the street to what he called 'downtown'. He had decided that since it was a nice day, rather than take the car we could walk and I could see more. "Where should we start," I asked.

Marcus shrugged. "Well, we could get you some new clothes, ones that are your own. Perhaps we can get you some earbuds to go with your phone, and maybe even a smart watch. You have more than enough money."

"Earbuds, smart watch," I repeated as a question.

"Yeah, the ear buds will make it so that you can talk on the phone, or listen to the videos, or music, or whatever and only you will be able to hear the sound. The watch will let you tell what time it is, but also it connects to the phone so you can control some functions of the phone with it."

I wasn't sure I saw the need for the watch, but the earbuds sounded useful. I could have privacy when using my phone, and that was appealing. Also, music was something I hadn't really thought about. "What is the music like now," I asked.

Marcus smiled. "Diverse. There are many different types, with many different words and meanings. Some have a strong message, some are just frivolous and fun to listen to. I'll get you set up so that you can listen to whatever you decide that you like."

"That would be excellent, thank you," I said with a genuine smile. Arthur wasn't sure that Marcus was an enemy, and as long as he was being friendly, I would enjoy his company while paying attention to his actions.

"Don't mention it," Marcus said, slapping me on the back.

"Why not," I asked.

Marcus looked at me for a second. "It's an expression. Kind of like saying 'you're welcome', just a different way of saying it."

"I see," I said. I didn't really see, why not just say 'you're welcome'? But, there was no point in thinking about that in a world where there were far greater differences to worry about.

We stopped at a store front, the sign claimed to have the best buys. "Let's get you some tech," Marcus said, a bit gleefully.

The store was bigger than anything I had ever seen. There were screens everywhere, from the phones to screens that were as big as some of the wall's in the home I grew up in. Sounds came from everywhere, and I closed my eyes for just a second.

"Are you okay," Marcus asked. "Do you want to come back later?"

I shook my head, clearing it a little. "No, we're here now and I don't think it would be different if I came back later, or tomorrow, or in a week. And, time is of the essence."

"Then let's get what we came for, and get out of here as quickly as we can," he said with a nod. We went to the section that had the earbuds, and he suggested a few different ones. In the end, I picked a pair that were blue because they reminded me of Tomren's eyes. We went over to the phones, and looked at the section that had watches. I was amazed by the fact that the screens were so small. I thought phones were small, but I was gobsmacked by the screens that could fit on one's wrist.

A pleasant woman approached us and smiled. There was something familiar about her hazel eyes. "These are sweet, aren't they? This one is the newest model, we just got it in yesterday," she said. "I think I've only got like two left. Which is perfect, because you guys could totally get one each and be matchzies."

'Sweet'? 'Mactchzies'? This woman made no sense. "How can they be sweet," I asked, incredulously.

Marcus coughed and quickly took the watch that she was showing and began examining it. "We only need one," he said, still examining the watch far closer than I thought was necessary.

The woman looked at me oddly. She smiled and said she would be right back.

Marcus got closer to me. "'Sweet' was just an expression. It means they are cool, or awesome, or-"

"Then why not just say that," I cut him off. I was surrounded by things that made no sense to me, people were talking in gibberish, and he was talking down to me like a damned child.

He stepped back a little, surprised by my tone. "It's just how people speak. Language evolves."

I suppose in some ways I was like a child. "I'm sorry," I said, a bit sheepishly.

Marcus sighed. "It's fine, I know this is a lot. Just let me do the talking and we'll be on our way."

The woman returned with a small box. "Do you gentlemen have more shopping to do, or will this be all?"

Marcus handed her the earbuds. "Just this today."

"I can take you over here then," she said, leading us to one of the screens at a desk.

"What's over there," I whispered to Marcus.

"That is where we will pay," he hissed.

The woman passed both items before the screen. "£327.83," she said.

"There is no way that those items weigh over three hundred pounds," I said.

The woman looked at me as if I were from another planet. Which, I suppose in some ways I was.

Marcus smiled awkwardly. "He's not from here," he said to the woman. He turned to me. "That's how much money it costs," he said, "£327.83. Did you bring your card?"

I reached into my pocket. I smiled as I handed the woman the card. She smiled back. "You can put it in the chip reader on your side," she said, pointing to the small screen facing me.

The screen said "Insert chip at any time". Was it a card, or a goddamned chip? What is wrong with this place? My heart started to race. I put the card in.

"Oh," the woman said, "you have to put the chip side in." I felt my face redden. And then I felt the air around me thicken, and the sounds slowed. Shit. Shit, shit, shit. I couldn't stop it. I turned to Marcus, and he was in the middle of blinking, and reaching towards me. I assumed he was going to show me how to use the card. I took a step back, and looked at the woman. She wasn't slowing.

"You need to calm down Sebastian, I can help you," she said, stepping around the counter and walking towards me.

Shit. I needed to get out of there. I needed to be outside, under the sun. This was not good.

I turned and ran, knocking into a shelf. Items began to fall from it as I ran faster to the door. I was outside, and beside the building before I calmed. Just before I calmed down, I noticed that there was a man smoking though not from a pipe, but from some sort of a stick. Suddenly, time resumed, and I stood a few feet from him.

The man yelped, and jumped back a bit. "Where the bloody hell did you come from?"

Shit. "I'm sorry, I was...running and needed a rest," I said, hoping that it sounded believable.

"Are you okay," the man asked.

I nodded. "Yes, I just need to catch my breath, I'm-"

"There you are," I heard Marcus call. I turned to see him approaching with a small bag. "I wondered where you had gotten off to."

"Yes, yes, I just needed a bit of air," I said. The man dropped what he was smoking and stepped on it. "Have a fine day," he mumbled and scurried off.

"Are you okay," Marcus asked, putting a hand on my shoulder.

"I'm better now."

"We should return home, you knocked over a whole shelf in there, scared the hell out of the people that were around. They are all confused as to what happened. They almost wouldn't let me buy the stuff," he said, lifting the bag.

I nodded, and we walked back to the house in silence.

31

Dinner was quiet for the most part that night. I was embarrassed, I felt lost, and I was scared. I didn't know how to control my powers. It was one thing to lose control in front of Marcus, it was another to do it in front of the world.

"I'm sorry," I said softly as I picked at my food.

Marcus set his fork down. "You have nothing to be sorry for. This is all understandably overwhelming for you. I shouldn't have taken you to such a busy place so soon. We need to move slowly, and we need to be careful."

"We can't move slowly," I said. "Tomren is in danger, the Brotherhood is either going to kill him, or already has," I choked on the words.

Marcus poured me some more soda. "What do you want to do? You just found out two days ago that you have the ability to slow time. You don't know how to control it, or if you even can."

"I don't know," I admitted. "But, I need to do something. I will not lose Tomren. He is all I have left. He was supposed to be safer with me gone."

"Tomorrow we should try to work on controlling your ability," Marcus suggested. "We can work in the basement, or if you prefer, we could head back to the castle. I assume there must be a beacon there still, one that you used to get here, and Arthur used to go back and forth?"

I nodded, and instantly regretted it. He hadn't known for sure that there was a beacon at the castle. Which means that Arthur had never told him where it was, nor had he told him of the church. "But, there is no need to go there. We can work on it here, in the basement."

Marcus shrugged, but he seemed to have tensed just a bit. "I just thought that maybe if you were closer to the beacon it would be easier to control."

"I don't think that is necessary. Here is fine."

"It's not far," Marcus continued. "We could drive there early before the crowds come, and we could get-"

"We're not going to the castle," I snapped, cutting him off. He was pressing the idea, and it made me uncomfortable. However, he may have been right about the beacon.

"Very well," he said, picking his phone up and tapping the screen aimlessly. I said nothing more, and as soon as I finished my food and put away my dishes, I went upstairs and closed the door to my room.

I was exhausted, and although a shower sounded like it would feel good, I simply laid down in the bed. Tired as I was, however, I could not sleep. Tomren was in danger, and Marcus had a sudden desire to find the beacon. Why? Did he honestly believe that it would make a difference in controlling my ability? That made sense on some level. I had never been able to slow time prior to making the trip here. Maybe this was normal. But, without Arthur here to help me, there was no one that had made the trip that could teach me. I could feel the beacon when I was close to it, I could sense its power. Perhaps that would make it easier to learn to control slowing time. But there was no need for Marcus to be there, and until I had some way to know that he was definitely a friend and could be trusted, I would take him nowhere near the church.

The sun had gone down hours ago. I looked at my watch charging on the nightstand. Four past midnight. It was a new day. I quietly got up, and put on a hoodie and jeans. Grabbing my watch and my phone, I slipped silently down to the basement. The lights came on when I opened the door, and I quickly closed it again, blocking any light from escaping. I went to the book. It was more of the same for today. King Osbert and his men were looking for Tomren. Nothing was said about finding him, whether safe or not. I didn't know how to access Marcus' computer, and I honestly didn't see the need anyway. I understand one day maybe looking closely to see if we could identify why the history changed, but it served no practical purpose to me presently. The only thing that mattered to me right now was finding Tomren. And I was tired of waiting.

I stood and turned to leave the room. I was done sitting by and looking to a book to tell me if Tomren was found or not, if he was safe, if he was even alive. I needed to go back, and I needed to find Tomren. I reached out to push the medallion and open the door, but I stopped just before I did. If there was even a possibility that Marcus was working with the Brotherhood, then it would be best if he didn't have the book. I went back and picked it up. Quietly, I slipped out of the basement and left the house.

I had walked only a few blocks in the direction of the castle, when I realized that I didn't actually know *where* the castle was. Arthur had given me the address to get to Marcus, but I did not know the way back. My heartbeat hastened in my chest. I needed Marcus to get back to the castle, but I couldn't trust him and he definitely wouldn't allow me to take the book. How was I going to find my way back to Tomren without Marcus?

I felt a strange tickle in the back of my mind. It felt the way it did when I could sense the beacon, but not quite. It was different, weaker. I reached for it. Suddenly I felt the air thicken, and I mentally stepped away from the feeling. The air felt light and cool again. I took several deep breaths, and closed my eyes. The feeling was still there in my mind. I reached for it again, and opened my eyes when the air thickened in response. I could no longer feel the soft breeze that had been blowing the trees only a moment before. I turned back towards Marcus' home. There were headlights from a car coming down the street. They were going so very slow. I reached out and touched the feeling in my mind, fully embracing it. At first, I thought the car stopped. But, as I walked closer to it, I saw that it was still moving. It was going so slowly that it was almost impossible to see any movement. I walked right in front of it, and looked at the driver. It looked like the woman from the store, and she was not slowed with everything else. She was saying something, but I couldn't make it out. She looked as if she was desperately trying to open the car door, but it was barely moving. I had a pang of a thought that she was close to my mother's age when she died, she even sort of looked like my mother. She didn't die, you killed her, a voice in my head said. It was the voice of Rorthan, still haunting my thoughts. Before I could think on it more, I jumped back. The car's movement was still so slow it was indiscernible, but the woman's hazel eyes were locked on mine now. She had stopped fighting with the door and was just glaring at me.

I ran as quickly as I could back to Marcus' house, and turned back to see the car still practically sitting in the silent street. I rushed inside and into the basement. The door didn't seem to move when I pressed the medallion. I pressed it again, and still nothing. I released the feeling in my mind just a little bit, and the door began moving slowly. As soon as it was open enough, I slipped in and put the book back on the desk. I was exhausted, and I released my hold on the feeling completely. The air felt normal again, but I only felt it for a moment before sinking into one of the chairs. Darkness claimed me.

***

I awoke to Marcus standing over me, shaking me gently. "Sebastian," he called. "Sebastian, are you okay?" I opened my eyes, and tried to sit up, but the dizziness that followed threatened to bring back the darkness.

"I don't know," I muttered. "What happened?"

Marcus frowned. "What were you doing down here?"

"I...couldn't sleep...", I sputtered, trying to form an excuse. "I wanted to check the book and see if they had found Tomren yet."

Marcus sat in one of the other chairs, and rolled himself directly in front of me. "Drink," he said, handing me a bottle of water.

I obeyed, drinking the cold water greedily. I instantly regretted it, as my head throbbed from the cold. "Thank you," I managed.

"You don't know why you ended up unconscious," Marcus asked. "Were you feeling unwell?"

Well, yes, after I managed to control my ability in a way we've never seen, I felt weak and passed out. "No, I was fine. I was just reading the book, and then you were waking me," I lied instead.

Marcus nodded. "We should take you to see a doctor."

"I'm fine," I said quickly. "No doctor."

"Okay," Marcus said. He turned on his computer, and the screen flashed to life. "I am curious though, as to what you were doing when you took the book and left?"

My pulse raced. I was already weak and light headed. This did not help. "What are you talking about," I asked.

He opened a video on his screen and it showed me taking the book and leaving out of the basement, it switched to another view and it showed me leaving the house. "You took the book. There are cameras all over," he said, pointing over his shoulder at the ceiling. "I saw the alerts on my phone this morning that the motion sensors...I suppose you don't know what they are. Motion sensors make the cameras start recording automatically when they sense movement."

He turned his chair back toward me. I swallowed, although my mouth felt like it was made of sand. "What is intriguing," he continued, "is that there was no sign of you returning. You just all of a sudden appeared in the middle of the room, and put the book back. And then, you collapsed. I ran down here as soon as I saw the footage, and found you. So, again, I have to ask, what the fuck were you doing?" He enunciated the question slowly, making each word into its own sentence.

I grabbed the bottle of water, and drank. I could feel the power tingling inside of me, but I dared not reach for it. I needed to recuperate from the last time, and I needed to learn why it had drained me. "I wanted to read it," I said slowly.

"Well, you know we shouldn't be reading it past the current day. Also why did you need to take it to read it?"

"I wanted some fresh air, so I took it outside to read," I said after a moment.

Marcus nodded. "Okay, say I believe that, which I don't really think that I do," he said, "what happened that made your ability trigger? Why did you suddenly appear? And why are you so weak?"

I shrugged, hoping that it came across as genuine. "I don't know. It just happened, and I ran back here when it did."

"I don't believe you. What aren't you telling me? Why are you lying to me," he said, his tone sharpening and his voice raising just a bit.

I didn't know what to say to convince him, and my head was still foggy. "Are you Brotherhood?". I blurted the question out without thinking.

Marcus looked as if I had slapped him. "What the hell are you talking about? Why would you ask me that?"

"Are you Brotherhood," I repeated, forcing a strength into the question that I didn't feel.

His eyes narrowed. "Are you," he practically yelled. "Of course I'm not a member of that bullshit cult. Arthur told you to trust me, Arthur led you here. Do you not trust Arthur?"

"Arthur said he didn't know if he could trust you, but he had little choice."

Marcus sat, practically fell, back into his chair. The look on his face seemed to be a mix of betrayal, hurt, and anger. "That's a lie. I've known Arthur for almost a decade. I've worked with him on everything. I offered to help him, and you. You're lying."

I shook my head. "I'm not," I assured him. "He said that he had found some things that made him question whether you could be trusted, and that he hoped he was wrong. He said he was going to try to find proof, but since he is dead, I have no way of knowing if he did or not."

"You're lying," Marcus repeated. The sharpness was gone from his voice, replaced only by pain. I could tell that he knew I was not lying, and it either hurt him deeply or he was an excellent actor.

"You don't believe that," I said.

"Fine. Leave," he said, anger returning to his voice. "But the book stays."

"No, the book goes with me. Arthur was clear that I was to take the book. What do you need it for anyway? If you aren't Brotherhood, and I am out of your life, what use do you have for it?"

"I am not Brotherhood," he said with spite, "and that is why the book stays with me. I don't trust that you won't end up getting captured, and they would be able to access the book. I don't trust with full certainty that you wouldn't be willing to trade the book for Tomren. They want your power, and they want the book. They believe it to be in the church, and have spent years, decades, centuries, millenia, searching for that church. They will not get the book while I live, and you will not either."

I felt for the power, but just reaching for it made my world start to darken again. I was still too weak. "It is not yours, and you will not stop me from taking it," I said, standing and using all of my strength to seem more confident than I was.

"That is not within your power to control. Now leave."

I stepped towards him. "It must have dawned on you by now that I controlled my ability last night? I will take the book, with or without your permission, I do not need you to agree."

"Sebastian, do not make it end this way," he said, almost pleadingly. "You may have controlled your ability, but look at what it did to you. You were unconscious and completely vulnerable. That isn't real control."

"The choice is yours," I said, taking another step towards him, and the book.

He turned back toward the desk and reached under it. A second later his hand became visible, and he was holding a gun. "Leave," he repeated. "Walk away, and let's not make this into something it doesn't need to be."

My pulse raced, and I felt the power inside thrum. Every fiber of my being was pushing me to reach out and touch it. I resisted. "Marcus, if you truly aren't Brotherhood, then don't do this," I said, taking another step towards him.

Marcus pointed his gun off to the side and pulled the trigger. The air took on that familiar heavy, stagnant calm. I stood there for a moment, shocked as I watched the barrel of the gun flash,

and the bullet slowly leave the chamber. I felt for
the power, and I knew it remained untouched. I
wasn't doing this.

"We need to go now," a voice came from
behind me. I whirled around to see the woman
from the car.

"Who the hell are you," I asked, my heart
still racing.

"Not your enemy," the woman said, "but I
can't hold this for long, and you are in no condition
to help. So, let's bloody go."

I had little choice. We both ran out of the
room. I stopped.

"What the hell," she asked with a hiss.

"The book," I said, running back into the
room. Marcus had barely moved, only his hand
with the gun coming back to where I had stood.
The bullet still moved slowly in the air towards the
wall, looking like it should fall. I grabbed the book,
and ran back to the woman.

We were outside of the house and in her car
before the air lightened again, the sound of the gun
firing finally coming from inside the house. And
then we were racing away from Marcus' home.

32

The car raced at a speed that was far too fast in my opinion. "Slow down," I said, more of a plea than anything.

"We need to get far away before he comes after us. Did he give you anything while you were there," she asked.

"These clothes," I said, holding out my arms. "A pair of earbuds. And a watch."

"The watch," she said, holding out her hand.

I took it off and handed it to her. She lowered the window, and threw it out.

"What the hell," I complained. "That was expensive."

She nodded. "£327.83 with the earbuds."

I looked at her. "How did you-". I had been right. "You were the woman at the store."

"Yes, at the store, last night when you hit pause, and when you first got here. Maurianne Lawlor," she said, extending her hand without looking away from the road.

"Hit pause? When I first got here," I asked, ignoring her hand.

"'Hit pause' is what I call it when we slow time," she said, pulling her hand back. "And, yes, when you ordered a ride to Marcus' house. You didn't know how to open the door."

"Shit," I said in disbelief. "You've been watching me." A dark thought hit me. "Are you one of the Brotherhood?"

She snorted. "Me? Brotherhood? You'd have been dead a week ago," she scoffed.

"Excuse me," I asked with a haughtiness in my voice.

"You would have been dead," she repeated. "I found you within minutes of your arrival. They could, and should, have too. So, either they are very inept, or..." she trailed off.

"Or Marcus really was with them, and they wanted something other than me dead," I finished.

"Yes," she agreed. "Either way, we need to stay far from Marcus. We need to get to the church, it is the only place that is safe from them right now."

"I'm not taking you to the church," I said quickly. "Just because I don't trust Marcus, doesn't mean I do trust you."

She snorted again. "You think I need you to take me to the church? I am perfectly capable of going there myself, thank you very much."

"You've been to the church?"

She sighed. "Yes. Arthur took me there for the first time when I was nine. I've come and gone freely ever since. I used to go there to hide from...well, it doesn't matter what I needed to hide from. The point is, it is a place that is more sacred to me than you will ever know, and while you were still tromping around in your medieval world, hell, before you were even born, I was learning how to use my powers."

"I mean, technically, I was born a millennia before you were," I retorted. "Why would Arthur have taken you to the church?"

She turned the car down a path, and I saw the familiar shape of the castle turret rising in the distance. There were a few busses ahead of us on the road.

"Because, I am his daughter."

"His daughter," I repeated. "He never said anything about a daughter."

"Why would he? Did you often have deep conversations about his family? His history?" I shook my head. "I didn't suspect you had. Besides, our relationship was," she paused, as if trying to find the right word. "Complicated," she finally said.

I was going to ask more questions, but she suddenly pulled off of the road, and drove down a small path into the trees. I could see the castle clearly. "We walk from here. Follow me, and do not leave the path that I take," she said as she turned off the engine. "Bring the book."

I grabbed the book and followed her. She cut into the trees and walked parallel with the castle. If we turned to the right now, we could walk directly to the castle, but she kept walking straight. "Where are you going? The church is in-"

"I know where the church is," she snapped, harshly but quietly. "There may be those watching however, that do not. There may also be those listening that do not. Keep your mouth closed until we are inside of the church."

I started to ask her who in the hell she thought she was, but the look that she flashed at me caused me to snap my mouth shut. I followed her as she led us past the castle, following the tree line. She stopped, and looked around.

"Here," she said, and walked from the cover of the trees to the castle grounds. I froze.

"What's wrong," she asked, looking around furiously.

I shook my head. "Nothing," I said, "there just used to be a bench here that I shared with Tomren once."

Maurianne rolled her eyes. "We need to focus on the task at hand, not whatever trysts you had with your lover boy prince."

I felt my face redden, though with anger or embarrassment I was not sure. "I know what we need to do," I snapped, "and I also know that the only damned reason I'm here is for the 'lover boy prince' as you so crassly call him."

She ignored me and continued leading us to the castle. From the path that we walked, the tour busses and those who rode them were nowhere to be seen. Finally, we reached the dilapidated remains of the once proud castle. The remains of what was once, albeit briefly, my home.

Maurianne walked to the entrance to the church, and pressed the medallion. The door slid away, and when I entered I felt a strong sense of being home. The lights in the church flicked on, and I sat down at the round table. As I looked at the faces frozen in a soundless scream, I remembered the first time I saw this room. I was amazed by the things I saw, amazed by the items that made no sense, the stories of 'flying transports'. Now here I sat, not only having seen the planes myself, but sitting in the same room at a time when planes crisscross the skies. I felt a wave of sadness coming when I thought about being here with Tomren, exploring and forming a bond that turned from friendship to love. That very bond had led me here, to a time and world that I knew nothing about, in an attempt to protect him. And yet danger still found him.

"Can we light the faces," I asked, without looking at Maurianne.

"Light them? The lights are on," she said seemingly confused.

I turned to her. "Have you never seen them with the fire? They are magnificent. They convey the pain that I feel."

Maurianne shook her head. "I have not. I did not know that they could be lit. I suppose if I'm being honest, I haven't spent much time in here," she said, coming and sitting beside me. She looked at the faces. "Who do you think they are?"

"Us," I answered without thinking about the question.

"Us?"

I nodded. "Those of us who have used the beacons, that have felt the burden of the knowledge in this room. Those of us that have fought against the Brotherhood, or have felt the evil touch that they bring."

"Maybe," was all she said.

"Maurianne," I said, turning to face her, "what now? What do we do? How do we get Tomren back?"

She sighed. "Call me Anne. I don't know. I don't know if we should go back to your time and try to find him, or if he's already been brought here. Hell, he may have even been taken to a different time." She looked at the book. "How far ahead have you read?"

I blinked. "Marcus said that Arthur was adamant that we should only read the current day. I hadn't looked past that."

"Arthur is dead, and Marcus...well, Marcus I do not trust," she said. "We have to make decisions now based on what we know. I want to destroy the

Brotherhood, and you want Tomren back. Those two things may cross paths here, and that book may be the best way for us to get ahead of events."

I hadn't thought about why she was helping me, or what her purpose was in doing so. I guess I just assumed that she was another part of Arthur's plan. "Why do you want to destroy the Brotherhood?"

"Because they are a disgusting cult that murder without discretion. And because they have hunted me my whole life. The same as they hunted for Tomren, though unbeknownst to them, the one they really wanted was you."

"But why? Why do they want anyone? Why do they care," I asked, almost begging her to help me understand why this was all happening to us.

"Because those who use the beacons are unholy to them. And those of us, and as far as I know it is just you and I, that are capable of controlling time are an abomination to be destroyed. They believe that we wield a power that only God should have."

"Which God," I asked, unsure why anyone would think that God wants them to murder another man.

"The God of their bible. The Christian God. Most other Gods have fallen to history. Their bible says that it is not for man to know the times and dates that God has set. They believe that our ability to travel to different times is a slap in the face of God."

"Christianity," I said, looking at the faces, "sounds terrible."

Anne laughed, but there was no humour in it. "It is, or rather it can be. It can also be beautiful, and give people hope. The same bible talks of love and peace, of treating others the same as you treat yourself."

"So the bible makes no sense?".

"It does to a great many people, and some of those people take the words and twist them to fit their own evil. I once followed the Brotherhood," she said quietly. "I thought that what I was doing was God's will."

"And now you don't," I asked, suddenly concerned that maybe she was not on my side.

"No, now I do not."

"Why? What changed?"

Anne looked at the faces frozen in a scream. "I was asked to do things that I was not willing to do. The more that I learned of both the Brotherhood of Time, and of the bible, I did not believe that they were doing God's work. They are animals, every one of them is simply a bloodthirsty animal. Some may believe, as I did, that they are blessed by God, but they do terrible things and they get pleasure from doing them."

"Like killing us?"

"Like killing anyone they want. Like torturing anyone they want. I've seen them torture and kill children that were not yet even teenagers. I've seen them rape, torture, and kill women, all the while saying that God was using them to punish the evil doers."

I was disgusted. "And this is all in their bible?"

"No," she said, shaking her head. "But the problem with the bible is that it can be twisted to meet the ideals of anyone. They can take the words, and twist and mutilate them until they seem to say what they want to hear. And so they do."

"So how do we stop them," I asked, quickly adding, "and get Tomren back?"

Anne smiled. "We read that book, and we find out where to take the fight to them."

33

I had read three weeks forward in the book, and there was still no sign of Tomren or the Brotherhood. I sighed in frustration. "This is getting us nowhere!".

"Then we keep looking," Anne said.

"You keep looking," I said, sliding the book to her, "I'm hungry, tired, and angry. My eyes can't read anymore."

I walked to Arthur's room, and looked in the refrigerator. Thankfully he had some sliced meats and cheeses, and plenty of water. As I ate, Anne came in and sat beside me. "I don't see anything in the book," she admitted with defeat.

"There has to be another way. I'm going to have to go back," I said.

She shook her head. "It's not safe for you there at all. At least here we can have some control."

"Control? I'm hiding in a church, that is not control. And," I snapped, "I could do that in my own time. This is just as secret then as it is now."

"But this is what Arthur wanted you to do, his plan was to have you-"

"I don't give a damn about his plan," I said, raising my voice. "He is dead. I watched him die right in front of me. The plan that he had is shit."

"And you think you have a better plan," she asked.

I couldn't tell if she was genuinely asking, or being sarcastic, but I answered just the same. "I need to go back. I need to find Tomren. The Brotherhood can wait until Tomren and I are safe. Hell, we can come back here to the church. But I need to find him.

"And if, which is the most likely possibility, the Brotherhood has him? How will you fight them?"

"I don't know," I admitted. "I suppose that if I can find them, I could hit pause and retrieve him."

"What happened when you hit pause the last time? What good will it do when you get Tomren, and then black out and the Brotherhood has both of you?".

"I don't know," I repeated. "What would you have me do? Sit here? Stay in this church for, what, the rest of my days?".

"We need to think of something," Anne said, "but running back with no plan is not going to do you or Tomren any good."

"Three weeks into the future they still haven't found any sign of Tomren. The longer we delay, the more likely that we will not find him at all."

Anne started to say something, but whatever she was going to say was cut off by the sound of Arthur's phone vibrating on the table across the room.

"What the hell," Anne asked, as we both stood and crossed to it.

The screen read "UNKNOWN NUMBER". "Do we answer it," I asked, picking up the phone.

"No one should have this number. It's possible that it's just a wrong number, I don't think we should answer it. Let them leave a message if they want to," Anne answered.

The vibration ended, and the screen showed a missed call before going dark. We both stared at the phone, as if it would do something. A moment later, the screen lit up again. There was a new text. I touched the screen, and it reminded me that it was locked. "How do we open it," I asked.

Anne took the phone. "I know his pin," she said, typing on the screen. A second later she showed me the phone.

"Call us back" a text said. Below the text was a video. I hit play. "If you want Tomren back before we kill him, call us back," a woman's voice said. The voice seemed familiar. "Either way, we will find you. The only question is, do you both die, or does your precious prince go on to live a long life?"

The camera turned to a hooded figure strapped into a chair. I knew from the clothes that it was Tomren, but when a hand pulled back the hood I gasped. He had clearly been beaten. His face was bruised, both of his eyes were dark purple and swollen shut. He tried to say something through the piece of cloth that they had gagged him with, but he was punched and he slumped down. He didn't move again. "You have one hour to return our call."

The video ended and I slammed my hand down on the table and screamed in anger. "They have him here," I yelled. "He is here, now. I need to find him."

"We need to think about this," Anne said calmly, putting a hand on my shoulder.

I shrugged her off forcefully, and looked at her. "There is nothing to think about. I will trade myself for him without any hesitation."

"They will kill you."

"They will kill him," I said. "I will not live out my time knowing that I let him die."

"Then let's make a plan of some sort," Anne said. "We can think of something, be prepared."

"You need not be involved," I said. "This is about me. You have no need to risk yourself."

"Of course I'm involved. They killed my father, and I won't let them kill my," she hesitated for a moment, "my friend. We will do this together."

"Fine," I nodded, "a plan. But I will call them in fifty seven minutes."

***

We spent fifty five minutes making a plan to get Tomren back. Anne hoped that I would not have to give myself up to make it work, but I was explicit with her that I would gladly do just that.

"It's not worth it," she argued, "they will just kill you both in the end."

"Perhaps, and hopefully it won't come to that. But I will not leave without Tomren being freed. If that means my own death, then so be it. I do not want to live with the knowledge that I could have saved him, but that I was too scared to do what needed to be done."

She started to argue more, but I held up a hand. "We need to call them now," I said as I picked up the phone.

I opened the text message, and called the number. The same female voice from the video answered after the first ring. "Meet us at the cave in one hour. If you're late you will never see Tomren again. If you are not alone, you will never see Tomren *alive* again."

The call disconnected. "I don't like it. The cave is far too easy of a location for an ambush. And you're not going alone," Anne said quickly.

"The cave is our only option. I have to go alone, you heard them, and I will not risk Tomren's life."

"Trust me, you're not going alone. I will stay out of sight, but you will not go in alone," Anne insisted.

"And how do you expect to stay out of sight in the cave? The path to the beacon is not very large, and it would be impossible not to be seen."

She sighed. "Then I come with you to the cave, and I stay outside. Arthur has some radios, we can stay in contact and I will come in if you need me. But I'm at least going to the cave."

"Radios," I asked, not sure what that meant.

Anne stood and went to the desk where Arthur used to sit. She opened a drawer under it, and pulled out a small box.

"Put this in your ear," she said, handing me a small earbud and putting one of them in her own ear. I followed her direction. "Say something," she said, and the sound came from the earbud.

"Whoa, that's different."

Anne smiled. "They work. We should be able to stay in contact now once you enter the cave."

"We need to start walking. It will take us at least forty minutes to get there. I don't want to run, so we should leave," I said looking at my phone.

"Um, we could just drive," Anne suggested.

I shook my head. "Through the forest?"

"Yeah, there are dirt bikes here. It would be a ten minute drive."

I had never heard of a dirt bike, but I knew that would not serve our needs. "I've never even heard of a dirt bike, and I certainly do not know how to operate one. So we would have to be together, and if we arrive together and they have a scout at the cave, well then-"

"They kill Tomren," Anne finished. "Very well. Let's go get our weapons, shall we," she asked, standing and heading back into the church.

She walked to the wall with all of the guns on it. On the wall hung a few sacks, she took one and handed one to me as well. I noticed now that the guns looked different than they had in my time. They seemed newer, better cared for. "I don't want a gun," I said flatly.

Anne looked at me sideways. "They will most definitely have guns. You should have one as well. You need to protect yourself."

I shrugged. "I don't like guns. They have always caused problems when I've been around them. Besides, I can always hit pause. That will be way more effective than a gun for me."

"Okay, but remember, don't hold it for too long. You need to stay conscious. If you need to pause then use that time to get out."

"I can't. Tomren will also be paused, and I can't run while carrying him and holding on to the pause."

Anne thought about it for a moment. "Okay, well, if you have to hit pause, let me know first. I'll come in and help. I can carry him, and I can take over the pause when you can't hold it anymore. At least take these," she said, handing me a knife and a flashlight.

I nodded. "That makes sense," I said. I looked at the wall of guns once more. "What are these," I asked, picking up one of the egg shaped devices that Tomren and I had wondered about.

"I'll take that," Anne said, quickly grabbing it from me. "It's a grenade. If you pull the pin, it will explode. You don't want to be around it when it does, so you pull the pin and throw it. It can eliminate multiple enemies at once."

"Good to know," I said. When she turned, I grabbed two of the grenades and shoved them in my sack. "We need to go."

34

We walked to the cave in silence, only stopping at the occasional sound. Anne had reminded me before we left that the Brotherhood may have put scouts at any point. The last thing we wanted to do was have them see that I was not alone. The last mileway or so we split up. After a few minutes I could no longer see Anne, nor could I hear her behind me.

"I'm still here," her voice said in my ear one of the times I turned around. I did not say anything in response, simply nodded once and went back to walking.

The cave entrance was somewhat more overgrown with vines and trees than I remembered, but inside it was exactly the same.

I took the flashlight out of my sack, and lit the way. It had only been a couple of months since Tomren and I walked this path for the first time. Though, it had also been over a thousand years. The thought made my head ache, and I forced myself to focus.

I followed the path until I reached the vast area that held the beacon. I could feel its power, the tingle inside of me pulsing.

"That's far enough," the female voice said.

I shined the flashlight to the source and froze. "Why," was all I could muster.

Sabina looked at me and smiled. "God's will, of course," she said. "You are an abomination, and those who use these beacons for anything other than God's will are heretics."

"You saved me from Rorthan. You protected me, why?"

Sabina laughed dryly. "I didn't know that you were the one. We always assumed it was Tomren. Had I known, I would have let the general kill you, and Tomren would have been saved from the agony of our...inquisition."

"Where is he," I growled.

"Now, now. You aren't exactly threatening to me. You aren't large, you aren't skilled with a sword, and while you have been lucky once or twice with a gun, you aren't a real threat. So I can keep my word, and reunite you with Tomren before freeing him. Or I can just kill him and take you back to the Grand Inquisitor."

I forced myself to calm. "Who is the Grand Inquisitor?"

She looked surprised. "Are you all really that ignorant of us? Do you not know what we want, what we have done, and what we are capable of?"

"He is the most efficient of their torturers," Anne said in my ear. *"He is known as being cruel,*

often torturing people even after they have answered his questions. Arthur thought he was probably near eighty years old, and we think he is from a time before yours. Perhaps even from one of the first beacons. We never learned his name."

I jumped when I heard Anne. I looked Sabina in the eyes. "Old dude? From before our time? Likes to hurt people? A total hypocrite, since you guys say that traveling through time is against 'God' yet he's gone further than I have."

Anger flashed on her face, and she slapped me. "He is the most devoted of us. You would do well to show him some respect. It may be a little bit easier for you if you do."

I rubbed my cheek. "Noted. Now, where is Tomren."

Sabina grabbed my collar and pushed me forward. "Walk."

"So you have no devotion to the king," I asked.

"King Hammond does not follow God. He allows the use of the beacons. Not only does he allow it, in fact, he embraces it. Bringing healers to our time, saving lives that God had destined to die. He protects the beacon. His allegiance is to the power he wields. He does not deserve devotion."

"*I'm close,*" Anne said.

"How close?"

Sabina shoved me in the back. "To Tomren? Not far."

"*I can see you, but do not look for me. So far they have not spotted me.*"

I nodded and kept walking.

"What will you do with us," I asked without turning around.

"I gave you my word, I will release Tomren alive in his own time. As for you, your life is over. I will deliver you to the Grand Inquisitor, and I will never see you again. He will either kill you, or torture you until you wish you were dead. Either way, you will not leave his dungeon once you have entered it."

"You might be-" my words cut off as I saw Tomren blindfolded ahead. "Tomren," I cried out and ran to him.

I put my arms around him, and he groaned. "Gently," he said as I took his blindfold off.

"I'm sorry," I said as tears streamed freely down both of our faces.

"You should not have come. You are more important than me, my father would have protected you."

I hugged him gently. "Be quiet my prince, I am worth no more than you. You are all I have, and I would risk all to save you," I said in between sobs.

Two men appeared from the shadows behind Tomren, one pulling him back, and one grabbing me.

"What do you want me to do with him," the man asked as he held my arm.

Sabina smiled. "We'll take him to his new home. When we have gone," she said, turning to the other man, "take Tomren back and drop him in his time. Meet us back when you're done."

"I won't leave Sebastian," Tomren said weakly.

Sabina turned to Tomren. She nodded at the man who held him, and the man punched him in the stomach. Tomren collapsed with a cry.

"Don't touch him," I said, reaching into my sack and pulling out a grenade. Before the man holding me could react I had pulled the pin.

"What the fuck are you doing? Put the pin back in that thing before you blow everyone up."

I threw the pin into the darkness. The man released his grip on me and I took a step back. "Let him go," I said, pointing to Tomren.

Sabina nodded. As the man released Tomren, she looked calmly at me. "There is no escape. There is no way out of this that will satisfy you. You either kill us all, or you see Tomren released and you sacrifice your own life. I'm prepared to die for my beliefs. Are you ready to die for your prince?"

"Someone else is here, they're coming."

I looked behind Sabina. "Who, who is it?"

"Who is what," Sabina started to ask, before she realized that I wasn't talking to her. "Grab them!"

The man closest to me grabbed me roughly, and I dropped the grenade. Suddenly, gunshots rang out. A lot of them, and they came rapidly. The man near me dropped, as did the man near Tomren. Sabina dove behind some rock formations.

"Time out now! The grenade, it's going to-"

Before Anne could finish, I reached for the power and timed out. I ran towards Tomren, and as I did, the grenade exploded in a bright flash. Small pieces of hot metal flew in every direction. I grabbed Tomren, and suddenly he was back to normal.

"What is happening," he asked.

"I'll explain later, just don't let go of my hand, we need to run."

And so we ran. Faster than the exploding metal.

Suddenly Anne was next to us. "How is he not timed out," she asked as we ran.

"I don't know, it must be because I'm touching him," I said through ragged breaths. "I can't hold this for long."

"I'll help," Anne said, and the air tightened even more around us. Smoke hung in the air as we ran past the men that had been shooting at the Brotherhood.

"Who in the bloody hell are they," Tomren asked.

"Americans," was all Anne said.

As we got near the cave entrance, I felt myself weakening. "I can't go-". That was when my world went black.

***

I woke up in the castle. Not the dilapidated, crumbling mess that I had last seen, but the actual castle. I sat up. I was in my bed, in my chambers. I felt weak, but otherwise whole.

"Tomren," I called out.

The door opened and Beltoch walked in. "The prince is in the throne room with the king. We have visitors. I was told to fetch you as soon as you awoke. Let's get you some decent clothes."

"Is he okay," I asked, rising to my feet as my thoughts went to his bruised and battered face.

Beltoch nodded. "He has been beaten rather severely, but he is okay. He will recover fully within a few weeks."

I sighed and sat back down on the bed. "I should've stopped them."

Beltoch cocked his head. "You could not have, sir. None of us could. But we are all grateful that you saved him from them."

That did nothing to help him now. He would have both the physical and mental scars of the ordeal that he went through. Beltoch put his hand on my shoulder as he set some clothes on the bed. "We are all grateful to have both of you back. Dress and join us, please." He paused at the door. "Welcome home."

35

I put on the clothes that Beltoch had left for me. The feeling of them struck me as strange. I had only been in the future for a few days, but I felt so comfortable in the clothing of that time, that I kept fiddling with and adjusting this outfit. I opened the door to my room, and was surprised to see it guarded by Leofrick.

"I will be accompanying you to the throne room," he said. "Since I had to demote Gilton after you lied to him, I will not be letting you out of my sight," he added quickly.

I sighed. "It wasn't his fault. I needed to leave. I'm sorry that it caused him grief."

"I agree, it was not his fault, it was yours," Leofrick sighed. "I do not blame you, I understand what motivated you and I am proud of you for having the courage to leave to protect the prince, and as a result you saved the prince. The King, however, blamed the guard and wanted him punished. I convinced him to allow me to simply demote him."

I swallowed. "Punished?"

Leofrick stopped and looked me in the eyes. "The king wanted me to have him lashed and sent to the dungeon. I convinced him to allow me to demote him, and sent him to the front lines of our general infantry."

Guilt washed over me. "To the front lines," I repeated. "He was one of the castle guards, and now his life is forfeit?"

Leofrick scoffed before beginning to walk again. "Forfeit? You think us so weak that our front line soldiers all die? No, but his life is much harder now. Away from his family, away from his home, and yes marginally more at risk. We have not had a battle in decades however, and I don't see our peace ending anytime soon."

"I'm sorry. I didn't intend for him to suffer."

"I'm sure you did not. As I said I understand your motivations, and as a result of your actions we have Prince Tomren home where he belongs." He glanced at me before adding, "For what it is worth, Gilton said that he would have let you go willingly had he known that you were trying to protect the prince."

"I would like to meet him one day and apologize personally to him."

"Perhaps. But, know this, young Sebastian, you do have people here that you can trust. Myself and the other guards, we would all die to protect the prince. And you, as the ward of the king, for that matter. You don't have to take unnecessary risks."

We neared the throne room. At the entrance, I stopped and turned to him. "The prince trusts you. I am grateful for your words, but I could not trust either of the king's generals. The man who called himself my father tried to kill me. His successor kidnapped and beat Tomren. Trust is not something that I can put in anyone right now." I turned back and entered the throne room before Leofrick could respond.

The king sat on his throne. Beside him sat Tomren, his face still bruised and swollen but bearing a smile that made my heart melt. Standing before the throne, three figures turned as I approached. Beltoch was there, as was Maurianne. The third person stopped me in my tracks. Marcus stood there. He was wearing some sort of uniform that I didn't recognize.

The king stood, and walked towards me. "Sebastian," he said, embracing me warmly. "I am so relieved that you are well." He stepped back, but kept his hands on my shoulders, looking at me through glistening eyes. "Thank you for again saving our prince. I will never forget that."

A genuine smile came to my face, my own eyes welling. "I would do anything for him, it is my duty and honor."

The king pulled me in for another embrace, before releasing me and going back to his throne.

"I understand that you all know each other," he said, gesturing at the four of us.

Everyone nodded. "Why is he here," I said, looking to Marcus with a scowl. "The last time I saw him, he was pointing a gun at me."

"A misunderstanding," the king said, frowning. "It would seem that you both suspected the other of working with the Brotherhood. I can assure you that neither of you fit that description."

I scoffed. "Then why the gun," I asked, turning to Marcus. "Why would you point a gun at me? Why didn't Arthur trust you?"

"I assume," Marcus began, "because he knew that I was lying to him."

His voice sounded strange. I did not recognize his accent, and I gaped at him. "Lying? How? Why? Who are you?"

"He can be trusted," the king cut in, "at least as far as he is not Brotherhood, and he is not a threat to us."

"Thank you, King Hammond," Marcus said. "I would not have shot you, Sebastian. I actually kind of like you. You are brave, and you are willing to do anything for those you love," he said looking to Tomren.

"You are all here because I trust that none of you are working with the Brotherhood. Beltoch, without your book, Marcus and Arthur would not have known the goings on of the kingdom from their time," the king started.

"Marcus, you have been watching the Brotherhood for nearly a decade, and more than once you have protected both of our times from the threat they pose."

The king turned to Maurianne. "Maurianne," he said, standing once more and coming down to her. He took her hand. "Please allow me to convey my deepest sympathies for the loss of your father. I had a complicated relationship with him, and I regret the years that I did not allow him here. He proved to be an ally, and I wish that we had more time to repair the mistakes that I made."

Maurianne bowed her head slightly. "I too had a complicated relationship with him. But he would have done anything for his," she glanced at me and paused, "for those that he cared about," she finished.

What the hell was that? 'For his' what? Before I could ask, the king nodded. "He gave his very life for those that mattered. He will not be forgotten."

The king turned to Marcus. "Mr. el-Kilahl, would you please explain your role?"

As Marcus cleared his throat, all eyes turned to him. "Sebastian, if I may before I start, I would like to apologize to you for how things ended in my time. I did not mean you any harm, and I would have never shot you." I simply glowered at him.

"Now, as far as my role," he continued, "I am not the individual that Arthur thought. He was not wrong to be suspicious of me, however, I do not work with the Brotherhood. I work for the American government-"

"Of course you do, bloody Americans," Maurianne interrupted. She put her hands up when the king scowled at her. "I'm sorry, continue."

"As I was saying," Marcus continued, "I work for the American government. We have been monitoring the Brotherhood of Time for nearly five decades. At first we thought that they were just a bunch of crackpot religious nuts. But they were well funded and well armed. So we watched them. It wasn't until about ten years ago that Arthur showed up on our radar. The Brotherhood were after a boy," Marcus looked to Sebastian. "And they were sure that Arthur could lead them to him. I was assigned to find a way to get close to Arthur, and so I did. Imagine my surprise when it turned out that the Brotherhood wasn't as crazy as we had thought."

"They are insane," Maurainne snapped, before putting her head down.

"They are," Marcus agreed, "but they are not crazy. They are actually very well run, and very smart. Once I got close to Arthur, we quickly began taking the Brotherhood seriously. While I was not honest with him, I can assure all of you that he was someone that I eventually considered a friend, and I would have protected him if I could have."

"What are you going to do about his murder," I asked, anger simmering just below the surface.

"Well, we are going to take down the Brotherhood. We are ready to move on the key leaders of the group. The problem is, there may still be much that we do not know. We have been interrogating Ms. Ayers, and we have what we believe to be enough information to bring down their entire operation. In fact, we've already started here, and will begin within a few hours in my time."

"Then what," I asked. "And what the hell is an 'American'," I added quickly.

"Then, you can live your life without having to worry about being hunted. We will watch you, of course. You have an ability that we do not understand. You don't scare me, Sebastian, but most people in my government that are aware of you are also scared of you. So, we will monitor you."

"You are going to spy on me?"

"Yes, though I would prefer for you to work with us willingly. I would much rather work side by side with you, than watching you from a distance," Marcus said.

"You didn't answer his question," Maurianne said before I could respond. "Perhaps you should tell him what an American is."

Marcus looked at her with a neutral expression before turning back to me. "America is one of the continents. I work for the United States of America. We do not have a king, but rather a President. And he is not the only voice in decisions that are made for our country. I could try to explain the whole thing to you now, but I would rather just invite you to come back with me and see for yourself."

"They are colonizers, they stole the land from sixty million people. They raped, tortured, and murdered until the number of native people on the land that they claimed fell to less than six million," Anne said, facing me. "Is that really the kind of people that you want to trust and work with?"

Marcus sighed loudly. "I am not proud of our dark history. That was hundreds of years ago, and yet we still do not treat the native population as I believe we should. But, we have tried to learn from our mistakes."

"Maurianne, I understand your distrust and dislike of the Americans," the king said. "However, this decision will lie with Sebastian. They have proven themselves our friends, and they did come, albeit a bit late, to help rescue my son. For the moment, they will remain friends.”

"Thank you,” Marcus said with a bow of his head.

"For now, there is a feast prepared in honor of all of you. You all played a role in returning my son to me, and I am grateful to each and every one of you. Please join me at my table for dinner.”

36

Dinner had been uneventful. I sat next to Tomren, but with the noise and bustle we did not speak much. I had not had the chance to really talk with him since we returned. Marcus and Anne spent most of the dinner in silence, flashing looks of disgust at one another. The king had stood and toasted us all, thanking us for saving his son's life and returning him safely home. The people cheered, and I couldn't help but wonder what they would think if they knew that Tomren and the rest of us had been in 2025, and that the two strangers that sat with us did not belong in this time.

I returned to my chambers as soon as it was respectful for me to leave. I had a bath drawn, gods what I wouldn't give for a shower, and sank into the water. The hot water reddened my skin, and I felt some of the aches ease. I closed my eyes and laid back.

How could I leave Tomren here and go to 2025? What did Marcus gain from me returning? If Maurianne was correct, and the Americans really were as despicable as she claimed, then were they just trying to use me for the ability that Marcus was now fully aware of? And what would I do there? I had a purpose when I went there before. I left to protect Tomren, and he still ended up in the hands of the Brotherhood. If they were truly being eliminated by the Americans, then what purpose did I have there? I did somewhat miss indoor plumbing. I certainly preferred the clothing. And the whole electricity thing was kind of nice I supposed. But none of that was worth leaving Tomren.

My eyes shot open and I sat up quickly when I heard the king's voice behind me. "You slipped away early."

"Your highness," I said. "I did not hear you enter, I would have dressed."

The king walked over to the bench across from the tub I was in. He looked around and smiled. "I've told you, it's Osbert when no one is around. And don't worry, I'm not looking." He became serious, his smile fading. "Do you love my son?"

I was taken off guard by this. Did he mean as a friend? As my prince? Or did he suspect that we were more? My heart sped up just a bit. "Of course, he is my prince and my friend."

The king shook his head and smiled at me. "That is not what I mean, and I feel as though you know that. I was young once," he said with a wink, "and I know when two young people have feelings for each other. Do you love him?"

The hair on my arms stood up as the gooseflesh covered them. "Yes," I said quietly. "I do, with everything that I am."

The king reached out and took my hand. "I am grateful that he has you. I am grateful for everything you did to bring him home to me. I would be lying if I said that it doesn't make my heart warm to see him happy." He sighed. "Unfortunately, you two can never be. You must know that there is no future with him. He is the heir of this kingdom. He is my only child, and the responsibility to continue his family line is a heavy one. As a father, I want only for him to be happy. As a king, I know that his happiness must come second."

I looked away, but I didn't remove my hand from the kings. Tears began to prick at the edges of my eyes. "I want you to go back to 2025, and go to America with Marcus."

I pulled my hand away quickly, wiping my tears as anger began to overpower the sadness. "Of course, get rid of me so that Tomren can focus on his duties as the future king."

"Sebastian, it's not like that," the king said, with compassion in his voice. It did nothing to slow my anger.

"It's okay, really," I snapped, standing out of the tub and grabbing a towel to wrap myself. I was so angry that my nakedness didn't even cross my mind. "My own father didn't want me, no one has ever wanted me except for Tomren, and of course the one person who actually wants me in his life is forced away from me."

"Please try to understand, I'm not trying to chase you away, and I do want you in our lives. Do not forget, I am the one that chose to make you my ward. That was my choice, because I care for you."

My mind was battling with my heart. The king had no obligation to be so kind to me, especially when I was being so disrespectful towards him. He was right, he did not have to take me on as his ward. Regardless of whether I saved his son in the cave or not. He could have chosen to just give me some coin, or land, or some other reward and let me deal with my own problems. But he chose to take me under his protection, he chose to allow me to stay here in the castle, he chose to give me access to everything that came with being the ward of the king. But now he was trying to send me away, to make me leave Tomren behind. He was choosing to break my heart, and it hurt even more than when the man that I thought was my father chose to try to kill me.

"I don't need your pity," I said quietly but with venom. "I have no one in this world, no matter the time, other than your son. And you are choosing to take that from me."

The king stood. "You misunderstand. I will not force you to leave. You are my ward, and you are welcome in my house until the day I die. If you do not wish to leave, then you do not have to."

I looked at him, face flushed with anger and eyes filled with tears. "And if I stay?"

The king sighed. "If you stay, you will be at worst my son's best friend. And at best, you will be his secret lover. He can never be with you. He will marry a princess, he will have babies, he will become king, and he will carry on the Hammond bloodline in this kingdom. That is his fate, and he has no more choice than I did."

The king turned and went to the door. "Sebastian, I do not lie, I do not say things that I do not mean just to make someone feel better. Without you, my son would likely be dead twice over. You have been dealt a shit hand in life, and I cannot make things the way that you want them. But I care for you, and I will give you anything that I can. I cannot give you my son."

I scoffed. "That is all I want."

The king nodded. "And I am genuinely sorry that it is not within my power to deliver it. Both for your sake, and for my son's. I assure you, seeing the way he is with you makes my heart warm with love. His mother," his voice cracked, softening my mood, "his mother would be pleased to see it as well. She would love you also. Sleep on it, Marcus leaves at noon tomorrow."

When the door closed, I went to the window and looked out. Lights from the town could be seen flickering in the distance. My tears came unbeckoned, and I wept. None of this was fair, and this life was not one I wanted to live without Tomren. I had not been alive until his love sparked my heart, and I would not go back to that lifeless existence. I draped my legs out of the window and sat on the sill. The fall was three floors, and I would likely die if I chose. A gun would be faster, easier, but I had no gun. I did have a window. I leaned forward, the same as I had almost a decade earlier when Arthur had pulled me back. My heart thumped in my chest, my ears filled with the sound of it drowning out everything else. If Arthur hadn't saved me that day, I would have died then. My father, rather Rorthan, would never have tried to kill me. I would have never had to see Arthur die in front of me. I wouldn't have grown up unloved, alone, and worthless.

But, I also would have never met Tomren. Sweet, kind, loving...handsome, Tomren. I would have never known what true love felt like, I would have never known the thrill of his touch. I would have never felt his lips on mine, his hands on my body. I could not live my life without those feelings in it. He is the only person that had ever made me feel alive.

I leaned forward. My weight shifted further towards the point of no return. Tomren's face filled my mind. His eyes full of tears when he received word of my fall. The painful scream that he would loose when he was told that I had died, no when he learned that I had chosen to die. My heart ached at that image, and I knew it was selfish to do that to him. I didn't care. I leaned forward, and slipped free of the ledge.

Except I didn't fall. Hands slipped under my armpits, and I felt myself being dragged back into the room. I fell backwards on top of Tomren.

"What the fuck are you doing," he cried. "What are you doing," he repeated, his voice shattered by emotion.

I rolled off of him, sitting on the floor. I scooted away from him, my face full of shame at what I had done. "I can't live this life alone, I can't be alone anymore," I cried.

He crawled towards me, both of us weeping heavily. "You aren't alone. But you would leave me alone? You would leave me to live my life without you? Do you care so little for me that you would rip my heart out? Because the day you die, I die. If you go, I go." His voice was loud, anger mixing with his pain. "I mean so little to you that you would kill me as surely as if you stuck a knife in my chest?"

"You will live your life without me," I all but yelled back at him. "You and I cannot be together. You have a duty to take the throne, to have children to carry on your name. I can't give you that. This was always going to have to end, we both knew that. You have your father, you will have a queen one day, and children, and people that love you. I don't, I have no one."

"You have me," Tomren said pleadingly. "You have me," he repeated, almost a whisper.

"Tell that to your father," I sneered, anger again welling inside of me. "He made it clear that I could never have you."

Tomren tried to come to me again and I scampered away, only to find that my back was against the wall. "You already have me," he said, reaching out for me. I looked at his face, twisted in pain and wet from tears. I had to get out of this. I reached for the power tingling inside of me. The air thickened, and Tomren slowed, his hands inches away from me. I stood and ran, leaving the room and racing to the church. The guards outside of my door stood perfectly still as I rushed past them. They would never even know that I had left. I could feel the power draining from me as I ran down the stairs to the church. I released the power as the door opened and I fell inside.

"What is wrong," Maurianne asked. She stood from a nearby table, and rushed to my side.

"I...need to...leave this time," I panted. I didn't want to leave this time, I wanted to die. But I knew after tonight that I would never put Tomren through that.

"Okay," she said calmly. "When?"

Before I could answer, I collapsed. I felt the drain on my mind from using my ability, and I let it swallow me whole, hoping against hope that I would not see the other side.

<h1 style="text-align:center">37</h1>

I did come out the other side. The darkness slowly gave way to light and sound. I could hear voices, Tomren, the king, Beltoch, and Marcus. I could not tell what they were saying however. I opened my eyes, my head pounding.

"Easy," Tomren said, instantly by my side.

"Where am I?"

"Your chambers," the king said. "Maurianne brought you here after you collapsed."

My head began clearing, and memory returned. I looked to Tomren, and he immediately looked away. "I'm sorry," I said, reaching for his hand. He didn't pull away, but he didn't take my hand as I had hoped. That was fair. I released my grip.

"As am I," the king said. "I was not thinking of the pain I would cause when I spoke with you. I still stand by what I said, you can never have the life you want with my son-"

"I don't even know what life I want," I interrupted. "I just want to live and experience life side by side with Tomren."

The king nodded. "And that is where I failed you. You are both young. You have time before Tomren must fulfill his duties as future king. I tried to pull the two of you apart, and I'm sorry for the hurt that caused. I believed that doing it now would be better than allowing you to get even closer to one another. I am not so sure that that was the best choice to make. The two of you clearly share a bond that is stronger than I thought."

"I have no one else, nor have I ever felt as close to anyone as I do to Tomren," I said. The expression on Tomren's face softened marginally.

"And I think that I have a solution. It is my hope that we can bridge the gap between our views, and do what is best for all of us."

"I hope that you mean that, father," Tomren said.

"I do," the king assured, looking at his son. "Please, join me for breakfast so that we can figure out the next step."

The king left with Marcus. Beltoch turned to me. "I do not know what it is that is causing you to have these episodes, so I cannot tell you how to treat them. I would say that if you are able to avoid them, that is probably for the best right now. If you ever need to talk, I am available."

I thanked him, and he left as well. Only Tomren and I remained in the room. He laid next to me on the bed. "Don't ever do that again," he said without looking at me.

"I won't," I said, moving closer to him. He propped himself up on his elbow and kissed my forehead, before putting his arm under me. I laid my head on his chest. "He's not wrong tho, you know that. We have no future."

"The future is always being written. We have now. And in ten minutes, which is the future, we will still have each other. Stop worrying about what may one day be. Live now, with me."

I said nothing more as we lay there. I closed my eyes and listened to the sound of his heart beating, his breaths slow and calm. I realized that I didn't know how to not have that in my life. Tomren pressed his head to mine. "I love you, Sebastian," he said. Before I could respond, he pressed his lips to mine and kissed me deeply. He stood. "I need to change my clothes, and you need to dress. Breakfast is soon."

When he left the room, I dressed. My head was already clearing, and I felt stronger. The voice in my head telling me that I had no worth to anyone, that I'd be better off to jump, was still there. But it was quiet. I now recognized that that voice belonged to Rorthan, to all of the years that he spent making me feel worthless. I was now more determined than ever to make sure that that voice did not win.

I walked to the dining hall wondering what 'solution' the king would have. Would he let Tomren be free to love whomever he chose, free to live his life as he wanted rather than as his duty demanded? I knew that would never happen. I also knew that nothing less than that would be a true solution.

The king was seated at the head of the table, Tomren on his right side already changed from the clothes he had been wearing. I was surprised to see Marcus seated at the table as well, one empty seat between him and Tomren.

"Sebastian, please come sit," the king said, waving me in. "We have much to discuss."

"Thank you," I said as I took my seat across from Tomren. I looked at him for only a second before quickly diverting my eyes to the food. My emotions were high, and I could feel the sadness pricking at my eyes.

"Eat, please, you need your strength. Eat, and listen. I have come up with a solution with the help of Marcus," the king said, gesturing to the other man. Marcus nodded but didn't speak. "I hope that it will satisfy both you and Tomren. But I need for both of you to understand that this offer is the only one I will make. It will not be negotiable. If you accept, the terms will be as I describe, and only as I describe."

Tomren and I nodded at the same time, preparing to hear the king's terms. "Sebastian, you have been a loyal friend to my son, you have now protected him at great risk to yourself twice. You will always have a place at my table, and in my home. However, as I have explained to both of you,

Tomren must wed and bear children to continue our line. I wish that I had another son that could take that burden from him, and free him to live his life as he chooses and with whom he chooses. Unfortunately, you both have felt the loss of your mothers and the solitude of being only children." The king wiped his mouth with his napkin, and I thought I saw him wipe his eye as well.

"However, my son is still young. There is no need for him to marry right now. He has time. This is where my proposal comes in. If you would like, I would have the both of you return to 2025 for one years time. I will say that he is traveling as an envoy for me somewhere. The people will be none the wiser. After one year, he will return and we will find him a suitable wife." The king turned towards me, and I fidgeted under his full attention. "You are welcome to return with him. You may stay here for as long as you like, or we can give you land and a home befitting your position as my ward. However, I will not have a scandal in my kingdom. After the year has passed, you will not be permitted to continue in an," he paused as if searching for the right word, "intimate relationship."

"So after a year I must pretend that my heart does not belong to Sebastian?"

The king and I both were taken back by Tomren's forwardness. My heart both welled with pride and burned with pain of unavoidable loss.

"Yes," the king said simply but sharply. "That is the offer that I extend to you. One year, and then you must resume your duties here."

"And what would we do in 2025," I asked. One year was better than none, and I would not sacrifice any time that I could have with Tomren.

"You would be under our protection," Marcus spoke up. "We would keep track of your location, and I would like for you to see some of our doctors. But you would be free to do as you please. Arthur left you a substantial sum of money, as you know. You could travel, you could find a place to stay where it is just the two of you, you could just live. Whatever you wanted to do."

"See your doctors," Tomren asked, for the first time looking as though his mood was lightening.

"Yes. Sebastian has abilities that we do not fully understand. We would like to learn more. It wouldn't be invasive, and it wouldn't be everyday. But, we would like to run some tests and see what we can learn. We would also offer a safe space for you to test your power, to practice," Marcus said, turning to me. "You will be safe and protected, and you will be free to live as you please."

"For one year," Tomren said, more of a statement than a question.

"Yes," the king said. "One year. Live, love, travel, learn. Do whatever you please. But in one years time, you are to return here."

"Very well, I accept," I said, looking at Tomren.

"As do I," he said. "Though I would note that I, we, deserve better."

The king nodded. "Indeed you do. But, duty is a heavy burden and it can strip away what you deserve and leave you with only what you get."

"When would we leave," I asked.

"Tonight," Marcus said. "I would prefer to do it after dark. You will not need to pack anything, though if you would like you can bring a small bag. As you know, the clothes will be different there, so no need for many belongings."

I slid my chair back, the wood screeching on the marble floor. "Very well. I will pack." I turned to the king. "Thank you, Your Majesty," I said before turning and leaving. He would never be 'Osbert' again, no matter what he said or did. One year was not enough, and if I was not good enough for his son then I did not deserve to call him by name.

I left the dining hall, and headed to the church. I was surprised when Beltoch caught up to me. "Young sir, if I may," he said, hurrying to keep up with me.

"I am no 'sir'. Just Sebastian," I said as I slowed for him.

"Very well, Sebastian. If I may, I'd like to give you this," he said, holding out a small book. I opened it and was surprised to see the pages blank.

"An empty book?"

"Yes. Much like the one that you read while in the future, I will write important things on this one, and you can review it in the future. It can be a line of communication, albeit one way, for you."

"Thank you, Beltoch. But, if I take this now, then it will not be waiting for me in the future. You must leave it somewhere for one day, somewhere that it will not be disturbed for a thousand years."

"But where," he asked, echoing my own wonderings. It couldn't be the church, because no one, not even Beltoch, could know about the church.

"I do not know. Allow me to think on it, and I will let you know before I leave. Is there anything else that I can do for you?"

The man shook his head, before telling me to make sure to see him before I leave to let him know what I decide. When he left, I continued to the church. It was time to prepare.

38

When I entered the church, there was already a fire burning inside of the faces. I walked over to the round table and sat. It felt like it had been a lifetime ago that I had seen this room for the first time. Tomren had brought me here, and neither of us could have imagined the life we were now living. The faces had struck awe in me the first time I had seen them. How many times had I now been here, in this 'room of faces'? Somehow the awe that I felt was gone. This room became little more than a hiding place. Silent and hidden for milenia, with only a small handful of people knowing its location. Arthur was dead, so that left three people that knew of this room's exact place. Myself, Tomren, and Maurianne. As if on cue, a voice behind me spoke. "Magnificent aren't they? Despite what they stand for, of course," Anne said.

I turned to her. "They are. I seem to forget that, walking past them without paying any attention. Everything has been so...fast since learning of all of this." I waved my hands around the room.

"Funny isn't it? We can slow time down, we can travel from century to century across milenia, but we still rush through life. Don't let this year with Tomren pass by without paying attention to each other."

I raised an eyebrow. "You knew of his father's plan?"

"I did. Marcus asked me to join you as well. I'm," she looked around, "undecided."

"You don't like Marcus much, do you?"

"It's not Marcus. Marcus may well be a fine individual. My father trusted him once, and although he grew suspicious he still put faith in him." She sighed heavily. "No, I don't like Americans much. Ironic, since my father is an American. But in my experience, even if an individual American is good, the whole of them are greedy, hateful, and bigoted. They don't like anyone that is different from them, and we," she put a hand on my shoulder, "are different from everyone. I worry about what the American government wants from you, from us. They do nothing without getting something in return."

"Marcus said they wanted to have me see some doctors, to run some tests."

"Yes, he said the same to me. But to what end. Do they want to find a way to copy our ability? Do they wish to find a way to stifle it? Perhaps even both? I do not trust them, and you would do well to be careful of them yourself."

"I will be. When will you decide?"

"Within a few days time. I will stay here. If need be I can use Arthur's beacon to come back. Not even Marcus knows where that beacon is."

I nodded. "Will you do me a favor then?"

"Perhaps."

I explained to her Beltoch's idea of the book. "And you need to place it here, in the church. But you don't want to expose the location to Belotch."

"Yes, I have no reason to doubt him, but once more people find out of this place, how long will we be able to protect it?"

"Not long. I will speak with Beltoch. I'll leave the book in Arthur's room, on his desk. How long must it stay?"

I shrugged. "I don't know. But I think just long enough for me to retrieve it in the future. A day should suffice. Once I have the copy in 2025, then the location of the copy here won't matter."

"It will already be written."

"Exactly. And any changes will show up in it as did the other book. Or, at least that's my guess."

"I will put it on the desk for one day then. Once the day has passed, I will return it to Beltoch. And then, I will likely come back to my own time. I will make sure to find you. Here," she said, putting a phone in my hand, "keep this away from Marcus. I will let you know when I'm back."

"I will," I stood and placed my hand on her shoulder. "Thank you, I would not have been able to get back here if not for you."

She looked at me for a moment. I couldn't read her face, but I felt like there was some sort of sorrow in it. She suddenly pulled me close and hugged me. "Be careful. There is much yet for me to tell you."

I returned her hug. "What is it?"

She pulled back, hands still on my shoulder. She shook her head. "Not now. Soon, maybe even when I get back. But not now."

"Then make sure you return," I said with a small smile.

"I will," she said, returning the smile.

I left the room, wondering when or if I would actually see her again.

***

That evening after dinner we said our farewells. The king held his son in a long embrace, and cried silent tears as he released him. When the well wishes and farewells were done, we left the castle to head to the cave. We traveled in silence, Marcus at first trying to make conversation, but giving up when all he got in response were grunts from Tomren and I. Neither of us wanted to talk.

When we arrived at the beacon, I felt it's pull in my mind. It's power thrummed inside of me as I drew closer, my body tingling.

"Are you both sure," Marcus asked.

I looked at Tomren, and took his hand in mine, lacing my fingers with his. "Yes," he said. "Let us go and begin our next adventure." His smile was warm, and it reminded me of our first meeting. He had promised adventure then, and an adventure we had certainly experienced.

"Let it be our greatest," I said, returning his smile.

And then we were lifting away from this time that we were both born in.